"ENERGIZE," COMMANDER WILLIAM RIKER ORDERED. . . .

Seconds later Riker, Worf, and Geordi stood facing a white dome in a clearing on the planet Hera. The sun was low on the horizon, but still bright in the clear blue sky. The air's warmth told Geordi it was late evening here rather than early morning. Thunder and lightning rumbled in the distance. "What the heck?" Geordi wondered; he had seen a lot of strange things on various worlds, but a storm in a clear sky was new to him.

Riker had his tricorder out. "It's a Klingon raid," he said. "They're invading."

Look for STAR TREK Fiction from Pocket Books

Star Trek: The Original Series

Star Trek: The Next Generation

Star Trek: Deep Space Nine

Star Trek: Voyager

INFILTRATOR

W. R. THOMPSON

POCKET BOOKS

New York   London   Toronto   Sydney   Tokyo   Singapore

This book is a work of fiction. Names, characters, places and incidents are products of the author's imagination or are used fictitiously. Any resemblance to actual events or locales or persons, living or dead, is entirely coincidental.

An *Original* Publication of POCKET BOOKS

POCKET BOOKS, a division of Simon & Schuster Inc.
1230 Avenue of the Americas, New York, NY 10020

STAR TREK is a Registered Trademark of Paramount Pictures.

A VIACOM COMPANY

This book is published by Pocket Books, a division of Simon & Schuster Inc., under exclusive license from Paramount Pictures.

ISBN: 0-671-56831-0

First Pocket Books printing September 1996

10 9 8 7 6 5 4 3 2 1

POCKET and colophon are registered trademarks of Simon & Schuster Inc.

Printed in the U.S.A.

INFILTRATOR

Chapter One

"THAT'S THE SHIP," Marla Sukhoi told her husband. She pointed to the white needle on the spaceport's flight pad. "The *Temenus*. It launches in eight hours."

Lee nodded. "Eight hours. They changed their plan. Do you think they suspect?"

Marla shook her head. The midnight air had made her black hair damp, and it clung to her forehead in loose strands. "Central's always suspicious, but it doesn't have a reason to suspect us."

Lee grinned crookedly, white teeth in a dark broad face. "I'm just nervous."

"You'd damned well better be," Marla said. Security around the spaceport was good, and Lee carried a half-dozen thumbnail bombs in his pocket. "Too many things can go wrong."

"Cheerful tonight, aren't you?" He reached out and stroked her cheek. " 'So lovely fair, that what seem'd fair in all the world seem'd now mean.' I'll be back for you."

"I know." The quote from Milton—Adam's descrip-

1

tion of Eve, another type of firstborn—warmed her as it always did. She kissed him. "Now get going."

"Right." Lee hurried down the slope. Despite his words Marla did not think she would see him again. His chances of sabotaging the *Temenus* were good, but his chances of survival were poor. A sense of loss and sorrow welled up in her, only to fade out before it could overwhelm her. Damn the originators, she thought. The changes that the genetic engineers had made in her people made it all but impossible for the people of Hera to sustain an intense emotion. She was able to view Lee's impending death with a sense of detachment that seemed to reduce the love she felt for him.

Marla turned away and jogged back to town. She was not afraid of being observed. Central Security had decided that extra surveillance would only alert the subversives to the start of Operation Unity, so Central had gambled by not increasing its activities around the spaceport. By the same token, only the people who had to know about Captain Blaisdell's secret orders had been told about Unity. Marla Sukhoi, who ran the Olympus Spaceport, was one of those people.

And now I'm a traitor and a murderer, she thought. So be it. When she had learned about Unity she had discussed its implications with Lee. They had concluded that if Unity succeeded it would provoke the primals into destroying Hera, and that would lead to the loss of their family, along with everything else. They could not count on the resistance movement to stop Unity, so they would have to do it themselves. Logic left them no other course.

Even so, she did not want to kill the *Temenus*'s crew. She wished that she were smart enough to think of an alternative.

Marla reached her home as the sun rose. She woke the children and got their breakfast ready. Gregor, the younger of her two boys, waited until Marla had her hands full before he brought up a problem. "I didn't finish my math homework last night."

Marla wondered why six-year-olds liked to leave their problems for the worst possible moment. "Anna, can you take care of this?" she asked.

"Okay. Come on, Geeker." Anna took her younger brother by the ear—a maneuver she had picked up in her aggression classes—and pulled him over to the dining room table. Marla watched in disapproval; the classes were supposed to teach children to suppress their aggressive instincts, not give in to them.

Anna put the boy's school pad in front of him and called up his calculus assignment. "What's the problem?"

"This one," Gregor said, jabbing a finger onto the pad. "Gotta integrate e to the minus x squared. I can't do it."

"Nobody can," Anna said. She spoke with all the authority of a ten-year-old. "It's an undefined operation. You have to sneak up on it. Write the Taylor polynomial for e to the x, substitute minus x squared for x, and integrate the polynomial."

"Teacher said we had to do it as an *integral*," Gregor protested.

Joachim, the older boy, blew air out of his cheeks. "Then write down that it's a trick question and solve it as a sigma series. They want you to learn to look at the questions, not just the answers."

Marla put breakfast on the table while her children squabbled over Gregor's homework. At least the talk kept them from noticing that their father was missing. It was not unusual for Lee to leave early; he was a field geologist, and the children probably reasoned he was out testing another new piece of equipment. After they had eaten, Marla bundled the children off to school, then went to the neighborhood tube station. The capsule that took her to the spaceport was empty, which suited her mood.

The capsule brought her to the spaceport entrance, where she nodded to the guard and walked to her office. On her way across the green she passed the marble column that commemorated the spaceport workers killed in a primal attack three years ago. A damaged freighter had made an emergency landing at the spaceport, and while repairs were made to the ship its crew had realized what the Herans were. The primals had gone berserk and killed several people with their phasers before they were stamped out.

Once inside her office Marla settled into her daily routine. The computer delivered reports to her in order of importance. Combat Operations had spotted a Romulan ship outside the Heran system; analysis suggested it was heading home after a routine exploratory flight. A primal ship was *en route* to the sector to lay a series of communication and navigation beacons; Operations wanted a warship readied to shadow it, in case the primals made trouble. The three robot warships of the Special Reserve were to be activated and deployed for maneuvers in deep space. The Hephaestus Institute needed to borrow a courier for a test of its long-range transporter system.

Marla ground her way through the work, half-expecting to see a security report. She found none, but that meant nothing. Central Security kept a tight lid on reports of sabotage and other forms of dissidence. Lee might have been caught at once, and her first hint would come when she was arrested.

A glint of light caught Marla's eye, and when she looked out her office window she saw the white needle that was the *Temenus* rising into the clear morning sky. A wave of guilt made her look away. If all went well, Lee's bombs would go off in six days and the ship would vanish. But if all went well, Central Security would never know if *Temenus* had been lost to an accident or sabotage—or an attack by the primals. The uncertainty should make them hesitant about trying Unity again.

Or so she hoped. She didn't understand the Modality. Over the past few years the Heran government had grown more secretive, more authoritarian. It had revived the originators' dream of conquering the old human race, and that threatened to bring destruction down on Hera.

Chapter Two

Captain's log, stardate 47358.1 The Enterprise has entered sector 11381, a reportedly uninhabited portion of the galaxy that the Federation is opening to colonization. Accordingly the Enterprise has been ordered into this sector to lay a series of communication and navigation beacons. As the beacons incorporate some experimental computer technology, we have been joined by a cyberneticist from the Daystrom Institute. Although quite young, Dr. Kemal comes highly recommended and has already shown a remarkable talent for enhancing the Enterprise's computer programs.

ASTRID KEMAL TRIPPED over her own feet as she walked into the Ten-Forward lounge. Most of Guinan's patrons politely ignored her as she stumbled, but Worf growled with embarrassment. He had invited the cyberneticist to join him and two of his security troops for lunch, and her clumsiness grated on his innate sense of dignity. A Klingon warrior was *not* seen in public with—he recalled a human word that one of his security ensigns had used—a *klutz*.

One of the two ensigns seated at the table with Worf showed less restraint in his reaction. "I *told* you so!" K'Sah crowed as he gave Sho Yamato a punch in the arm. "Pay up!"

Worf growled at K'Sah while Yamato rubbed his upper arm. The massive Pa'uyk resembled a poisonous, shaggy spider with pincerlike hands at the ends of its four arms, but Worf felt unintimidated by the creature. "I dislike your gambling," the Klingon rumbled.

K'Sah ignored the hint. "How could I pass up a sucker bet?" he said. The chitinous tips of his four legs tapped merrily on the deck. "Besides, Sho's buying *you* a drink, too."

"A bet is a bet," Yamato said in agreement. He signaled one of the bartenders, then looked at Kemal. She stood at the bar, ordering a drink from Guinan. "Lieutenant," he wondered, "is Dr. Kemal always this . . . artless?"

"No," Worf said curtly. That was literally true. She had been on the *Enterprise* for over a week, and he knew of one occasion on which she had not stumbled. That had been when she entered his security office today to work on his computer subsystems. He regretted that he had no witnesses. "Do not accept any more bets on her performance," he warned Yamato.

"Yes, sir," Yamato said, and looked at K'Sah. "I thought that bet seemed peculiar," Yamato remarked.

K'Sah clacked his serrated mandibles in mockery. "Let that be a lesson to you. Never bet against me." Despite his friendly tone his words seemed threatening. Worf told himself that must be a false impression. The Pa'uyk world had only recently contacted the Federation, and no one seemed to have much knowledge of their customs and manners. K'Sah himself would say nothing useful about his people, even though he was temporarily under Worf's command as an exchange officer from the Pa'uyk military; K'Sah took the reasonable (to him) position that he was the one who was to do the observing, not Worf.

A bartender arrived with a tray laden with drinks: synthehol for Yamato, some sort of reeking meat juice for K'Sah, prune juice for Worf. As the bartender walked away Kemal joined the party at the table. She was a tall woman whose deep voice matched her robust physique. She was as dark as a Klingon, showing the mixed European, Asian and African heritage common to many human colonists. She was also uncommonly strong; Worf had seen her lift a navigation beacon with her bare hands, a feat that would have tested his strength.

As Astrid sat down Worf saw that her glass was filled with a bright orange liquid. "Sorry I'm late, Worf," she said.

Worf gave a noncomittal grunt and took a swallow of prune juice. Its alien biochemicals had a soothing effect on the Klingon metabolism, and Worf felt his temper subside. "Ensign Yamato, Ensign K'Sah," he said, nodding at his men to introduce them.

His good mood did not last. "Sho's paying for this round, thanks to you," K'Sah said to Astrid. "Those two left feet of yours are the best money-maker on this ship."

Worf growled. "You will cease making these bets, Ensign."

"It's all in fun, Lieutenant," K'Sah said. "Hey, Kemal, why don't you come in again and give Sho a chance to even the score? I bet you won't trip this time."

"Cute, K'Sah," Astrid said in disdain. She took a sip of her drink, then looked at Yamato. "Your first name is Sho? I'm Astrid. Let me buy the next round, to make up for that bet."

"No fair!" K'Sah protested. "How am I supposed to enjoy my drink if I can't force someone to pay for it?" He rested the elbow of one of his upper arms on the table with his hand out, challenging Yamato to arm wrestle. "Come on. Loser buys the next round."

Yamato raised an eyebrow at the spikes that protruded from the coarse fur on K'Sah's arm. "Didn't you just say I should never bet with you?"

"Dullard," the Pa'uyk sneered. "Are you going to believe *everything* I tell you? How about you, Asteroid?"

Astrid shook her head. Worf thought she seemed untroubled by a nickname that was clearly meant as a dishonorable comment upon her size. "I've heard about you. You'll cheat."

"Aw, c'mon, human!" K'Sah's faceted eyes gleamed as if he felt delighted by the accusation. He pushed a bristly arm toward her. "I can fight clean. Honest!"

Worf watched her, idly curious as to whether or not she would accept the challenge. While human females were not noted for their aggressiveness, he wanted to think that this woman had a certain degree of spirit. Equally important, a dozen people had clustered around the table to see what would happen. It had been bad enough that they had seen Astrid stumble as she entered Ten-Forward. Worf did not want them to think that he had made the acquaintance of someone who would back away from a challenge.

Astrid glanced at Worf as though reading his mind. She put her elbow on the table and cautiously clasped K'Sah's chitinous, spiky hand. She let out a slight grunt of exertion which told Worf that the contest had begun. "Not bad," K'Sah admitted in a voice that showed no strain. Millimeter by millimeter he pushed her hand toward the tabletop. "For a human you've got muscle."

"Charming, isn't he?" one of the human onlookers muttered.

"You mean 'obnoxious,'" Worf grumbled. Even by Klingon standards K'Sah was a rude spawn of a tribble.

K'Sah snickered at Worf. "I love recognition," he said. With one of his free hands he took Astrid's half-finished drink, poured it into his mouth—and spewed it out. "What *is* this slop?" he demanded, while several onlookers backed away from the orange mist.

"Orange juice," Astrid gasped. Her face showed the strain as she fought to keep her hand above the tabletop. Worf did not mind that she was about to lose. He honored anyone who would enter battle, even though defeat seemed inevitable.

"'Orange juice,'" K'Sah repeated in disgust. He tossed the glass aside and looked at their hands. "This is taking too long," he decided. There was a thump under the table, and Astrid let out a surprised yelp. At once she shoved K'Sah's hand up and over, and there was a sharp *crack* as the back of his hand slammed onto the tabletop.

Astrid released her grip. K'Sah jumped to his feet and clutched at his injured hand with his other three hands. While he hopped around the lounge and howled curses in his native language Astrid leaned over and looked at her lower leg. "Are you hurt?" Worf asked her.

"He . . . he kicked me in the shin." Worf had never seen anyone who looked so thoroughly flustered. "I thought he said he'd fight clean."

K'Sah glared at her while one of the onlookers, a medical technician, examined his hand. "I said I could," the Pa'uyk said, speaking through gritted fangs. "I didn't say I would. Do I look like an idiot?"

The technician snorted. "What you look like," he said, "is somebody with a broken hand. Let's get you to sickbay."

K'Sah followed the orderly to the lounge door. He stopped after a few paces, turned around and looked at Astrid. "Hey, Kemal," he rasped. "Best two out of three?" Then the orderly pulled him through the door.

Guinan came to the table with a fresh tray of drinks. The lounge hostess's smile suggested she shared a wonderful joke with the universe. "I'm putting this on K'Sah's tab," she said as she handed out the glasses. "Sake, prune juice, orange juice. That was quite a show," she added, and sat down. "You didn't strain any muscles, did you?"

Astrid shook her head. "The truth is, I got lucky. He slipped."

"I'll say," Guinan said. Worf heard the amusement in her voice—and something else, as if she were trying to insinuate a second meaning into her words.

Astrid ignored her words. She raised her glass and looked at Worf. *"Ghlj get jagmeyjaj!"* she snarled.

The Klingon words brought a pleased look to his face. He seldom encountered a human who spoke his language with such flawless pronunciation. Picard and Riker spoke Klingon, but they always made the language sound, well, *polite.* "And may *your* enemies run with fear," he said, returning the toast. He allowed himself a faint smile. "As K'Sah did."

Yamato eyed Astrid's glass. "'Orange juice'?"

"I like orange juice," Astrid said. "And Guinan serves the best I've ever tasted. I wish I knew how she gets this much flavor out of a replicator."

The intercom sounded before Yamato or Guinan could respond to that. "Lieutenant Worf, please report to the bridge."

"On my way," he said, standing up.

Worf left the lounge and went to the turbolift outside its door. He thought about Kemal as he rode the elevator to the bridge. She was strong and healthy, and she handled computer tools with great dexterity. He did not understand her clumsiness, and he was suspicious of things he did not understand.

The turbolift stopped and Worf stepped onto the bridge. Captain Jean-Luc Picard nodded to Worf as the security chief went to his post. "We've picked up a distress signal, Lieutenant," the captain said in his resonant voice. "It's an automated beacon. We'll rendezvous in fifteen minutes."

"Aye, sir," Worf said, looking at his instruments. "I have the beacon. Getting a sensor lock now."

Data, the android systems officer, left his helm station for the science officer's post. "I am reading signs of a ship, Captain, and humanoid life-forms."

"'Humanoid' covers a lot of ground," Will Riker said. *Enterprise*'s executive officer pulled thoughtfully at his short dark beard. "Can you get anything more specific, Data?"

"No, sir," Data said. "There is heavy interference

from the ship, indicative of a major reactor accident. Readings suggest that the reactor core has been jettisoned."

"Hail them, Mr. Worf," Picard said.

Worf sent a general signal, then scowled at his instruments. "No response, sir."

"I have an image now," Data said.

"Put it on the main viewer," Picard ordered.

"Aye, sir." The main viewscreen at the front of the bridge showed a starfield and a small, elongated ship. The hazy, unsteady image told of the intense radiation surrounding the vessel. Its slow tumble announced that it was out of control.

"I don't recognize the configuration," Picard said. He turned to Deanna Troi, who sat at his left hand. "Do you sense anything, Counselor?"

The Betazoid empath nodded. "There's at least one person still alive out there, Captain," Deanna said. "He's . . . annoyed. Very, very annoyed."

"'Annoyed'?" Picard raised an eyebrow. "That's a rather mild reaction to a space disaster."

"Unless . . . perhaps the pilot is a Klingon," Worf said.

"But I don't sense a Klingon," Deanna said. "This is a human, but with a very deliberate, formidable personality. It's as though whatever happened is merely a nuisance."

"A reactor accident is more than a nuisance," Picard noted. "Mr. Data, is it safe to transport aboard that ship?"

"Not without environment suits, sir," the android said. "The radiation levels are too high for crew safety. I would suggest beaming aboard survivors as soon as we are within transporter range."

"Make it so," Picard said. "Mr. Worf, I want you to supervise the rescue operations. See if the survivor can tell you what happened."

"Aye, sir." Worf touched the intercom control. "Dr.

Crusher, report to transporter room three. Possible radiation injuries." Worf turned toward the turbolift.

Deanna spoke quickly to the captain, then hurried into the elevator with Worf. She waited until the door had slid shut before she spoke. "Something's bothering you, Worf."

He growled as the turbolift glided down its shaft; he disliked his inability to keep secrets from the counselor. Her large, dark eyes only added to the impression that she could discern his every thought. "Have you met Dr. Kemal?"

"The cyberneticist?" Deanna shook her head. "I haven't had the pleasure. Why? Do you have a problem with her?"

"I would like to know why she cannot enter a room without falling down," he said. "It does not fit what I know of her."

Deanna smiled. "And that makes you suspicious?"

"Everything does," Worf said, annoyed that she felt amused by a natural Klingon attitude.

"It's an intriguing point," the counselor said as the turbolift stopped. "I'll see if I can have a few words with her."

Worf nodded and stepped out of the elevator. He walked into transporter room three, where Beverly Crusher, the ship's chief medical officer, was already present with a pair of orderlies and two stretchers. "Oh, Worf," she said. "You can't have K'Sah back until tomorrow morning."

"Why so long?" Worf asked.

The doctor brushed a tumble of auburn hair from her face. "Because along with five broken bones and a shattered wrist-spike he has two torn ligaments, a lacerated vein, and considerable soft-tissue damage in his hand and forearm. He won't be fully healed until tomorrow."

Worf accepted that with a nod. He felt pleased that Astrid had done so much damage, even if by accident. "Is he in much pain?"

Crusher shook her head. "No, not anymore."

"Pity," Worf said. "Perhaps this will cure him of gambling."

"I wouldn't bet on that," Crusher said, a comment that drew groans from her orderlies. "He tried to bet Dr. Par'mit'kon ten credits that he'd be fully healed by midnight."

The transporter technician spoke to Worf. "Lieutenant, we're in transporter range of that ship. I've locked on to two survivors; they're sealed into an escape pod. I can't detect any other life."

"Bring them aboard," Worf ordered.

Light shimmered on the round transporter stage, and two men materialized on its surface. One lay flat on his back, unconscious, while the other knelt by his side. The kneeling man looked around as Dr. Crusher and her orderlies surged onto the stage. "This must be the *Enterprise,*" he said.

"Good guess," Worf said.

"I'd heard you were operating in the area," the man said, while Dr. Crusher scanned him. "And no other Federation ship has a Klingon crew member. I'm Gustav Blaisdell, master of the *Temenus*. This"—he gestured at the unconscious man—"is Vlad Dunbar, my navigator."

"Are there more survivors aboard your ship?" Worf asked.

"No, everyone else died." Blaisdell rose to his feet. He was a large man with an olive complexion; Worf estimated that he was two meters tall and massed a hundred kilos, which made him only slightly larger than the Klingon. He carried a rucksack slung over one shoulder. "The rest of my crew was beyond my reach, but I got Vlad into an escape pod before the life system failed."

"And just in time," Crusher said. She injected something into the unconscious man. "Your friend has a near-lethal amount of tetrazine in his system, and you've both taken a large radiation dose. Let's get you to sickbay."

Dunbar was every bit as massive as his captain, and Crusher needed the help of Worf and the two orderlies to

wrestle him onto a stretcher. One of the orderlies activated its antigrav suspensors, and they floated Dunbar
out into the corridor. Worf walked alongside Blaisdell.
"What was the nature of your accident?" Worf asked.

"I don't know," Blaisdell said.

"You must have some idea," Worf insisted.

Blaisdell shrugged. "Everything just blew."

"There was no warning?" Worf asked.

"I heard a few thumps when the power died," Blaisdell said. "After that I was too busy staying alive to
notice much else."

"Yet you had the time to gather your luggage," Worf
said, eyeing the man's rucksack.

Blaisdell sighed noisily. "It was within reach."

"And you did not eject?"

"In a short-range pod?" Blaisdell shook his head.
"Staying with the ship seemed a better idea. We were still
drawing power from the emergency system."

"That's enough talk for now," Crusher said firmly.
The group came to a turbolift. Worf remained in the
corridor while Crusher and the others crowded into the
lift. "I'll let you know when my patients are ready for
questioning, Lieutenant," the doctor said, before the
door slid shut.

Worf scowled at the door. He found Blaisdell to be
exactly as Deanna Troi had described him: deliberate
and formidable, and unfazed by his experience.

He was also a liar. Worf felt certain that Blaisdell knew
exactly what had happened to his ship, and that it was no
accident.

In Greek mythology Temenus had served the goddess
Hera, and that was enough to tell Astrid Kemal that the
ship was from the planet Hera. She sat at the computer
terminal in her quarters and viewed everything she
could find about the planet. At five thousand words per
minute, the terminal's maximum display rate, that did
not take long. She found nothing useful, however. All of

the information on Hera was consistent and innocuous. There was nothing she could point out to Worf and say, sir, this proves the Herans are a threat to the Federation.

That left telling the truth.

Astrid shut down the terminal and closed her eyes. It would be nice to stop lying and hiding, and the Federation *had* to know about the Herans. They were genetically engineered supermen. Their average intelligence was seventy percent higher than human-normal, and their strength and endurance were superior to that of a Klingon. Their senses and reflexes were just as superior, and they were immune to all known diseases. They also believed that they had a right to dominate the galaxy; that was why they had named their world after a mythological goddess of the heavens.

She could see herself explaining that to Worf. He would nod, once, deliberately, and ask her how she knew this. Then she would have to explain that she and her parents were Heran refugees.

Her parents had warned her what would happen if any of the old humans ever found out what she was, and the prospect chilled her. A few years ago an *Enterprise* crew member had been expelled from Starfleet when it was learned that he was part Romulan, and not part Vulcan as he had claimed. Compared to what could happen to her, ex–Medical Technician Simon Tarses had been fortunate. After four centuries the human race still remembered Khan Noonien Singh's conquests, and they feared that genetic supermen like him would attempt to dominate humanity again.

Astrid lay down on her bunk and tried to figure out what to do. Every alternative frightened her.

Chapter Three

"I FEEL LIKE SOMETHING out of an old space opera," Geordi La Forge said as he struggled to climb into the environment suit. It was a bulky garment, a thick white coverall with a bubble helmet and a clumsy backpack. It looked like a twentieth-century moon suit, and the *Enterprise*'s chief engineer felt sorry for anyone who had explored the Moon in anything so hideously uncomfortable.

Evidently the other members of the away team shared his sentiments. "I'd like to catch the sadist who designed this monstrosity," Will Riker said, a comment that drew an agreeable growl from Worf and a sour laugh from Reg Barclay.

"The designers were not sadists," Data said. "They were all members of the Vulcan Science Academy, and as such possessed well-balanced personalities."

"Vulcans," Barclay grumbled. Geordi's assistant struggled with his suit's backpack. He was a tall man, as thin as a guitar's neck and with nerves perpetually stretched as tight as a guitar's strings. "It, it figures. Comfort is illogical."

"Let's get this over with," Geordi said. He closed his helmet and checked the tiny readouts in front of his chin. They showed normal, which was reassuring, as was the faint susurration of air inside the glass bubble.

What the engineer saw through the glass did not reassure him. Geordi had been blind since birth, and his vision came through a wraparound gold VISOR. The sensors built into his VISOR allowed him to sense almost the entire electromagnetic spectrum, along with a variety of esoteric radiations—few of which were transmitted by the helmet. The radiation-proof glass would pass only the so-called visible portion of the spectrum, and Geordi felt crippled by the sudden limitation of his sight.

Well, he thought, if other people can live with this, so can I.

The away team stepped onto the transporter stage. Riker gestured to the technician, and a moment later they materialized in a narrow corridor on board the *Temenus.* The air was filled with smoke, and the only light came from the blue glow of emergency lamps. The artificial gravity was still operating, but at one-tenth normal. The feeble tug made Geordi feel giddy.

Geordi whistled at his readouts. "It's pretty hot in here," he said. "Ten minutes would kill an unprotected human—call it ten minutes and five seconds for a Klingon," he added, unable to resist teasing Worf. "Let's see if we can find a purge system."

"We should find the proper controls in the engineering section," Data said. He walked to one end of the corridor, which was blocked by a sliding door. The door did not respond when he tried its control pad, but it slid aside when he pushed it. Geordi was glad for the android's enormous physical strength.

The door admitted the away team to the ship's engineering section. "Nice," Geordi said as he looked around. *Temenus* wasn't much more than a starfaring yacht, but her reactor and warp unit reflected a brilliant sense of design. "Very nice."

Riker chuckled. "You sound like a man in love."

"Just about," Geordi conceded. He found a control station, and in a moment he had an emergency power system on-line. The main lights came on and the control panels lit up. "I'll need an hour to purge all the radiation and coolant from the life support system," he told Riker, "but that shouldn't be a problem."

"Good." Geordi saw Riker's suited form twist around. "Riker to Dr. Crusher. We have three bodies here."

"Understood," Beverly Crusher answered. "I'll perform autopsies after you've secured that ship."

Geordi looked at the nearest body on the deck. The intense radiation and tetrazine coolant had done a lot of damage to the corpse, which barely retained a humanoid shape. "I think a postmortem would be pointless," Geordi said. "The remains are pretty badly burned." On his way to a control station, Barclay gingerly stepped around one of the bodies as though fearing it might rise up and grab him.

Data accessed the ship's computer while Geordi and Barclay began the life system purge. It was hopelessly dead. The android found the flight data recorder, opened it and removed its synthetic diamond cartridge, which he scanned with his tricorder. "There are no indications of impending trouble in the recorder," Data stated. "The primary, secondary and emergency reactor cooling systems all failed simultaneously, and without warning."

"They had *three* critical failures in the space of a few seconds?" Riker asked in disbelief. "Impossible."

"No," Worf said. He had climbed atop the warp coil casing. He gestured to Geordi, then pointed to the cabin ceiling. "Sabotage."

Geordi followed Worf's gesture and whistled in awe. Three separate units nestled amid the piping had small, blackened holes carved in their shells. "I see what you mean. Shaped charges?"

"Yes," Worf said. "This is the work of an expert."

"I'd like to know the motive," Riker mused. Geordi saw him raise his hand to his helmet, as if to stroke his beard. The glass bubble blocked him. He looked at a hard-copy instruction manual on a work shelf. "'SS. Temenus, Hurran Institute of Astronautics.' There's no 'Hurra' in the Federation, is there?"

"Heera, Commander," Data corrected. "The name is Greek, and that language employs the long 'eta' form of the letter e rather than the short 'epsilon.' There is an independent, human-colonized world by that name at coordinates—"

"Okay," Geordi said. It was only coincidence that Hera was the name of his mother's ship, still missing in space and presumed destroyed, but the coincidence stirred uncomfortable memories of the loss. "Data, does the log say anything about the ship's mission?"

Data consulted the computer station. "The Temenus departed Hera eight days ago on a mission to Aldebaran Two to purchase computer components."

"At Aldebaran?" Barclay asked in surprise. "W-why not Benzar? It's a lot closer, and, and it's the place for computers. Aldebaran is just a b-big shipyard."

"You are correct," Data said. "However, the log mentions one Khortasi, a Ferengi sales agent with an office located adjacent to the New Aberdeen Naval Yard."

Geordi chuckled. More often than not, "Ferengi sales agent" meant "fence." "So Blaisdell may have been shopping for stolen computer components."

"That is the most likely explanation," Data agreed.

Riker snorted in contempt. "This entry smells like a cover story. Nobody records criminal activity in their ship's log."

"Indeed," Worf rumbled. "I will discuss this with Captain Blaisdell."

Deanna Troi smiled as Astrid Kemal bumbled into the doorway of the counselor's office. As Deanna had expected, the young woman's clumsiness was an act.

Deanna thought she had already guessed the reason behind it.

Deanna had a desk in her office, but it was hidden in a corner and almost lost between two exuberant potted ferns. She did her real work sitting on the comfortable chairs that dominated the floor. She sat on one now, and as Astrid entered the office Deanna gestured for her to take a seat. Deanna's empathic sense told her how uneasy Astrid felt in her presence. "You wanted to see me, Counselor?" the cyberneticist asked.

"Lieutenant Worf asked me to see you." Deanna held a versina paperweight in her hand. As Astrid slid into her seat Deanna chucked the glittering green crystal straight at her. Astrid's hand snapped out as she fielded the crystal. "Very good," Deanna said. "The clumsiness is an act, isn't it?"

Astrid nodded as she returned the paperweight to Deanna. "And you want to know why I do it."

Deanna shook her head, making her wavy black hair shimmer. "I think I can guess why. It's protective coloration, isn't it?"

The woman's uneasiness increased; Deanna watched her clasp her large hands over a knee. Her dominant emotion was guilt at being caught in a lie. "Not much gets past you, does it, Counselor?"

"Your behavior isn't unusual," Deanna said, placing the versina paperweight on an end table. "You're like a man who's afraid of being thought a coward. He'll constantly start fights to prove he's brave. You're trying to prove you're harmless, so people won't feel intimidated by your size and strength."

Deanna sensed Astrid's surprise as she nodded. "It's an old habit, Counselor."

"Do you think it's a necessary habit?" Deanna asked.

"It was when I was a girl," Astrid said. "Some of the kids I knew were scared I might beat them up, and some of them were jealous because I was a good athlete, so I acted klutzy to even things out. It made it easier for me to get along with everyone."

"So why do you keep it up?" Deanna asked. She sensed the woman's sincerity, but her explanation sounded thin, as though she were hiding something—most likely from herself, Deanna reflected. Astrid might be unaware of the true reason for her behavior, but some judicious nudging could bring it to light. Deanna shifted around on her chair, assuming an open posture that all but shouted *See? I'm comfortable in your presence.* "Such an act may have been necessary with children, but I doubt that you intimidate anyone on this ship."

"I think I do." Astrid was actually fidgeting in her chair. "It's hard to explain—"

"But you're so convinced that you make people nervous," Deanna concluded, "that you see proof of this even when it may not be there. You're a young woman, Astrid—twenty-two, aren't you? You wouldn't want to spend the rest of your life putting on an act."

Astrid looked as uncertain as she felt. "Maybe you're right."

"That's been my experience." Deanna felt exasperated; Astrid Kemal was as tight-lipped as Worf. That made probing her difficult. Counseling was a process that needed the patient's cooperation. "You see, I have a problem similar to yours. Before I left home I was afraid that my empathic sense would disturb non-Betazoids. I'd heard about alien ideas like privacy and lying, and I didn't know how aliens would react to my presence. I was pleasantly surprised to find that most people could take an empath in stride.

"Of course, a few people still have trouble with me," she went on. "They're afraid I might be a telepathic voyeur, or that I might reveal their deepest secrets. I handle that head-on, by letting them know my talent's abilities and limitations—*and* by making sure they know what sort of a person I am. As you're beginning to notice, that makes people more comfortable around me."

Astrid smiled weakly. "I thought I was handling myself pretty well."

"You are," Deanna assured her. "My point is that I take it for granted that people will like me as I am. When there's a problem, I don't smooth it over by pretending to be something I'm not."

"And that works for you?" Astrid asked.

"It works very well," Deanna said. "I think you should walk into Ten-Forward, *without* tripping, and see what *doesn't* happen. Do it now," Deanna suggested. "I'll check on you in a few days, to see how you're getting along. And you needn't feel guilty over what you've done. You'd be surprised at how common the 'little white lie' is in human society."

"Yes. Thank you." That only increased Astrid's sensation of guilt, but Deanna expected it to fade in time. Deanna watched her get up and walk out of the office. After a moment Deanna reached out and picked up the versina paperweight. As she peered into the crystal she saw how its facets and internal structure shattered the simple image of her office into a hundred random fragments. Looking into the crystal was like looking into a human mind.

Deanna put the crystal aside and went to her desk. Worf had given her a larger problem than he had realized, and she wanted to do some research before she approached Astrid Kemal again. The woman's problem went deeper than a simple anxiety to please people. Despite her outward calm, she was in a state of terror.

Chapter Four

WORF STRODE INTO SICKBAY not long after his return to the *Enterprise*. Dr. Crusher was just finishing her treatment of Dunbar. The large human lay unconscious on the biobed, but the indicator needles on the display above his head suggested that he was out of immediate danger. Blaisdell loomed behind the doctor, a look of amused curiosity on his face as he watched her work.

"Hey, Klingon!" K'Sah reclined on another bed, one of his shaggy forearms encased in a regenerator. "If you're shopping for recruits, we've got a couple of live ones here. Sign 'em up before they come to their senses."

"Be silent," Worf said curtly.

"Hell, look at them." The human-sized spider gestured lazily at Blaisdell. "Big, strong, halfway intelligent—they've got potential, even if they're only human."

Worf considered breaking K'Sah's other hands, but decided it would accomplish nothing. "Doctor," he said, "when may I speak with Blaisdell?"

"Whenever you like, Lieutenant," she said. The doctor started putting her instruments away. "He's fully recovered. I discharged him a half hour ago—"

"And I've been in the way ever since," Blaisdell said. "I imagine that you have more questions for me."

"I do," Worf said.

"Just be careful around him, human," K'Sah said. "The Klingon will talk both of your round little ears off."

Blaisdell eyed K'Sah in disdain. "Pain has a bad effect on this creature."

"He fights well," Worf said, nettled at having to defend K'Sah. "That excuses much. Come with me."

Blaisdell picked up his rucksack, slung it over his shoulder and followed Worf out of the sickbay. "Your ship is still contaminated," Worf said as they walked down the corridor. "We will supply you with quarters until it is spaceworthy again. Our engineers will replace its reactor core."

Blaisdell nodded. "That sounds expensive."

"Starfleet does not ask payment for emergency services," Worf said.

"But you'll still expect answers to your questions."

The man's condescending tone annoyed Worf. "What is your business on Aldebaran?" he asked.

"Exactly what it says in my ship's log, which I see you've read," Blaisdell said. "Khortasi claimed to have certain Romulan military codes. Hera has had trouble with Romulan raiders, and our defense forces—but I'm sure a Klingon understands strategy."

Worf mulled that over as the two men entered a turbolift. It was plausible, and even possible, yet there was that damnable condescension again. "Deck twelve," he told the turbolift. "The Federation does not approve of such dealings. They might provoke the Romulans."

"Hera doesn't belong to your Federation," Blaisdell said as the lift began to move. "I suppose you're going to keep me from visiting Khortasi?"

"No," Worf said, "but you would find the visit fruitless."

"I imagine that Federation Intelligence is already questioning Khortasi," Blaisdell said.

"You may assume that," Worf said. In fact Federation security forces had not had the time to respond to the query Worf had sent them, but Worf saw no reason to mention that to Blaisdell.

Blaisdell nodded. "Your next question will be about the accident. To answer it, I still don't know what caused it."

"We know its cause," Worf said. "Your ship was sabotaged."

"Was it, now?" Blaisdell asked. "That would explain the lack of warning."

"You claim to be on a government mission," Worf said. "Why would anyone wish to sabotage you?"

"I can't explain that," Blaisdell said.

"Why am I not surprised?" Worf muttered. The turbolift stopped and opened its doors. The two men stepped into the corridor. "Your quarters are this way," Worf said.

Blaisdell raised an eyebrow. "No more questions?"

"You seem to have no answers," Worf said. He stopped at an unoccupied stateroom and the door slid open. "Regulations require me to inspect your luggage," Worf said as they entered the quarters.

"Or *allow* you to inspect them?" Blaisdell smiled as he passed his rucksack to Worf. Worf carried it to the stateroom's table, opened it and spread out its contents. He found an old-style hand communicator and a tricorder. "No weapons," Blaisdell told Worf.

"So I see." Worf held up the tricorder. "This is an unusual design."

"It's been modified to carry secure messages," Blaisdell said. "It can rebuild its physical circuit structure to defeat hacking efforts."

"What message does it carry now?" Worf asked.

"A map of Cardassian space," Blaisdell said.

That surprised Worf. The Cardassians were major

rivals of the Federation, and whatever their faults, they had an admirably efficient security system. "Your spies are good," Worf conceded. "Why do you carry this map?"

"We were going to barter with Khortasi for his information," Blaisdell said.

"By trading information which would be useful to pirates," Worf said.

"Or to the Federation," Blaisdell said, and shrugged. "We don't care who he planned to sell it to. But if we can't deal with Khortasi, maybe we can do business with your people."

"I think not."

Blaisdell smiled. "You don't trust us?"

"Of course not." Worf felt his suspicions deepen. Whatever business Blaisdell had with Khortasi was surely a cover for some other activity.

Worf turned his back on Blaisdell and left the stateroom. He wished that he could lock up the Heran and confiscate his property, but Blaisdell's activities skirted the law without breaking it. Suspicion was not an adequate excuse for an arrest, at least not in the Federation.

But suspicion made a good starting point.

"Boy, am I glad to get out of that suit," Geordi said as he entered Ten-Forward with Data and Riker. He worked his shoulders up and down; he could still feel where the backpack supports had dug into his flesh. "Data, if the Vulcans who designed that monstrosity were normal, I'd hate to meet a *crazy* Vulcan."

"That is an unlikely event in any case," Data said, serious as ever. "Vulcans are noted for their strict observance of mental health principles."

"Which explains why they don't wear their own E-suits," Riker said.

The three men stepped up to the bar and ordered drinks from one of Guinan's bartenders. Geordi had just accepted a Saurian brandy when Astrid Kemal walked into the lounge. For once the woman didn't trip, which came as a pleasant surprise. Geordi had worked with her a bit over the past week, and he enjoyed her company. Despite her size and strength she was quiet and a bit shy, and she liked to talk shop with him. The engineer found all that appealing. It didn't hurt that she was pretty, spoke in a warm voice, and had an absolutely terrific sense of humor. She smiled as she saw Geordi, which struck him as a good sign.

Riker seemed uninterested in her as she approached the bar and asked the bartender for an orange juice. "If you think the suits make you uncomfortable," he said, "imagine what Worf's going to do for the Herans."

"Yeah, they're on his list, all right," Geordi said.

"What's the problem?" Astrid asked.

"It's that distressed ship we found," Riker said. "It was sabotaged, and part of the crew died. Worf's just hoping for trouble."

"It's more than that," Geordi said. They took their drinks and went to an empty table. Geordi was glad that Astrid joined them. "He crawled over every millimeter of that ship while we ran the decontamination protocols. You don't run a search like that while you're wearing an environment suit, not unless you've got a good reason."

"That log entry was pretty fishy," Riker said.

Geordi nodded as they sat down. "I know, but when I asked Worf what was up—" Geordi shrugged. "He just growled and beamed back to the *Enterprise.*"

Astrid looked thoughtful. "I guess something made him suspicious," she said. "He must have a good reason."

"Well, I didn't see one," Geordi said. He thought it over as he took a sip of his drink. As puzzles went, this wasn't quite the same as tracing down a glitch in one of the ship's subsystems, but it still intrigued him. "Data, what do you know about Hera?"

"Hera is the third planet of 492 Lyncis, a class G-2

subdwarf star approximately twelve hundred and seventeen light-years from Earth," Data said. "It is a class M planet, settled by Terran emigrés in the late twenty-first century. The original colonists adhered to a doctrine that advocated the selective breeding of humans to eliminate undesirable genetic traits and raise the quality of the race to a new level."

"More damned superhumans," Riker muttered. "They sound like some of Khan Singh's human followers."

"That is possible," Data agreed. His drink was a mixture of lubricants and nutrients, concocted to maintain his organic components in perfect balance. He took a measured swallow before he continued speaking. "The Khanate had many imitators after its destruction. Some of them attempted to establish themselves in extrasolar colonies, as did Khan Singh."

"And dreamed about lording it over us mere humans," Riker said contemptuously. Khan Singh had been a genetically engineered superhuman, created by a group of human scientists in the late twentieth century, and he and his fellow creatures had conquered a quarter of the Earth before they were defeated. Khan was the last great tyrant of human history, and after four centuries his name remained a synonym for arrogance and injustice. "It looks like Worf's instincts are still good," Riker went on. "If these Herans think they're superbeings we could have a real problem on our hands. They'll have to do something to prove their superiority."

"If that's what they are," Geordi said. He disliked eugenicists, who all seemed to think it was immoral to let a blind man live, but he told himself that his feelings weren't that extreme. "Selective breeding can't improve human beings," he said. "They probably gave up on that a long time ago."

"They probably moved on to more effective techniques," Riker argued. *"Homo arrogans* never knows when to quit."

"Yeah, I guess not," Geordi said. He decided to change the subject. "You're from Zerkalo, aren't you?" he asked Astrid.

She seemed startled; she had been quietly toying with her glass while the others talked. "That's right," she said.

"I guess us Earth natives can get pretty boring when we talk about ancient history," Geordi said. "All this stuff happened centuries before they colonized your planet."

"Earth history always seems so complicated," she agreed. "Ours is a lot simpler—the second thing we did after we landed was to overthrow the government. End of history."

"I am unfamiliar with this version of Zerkalan history," Data said. "What was your first action after landing?"

"We set up a government, of course," she said. "If we hadn't, we wouldn't have had anything to overthrow."

Data looked puzzled as he worked through her logic. "I fail to see the purpose in this chain of events," he said.

"It's one of our jokes," Astrid said. She gave a philosophical shrug. "Now you know why you've never heard of any famous Zerkalan comedians."

"Zerkalans are anarchists," Riker told the android. "They don't believe in organized governments. That's why they haven't joined the Federation yet."

"Ah," Data said. "Then your joke is a humorous way of expressing this principle."

Astrid nodded. "We aren't perfect anarchists, although our post office really tries. We've got a few things—a judicial system, a public health agency, diplomats, a weather service—but we like to keep the government to a minimum. No public records, no taxes, no military."

"It sounds almost too simple to work," Geordi said.

"It is," Astrid agreed. "It takes a lot of effort to keep an anarchy in running order, but we don't expect much from our government and it always delivers."

"So how does a Zerkalan end up working for the

Federation?" Riker asked. "A law-and-order outfit doesn't seem like the right place for an anarchist."

The woman spread her hands helplessly. "What can I say? I always was the white sheep of my family."

Geordi chuckled. "Don't tell me you got run out of town because you were on the right side of the law."

"It would appear that Zerkalan humor depends on inverted logic for its impact," Data observed as Geordi laughed.

"Was I being humorous?" Astrid asked. "I didn't mean it."

"Indeed? Geordi's reaction indicates—" Data paused. "Ah. This is another Zerkalan joke."

"Humor has a disruptive effect on Data's logic," Riker told Astrid.

She looked abashed. "Oh, I'm sorry. We anarchists try to be careful about creating disruptions."

"You'd have to be," Geordi said. "I mean, you could reduce the entire universe to chaos, and what would anarchists do without any order to destroy?"

"Good point," she said, "although I still think total disorder is a neat idea. Speaking of disorder, there's a balky beacon waiting for me to reprogram it." She stood up.

"Yeah, hey, I'll see you later," Geordi said, a questioning note in his voice.

Astrid smiled and nodded. "Okay, great." She turned away and walked out the lounge door.

Riker chuckled. "You two hit it off pretty well," he said.

"I guess so," Geordi admitted. "Say, Data, what do you know about Zerkalo?" he asked.

Riker chuckled again, and Geordi smiled weakly as he braced himself for some good-natured razzing. "Maybe you should ask Kemal," Riker suggested. "She might be more, ah, 'informative.'"

"Okay, so I'm transparent," Geordi said. "How about it, Data?"

"Zerkalo is a class L planet," Data said. "It orbits

Gyre's Star, a class K 5 subdwarf star near Geminga, and has two large natural satellites named Waybe and Tove. As Commander Riker noted, it is not a member of the Federation, although there are negotiations under way to bring it into the Federation."

"Anarchists in the Federation?" Riker asked. "What's the attraction?"

"There are certain economic and cultural benefits to Federation membership," Data said. "There would be an increase in trade and information exchange. To continue, although Zerkalo's first settlers were Tellarites and landed in 2238, Zerkalo has also been colonized by humans, Vulcans, Kalars, Derevos, Tiburons, Andorians, Zhuiks, Saurians and members of nine other races. No single species dominates the population, which is estimated at twelve million."

"'Estimated'?" Riker asked.

"Anarchists wouldn't care for censuses," Geordi said. "They give too much information to tax collectors and bureaucrats."

"You sound like a natural anarchist, Geordi," Riker said. He leaned back in his chair and swirled the remains of his drink around in the glass. "Kalars. That would explain a lot about her."

"Big, strong, even-tempered . . ." Geordi shrugged. It didn't seem unlikely that Astrid would have some Kalar blood in her veins.

"I don't know," Riker said. "She doesn't look like a Kalar."

"I must agree with that assessment," Data said. "Although several Kalar subgroups are both tall and muscular, Dr. Kemal shows none of the other characteristics indicative of Kalar ancestry, most notably their cranial structures."

Geordi shrugged again. "It really doesn't matter."

Marla Sukhoi was at work when two Central Security agents arrested her. The man and woman walked into her office at Olympus Spaceport and flashed their blue-green-and-red Security sigils. "Marla Sukhoi?" the woman asked. "You're under arrest for treason."

She nodded and switched off her desk. "You caught Lee," she said as the man cuffed her hands behind her back.

"Lee Sukhoi died six days ago," the woman said. "It's taken us this long to identify the remains."

"I see." Marla had hoped that Lee had survived, but with each passing day that had seemed less and less probable. Even so the confirmation of his death left her stunned.

But—six days. They had killed him after *Temenus* left. He might have succeeded.

The two agents marched their prisoner out of the spaceport's office complex and took her to the tube station. A capsule took the three people from the spaceport to the Modality District in ten minutes. The agents did not speak to her; there was no need. Central had some reliable interrogation drugs, and no qualms about using them to establish a suspect's guilt or innocence. A preliminary questioning would only have wasted time.

The capsule stopped outside the Central Security Building, and Marla was taken into the basement. The two agents took her into a holding room, where the walls, floor and ceiling buzzed with the low-frequency sound of active force barriers. Then the man gave her an injection.

The agents pushed Marla into a chair as the drug spread through her body. She was glad for the seat. The strength seemed to drain from her knees, and she began to shiver as the room turned ice-cold. There was a strange sensation in her stomach and she felt dizzy. A corner of her mind recalled something she had read in a history book. This was how primals felt when they were contaminated—wait, the proper word was *infected*— with a disease-causing organism. She wondered if the Unity virus would make primals feel this way.

A new man entered the room; he looked familiar, but the drug-induced haze made that of no importance now.

He questioned her, drawing her out of her fevered reverie. Feeling distant and detached, Marla explained everything she and Lee had done. She had told Lee about Operation Unity when she learned about it. They had decided it was a threat to their family and had to be stopped before it provoked the primals into attacking Hera. Without that provocation the primals would leave Hera alone; the creatures weren't all that dangerous.

"That's about what I expected," the woman agent said.

"Yes, but I wonder why the Sukhois have such a high opinion of the primals," the interrogator said. "They should hate them. Have you seen the originator file?" he asked.

"The what?" Marla asked. Her body was fighting the drug, slowly throwing off its effects. She felt half-awake now. "I don't know what that is."

"Don't you?" he wondered. "Tell me what you think about the originators."

"Evil, murdering—" She almost choked on her sudden rage.

"She hasn't seen the file," the interrogator said dryly. Now Marla recognized him: Carlos Ulyanov, Senior of the Modality. In a grim way it flattered her to think that the leader of the Heran government had taken an interest in her. "We won't squeeze any more information out of her. I'll schedule her execution myself."

Ulyanov paused and sighed. "I'd rather not do this, but she knows too much about Operation Unity and about the originator file, now. If she talked to anyone, she could turn even more people against the Modality."

The woman agent sighed. "If we're so smart, why can't we find another choice?"

"We're not gods," Ulyanov said. "This is like our struggle against the primals. It's unpleasant, but we've no choice. The alternative is to endanger our people, and these radicals are as much of a threat as the old humans."

"At least the Sukhois can't be entirely blamed for their

fears," the woman agent said. "If they knew how good our defenses are, they wouldn't have feared a primal attack. Maybe we should lift the security restrictions and tell everyone about our preparations. That would convince everyone we're safe."

"No," Marla said. She felt almost fully conscious now. "One planet against the galaxy is suicide."

Ulyanov looked at her. "At worst we would only fight the primals, not the entire galaxy." His voice sounded intent, and Marla realized he was conducting an experiment. He wanted to see if he could persuade this radical to change her mind. "And our eugenics plan would avoid war and turn the primals into healthy people. They would thank us if they could understand it. It has to be done; the primals are ready to colonize this sector, and we won't be able to conceal ourselves much longer. Our survival demands drastic measures."

Marla thought about possible answers and rejected them. Her captors were arguing from a position of power, not logic. Nothing would persuade them that the chance they took was too great; they didn't want to believe anything could go wrong. "Lee was right," she finally told him. "The Modality thinks it's all-powerful. And power makes you stupid."

Chapter Five

WORF HAD SENT several messages to Starfleet Intelligence, and a reply came early the next morning, while Worf was eating breakfast in his quarters. His quarters were quiet. His son, Alexander, was vacationing on Earth with Worf's foster parents. Worf missed Alexander, yet today he was glad the boy was not on the ship. The Herans seemed threatening, and while it was a shameful thing for a Klingon to admit this, Worf did not want to expose his son to danger. After all, the boy was too young and inexperienced to have a chance to kill his enemies in honorable combat.

The message said that Khortasi had died forty-seven standard days ago. A Tellarite had been detained on charges of murdering him; the motive involved a dispute over black-market computer components. There was no trace of any Romulan codes.

Worf wished he knew what to make of that information. His next move was clear. "Computer, locate the Herans."

"Vlad Dunbar is in sickbay," the mechanical voice responded. "Gustav Blaisdell is in his quarters."

Worf checked the charge in his phaser before he left his quarters. At the moment he had only questions for Blaisdell, but with any luck his questions would provoke trouble.

Worf went to deck twelve. When he entered Blaisdell's stateroom he found the human seated at the table, where he worked with his tricorder. "I assume you have more questions," Blaisdell said.

"Yes." Worf watched the man slouch in his chair. Blaisdell seemed amused by Worf's presence. "You claim that Khortasi has Romulan codes. How do you know of this?"

"I don't," Blaisdell said. "It's just a reliable report."

"And do you know anything of Khortasi's reliability?" Worf asked. "Am I to believe you made this journey on the basis of a rumor?"

"Your beliefs are your business." Blaisdell turned off his tricorder and slid it into his rucksack. "I spoke with Khortasi before we left Hera. His meaning was clear, even if his words were guarded."

"Why would you need to speak with Khortasi?" Worf demanded. "Do you command Heran security?"

"Khortasi needed to see me so he could recognize me. What do you care?"

"We cannot find these Romulan codes," Worf said.

"That's not my problem."

"Your problem is sabotage," Worf said.

Blaisdell smiled. "That's not your problem."

"The sabotage occurred in Federation space," Worf said.

"On board a Heran ship."

Worf growled and left the stateroom. Once he was out in the corridor he permitted himself to smile. Blaisdell had spoken with a dead man? Catching the Heran in a lie made Worf feel better. It put his suspicions on firmer ground.

K'Sah, Yamato and Kellog were all waiting for Worf in the security department's main office, and all three stood to attention as he entered the compartment. "I want somebody on board the *Temenus* at all times," Worf told them.

"Yes, sir," Kellog said. "Is there anything special we should watch for?"

"Watch for everything," Worf rumbled. "Computer activity, transporter activity, further evidence of sabotage. Kellog, you will take the first watch."

"Yes—" Kellog stopped, cleared her throat and coughed. "Yes, sir," she said.

Worf thought her voice sounded rough. "Are you well?" Worf asked.

Kellog nodded. "My throat's just a bit scratchy, sir."

"Humans," K'Sah grumbled to the ceiling. "Coddle them, filter out all the bugs, and they *still* get sick."

"Report to sickbay," Worf told Kellog, as he clamped down on his temper. "Yamato, you will take the first watch. K'Sah, we shall talk."

The two humans left the security office. Worf glowered at K'Sah for a moment. The Pa'uyk stood at attention as Worf walked around him, looking him over. "Explain your behavior," Worf ordered.

"Sir?" K'Sah asked.

"Why do you constantly offend humans?" Worf demanded.

K'Sah looked puzzled. "Do I do that?"

"Do not feign ignorance!" Worf roared. "You greet them with insults, you converse with them in insults, you bid farewell to them with insults—"

"Sir?" The shaggy spider seemed baffled. "I talk to humans the same way I do to real people. If I wanted to insult them, I could be so rude that even a Klingon would notice."

Worf growled before he found his voice again. "You are restricted to your quarters."

"Sir? What for?"

"And you are on report!"

K'Sah's bewilderment deepened. "Was it something I said?"

"Out!" Worf bellowed.

K'Sah hastened out of the office. Worf briefly regretted the fact that the *Enterprise* was not a Klingon warship. Klingon law allowed the summary execution of insubordinate junior officers. It would have delighted Worf to strangle K'Sah.

Worf left to find the captain. He wanted permission to keep a close watch on the Herans. Humans thought there was something dishonorable about suspicion, and they would only permit surveillance after going through certain awkward legal formalities, if they agreed to it in the first place. Fortunately, Worf assured himself, the captain could be reasonable when his ship's safety was at stake . . . and even a human would be suspicious of the Herans.

Beverly Crusher glanced at Riker as he walked into sickbay. "Don't tell me, let me guess," she said. "You've got the sniffles."

"Just a little fever," Riker said. He looked at the woman seated on the biobed. It was Kellog, one of Worf's security troops. She looked a bit sweaty. "Is something going around?" Riker asked her.

"Caught a bug somewhere, sir," Kellog said.

"It's nothing serious," Crusher said. She sprayed something into Kellog's arm. "It's just a minor viral infection. Will, have a seat and I'll be with you in a moment."

Riker perched himself on a bed. It felt good to take the load off his feet. "Where's your staff?" he asked.

"They're out immunizing the rest of the crew," Crusher said. "Ensign, go to your quarters and get about twelve hours of sleep."

"Yes, sir." Kellog left the sickbay.

Crusher went to Riker and scanned him. "You've got

the same virus," she said. "It's a bit odd; it contains a lot more genetic material than normal, and it's highly contagious, but it doesn't have much effect on the human metabolism."

"Except that I feel worn out," Riker said.

"That's a typical fever symptom." She traded her tricorder for a hypospray and administered an injection. "You should feel better in a few minutes, although you'll feel tired for a while."

Riker nodded. "This won't keep me from playing poker tonight, will it?"

"No, although I'm going to be late for the game," Crusher said. "I want to run some tests on this virus, and then I have to set a couple of broken legs."

"Who had the accident?" Riker asked.

"Whoever brought this virus on board," Crusher said. "It's probably someone in engineering. They used the shuttles at our last planetary stop, and shuttle quarantine procedures aren't as reliable as the transporter biofilter."

"I'm surprised this bug didn't show up earlier," Riker said. "We left Deneva two weeks ago."

Crusher smiled and shrugged. "Plenty of diseases have even longer incubation periods. In any case, I suspect this virus comes from Deneva; it only infects humans, which suggests that it's of human origin."

"I see," Riker said. Deneva was a human colony world, and its first colonists had unintentionally brought along an assortment of harmless viruses and bacteria when they left Earth. The organisms had colonized Deneva as readily as their human hosts, and from time to time they left their adopted world. "We're lucky this virus didn't mutate into something serious. Is there anything special I should do while I'm waiting for this shot to take effect?"

"Just the usual." She put the hypospray away. "Get some rest, drink plenty of fluids, and bring lots of money to the game tonight."

Riker grinned and got off the bed. "Okay." He walked

toward the door, then stepped back as Picard entered sickbay. He looked a bit under the weather. When Riker greeted the captain, Picard grinned crookedly and tapped his throat.

"I'd say it's done," Geordi told Gakor as he shut off the melder. The new reactor core was a set of dilithium crystals encased in a gallium-arsenide sphere barely fifty centimeters in diameter. Only a single control socket marred the core's mirrorlike surface as it reflected the scene in the engineering shop. "Pretty, isn't it?"

"Pretty dangerous," Gakor said. The Tellarite leaned closer to examine the core. The reflective surface distorted his pink, snoutlike face as he studied it. "It'll probably blow the nanosecond you engage it."

"Where's your confidence?" Geordi asked. He knew better than to take Gakor's warning seriously. Tellarites would argue every possible topic. "The design's so simple, it's sophisticated. I don't think it *can* blow."

"I'm glad you appreciate the design," Dunbar said. The deck seemed to thud beneath his boots as the massive man walked into the shop. He had been in and out of engineering several times that day, assisting Geordi and his team with their work on the reactor core. Geordi had learned that Dunbar was a good engineer; show him an unfamiliar piece of equipment, explain its operations, and the Heran could immediately handle it like an old pro. He also looked fully recovered from his injuries. "I see you've finished on schedule," he said to Geordi.

"I said I would," Geordi told him, and nodded toward Gakor. "Having a good team helps."

"Yes, it would make up for your deficiencies," Dunbar said.

Geordi faced him. "What deficiencies?"

"Just the obvious one," Dunbar said. "Or two."

"You mean my being blind?" Geordi grimaced at his own angry tone. Ordinarily he would have let Dunbar's comment pass, but the man rubbed him the wrong way.

Well, too late now, he thought in self-annoyance. "None so blind as they who will not see," he muttered.

"Including those who won't see what careless breeding does to humanity?" Dunbar asked. "Messing up the gene pool, driving us to ruin—"

"What happened to me was bad luck," Geordi said. "And if you're going to criticize what my parents did—"

"I am," Dunbar said, "because I know what people like them did to my world. They brought all sorts of filthy mutations from Earth. After a few generations that nearly destroyed us."

"I hear that mutations help a species evolve," Gakor said. He squinted myopically at the Heran. "In fact, there's evidence that weakening the senses forces the brain to develop as an aid to survival. Contrariwise, isn't it true that Terran owls and eagles have astounding vision, yet Terrans make disparaging comments about 'birdbrains'?"

Dunbar looked down his nose at the Tellarite. "A foolish argument, but about what I'd expect from something that can barely walk upright."

Gakor was opening his mouth to retort—or continue the argument—when Dr. Par'mit'kon entered the shop. His lidless yellow eyes seemed to take in the entire compartment at once. "Any humans in here?" the Saurian physician asked, oblivious to the tension.

"Just me and our guest," Geordi said, glad for a reason to end the argument. "What's up?"

"We've got a minor epidemic on our hands," Par'mit'kon said. He ran a tricorder over Geordi, then held it close to his fishlike face to read it. "You're clean. I'll just immunize you."

"What is the nature of the epidemic?" Dunbar asked.

"It's some sort of creeping crud," the reptilian doctor explained as he gave Geordi an injection. "It's human-specific and it spreads fast."

Dunbar looked amused. "Does this happen often?"

"Not on this ship, pal," Par'mit'kon said. He turned to

Dunbar and started to scan him—and yelped as Dunbar slapped the tricorder from his hands. "Hey!"

"I had enough of your probing in that obscenity of a sickbay," he said.

"You'll take more of it," Par'mit'kon said. He picked up his tricorder. "I'm the doctor here, pal."

"Where I come from—" Dunbar began.

"—ain't the *Enterprise,*" Par'mit'kon finished.

Dunbar glowered at Geordi and Gakor as he was scanned. "Do you have to do that in front of people?" he demanded. "As though I were a sick weakling?"

"Swallow your embarrassment," Par'mit'kon grumbled, and finished his scan. "Healthy as a snake. In fact, I can't find a single bug in you, except for the usual intestinal flora." He sounded puzzled. "And your immune system is going like a reactor. I've never seen anything like it, and I don't see how we missed it on the sickbay instruments. I'm tempted to drag you back into sickbay—"

"Don't waste my time," Dunbar said.

"—but I can resist the temptation." The doctor traded his tricorder for a hypospray. "Stick out your arm and say 'ah.' Unless you want to get sick?"

"How about me?" Gakor asked as the doctor immunized the Heran.

"Don't worry," Par'mit'kon said, "you're naturally immune. It has to do with alien metabolisms, or living right, or something. I never was any good with mammalian physiology," he added, giving Dunbar a cold glance. "But I'd sure like to know why you're so healthy."

"Good health is common on Hera," Dunbar said. "I never give it much thought."

"Maybe you should." The doctor got his tricorder out again. "I'd like more thorough readings. You're a textbook case of perfect health."

"Then I should hardly matter to a doctor, should I?" Dunbar said. He strode out of the shop before Par'mit'kon could scan him again.

"That egg stealer really scorches my scales," the reptilian doctor griped. He gestured with his tricorder. "And we didn't get these readings on him in sickbay."

"They're really weird, huh?" Geordi asked.

Par'mit'kon dipped his head in agreement. "They're textbook-perfect. Seeing them in real life is about as likely as getting a royal flush when Riker is dealing the cards."

"Maybe something's wrong with your tricorder," Geordi said. "Get Reg Barclay to check it. Gakor, let's get this core installed." Par'mit'kon left, and Gakor produced a set of antigrav clamps and attached them to the core. Geordi grasped a handle and pulled the sphere free of the workstand. "Transporter room," Geordi said.

"Yeah." Gakor snuffled as they guided the unit out of the shop. "What's with that Dunbar, anyway?"

"His planet was colonized by people who believed in eugenics," Geordi said. "That's this weird idea some people had for improving the species. You take the 'best' people—which usually means people who agree with you—and eliminate everyone else from the gene pool."

" 'Eliminate'?" Gakor repeated. He shuddered as Geordi drew a finger across his throat like a knife. "Yech. So why'd he freak out when the doctor scanned him?"

"If you want my guess, he thinks that only 'inferior' people get sick," Geordi said. "Scanning him implied he could get sick, which must come across as an insult on Hera. Although I'll tell you, I don't intend to visit the place and check out my guesses."

"Can't blame you," Gakor said. He patted the reactor core. "You know, for somebody who's dependent on the help of 'inferior beings,' he's got a big mouth."

Geordi nodded. "Well, that kind of arrogance fits with eugenicists. He wouldn't think our feelings matter."

They carried the warp core into the nearest transporter room, and a moment later they materialized inside the *Temenus*'s engine compartment. Without an environment suit's helmet to obscure his vision Geordi could see perfectly. His VISOR picked up a variety of sights that organic eyes would have missed. Computer pulses chased one another through circuit guides, and the antigrav plates in the deck polarized the light reflected by the floor. The coolant lines had been repaired so expertly that he could barely spot the weld points—good, solid work, he noted in approval. His engineering team might have loathed the Herans, but they hadn't let their emotions interfere with their work.

Geordi and Gakor opened the reactor shell and peered into it. "Impressive," Gakor admitted. "Their designers were really on the ball."

"We could learn a few things from them," Geordi agreed. The design looked simple, but Geordi was a-mazed by the sophisticated layout of the superconducting coils. The coils that generated the containment field were layered to interact with one another, automatically varying their field strength as the reactor's power levels rose and fell. It would be impossible to push the reactor into an overload; the rising magnetic fields would automatically pinch off the flow of ionized antimatter into the dilithium crystals as the reactor approached the danger level. "Well, let's get to work."

The installation was halfway finished when Worf materialized in the compartment. Geordi's VISOR showed a familiar infrared pattern rippling across the Klingon's face and wrinkled scalp. He was like a hunter stalking his prey, or a detective ferreting out clues. "Welcome to the scene of the crime," Geordi said.

Worf gave a hopeful grunt. "You have found evidence?"

Geordi chuckled. "I was just making friendly conversation. Are the Herans giving you trouble?"

"They are not giving me information," Worf said.

"You're not the only one with that complaint," Geordi said. "Dr. Par'mit'kon got some odd readings on Dunbar. Dunbar got testy and refused to let him take any more readings."

Worf grunted and looked at the reactor core. "Something is wrong with this unit," he declared.

"Impossible!" Gakor snapped. "We've spent all day on this thing. It's perfect! It's brilliant! It's—"

Worf snarled at him.

"—going to need more work," Gakor finished quickly.

Geordi saw what the Klingon wanted: time. "How long will it take us to fix things?" Geordi asked in resignation.

"As I am not an engineer, I cannot say," Worf answered. He touched his combadge. "Worf to *Enterprise*. One to beam back."

Chapter Six

THE AFTERMATH OF THE INFECTION left Captain Picard looking fatigued, but Deanna Troi sensed that he was as alert as ever. He watched Gustav Blaisdell as the Heran sat down with Picard, Worf and Deanna in Picard's ready room. Blaisdell's eyes scanned the office, and Deanna realized he was looking for clues to Picard's personality. The office was furnished in an austere style, and its most prominent decorations were a model of Picard's old ship, the *Stargazer,* and a painting of the *Enterprise.* To anyone who did not know Jean-Luc Picard, those clues would have suggested he was an unimaginative martinet.

Deanna knew better. The room's stark style helped the captain to concentrate. The model of his old ship, which he had lost to an unprovoked Ferengi attack, reminded him that a starship commander carried a heavy burden of responsibility; the painting only emphasized the point. Like a mirror, the room was far simpler than the mind it reflected.

"We've a great deal to discuss, Captain," Picard said

to Blaisdell. "You can understand that I'm curious about the sabotage on your ship."

"Of course," Blaisdell said, turning his attention to Picard. "A crime has been committed in Federation space, although I'd like to point out that my government claims exclusive jurisdiction over its ships."

"I don't dispute that claim," Picard said, "but surely it's to our mutual advantage to find the perpetrators."

"Yes," Blaisdell said. Deanna sensed his reluctance to speak. He had a brilliant, well-controlled mind. His emotions gave her a sensation that somehow made her think of Astrid Kemal, and she sensed that he was planning strategies to avoid revealing any facts. That seemed connected to an odd sense of guilt, as though he were somehow failing in a vital duty. "I'm sure your people have inspected the *Temenus*," the Heran went on. "What have you found?"

"Little," Worf said. "Each bomb used five grams of parmaline, sealed in tritanium discs and hidden within different control units."

"All of which would make them virtually undetectable," Picard said. "Does this suggest anything to you, Captain?"

Blaisdell shrugged. "Parmaline is a standard industrial explosive," he said. "Anyone can obtain it."

"You were on a mission to obtain Romulan codes," Worf said. "This would benefit your people. Why would anyone sabotage your ship?"

"Politics," Blaisdell said. "All of our leaders want to defeat the Romulans, but each of them wants to be the hero who does it. Some of them don't want to see their rivals succeed—but a Klingon doesn't need to hear about treachery from me."

Worf bridled at that, but Deanna saw that the Klingon's glower did not intimidate the Heran. Picard had frowned at Blaisdell's mocking tone, but he let the comment pass. "So you were sacrificed as a pawn in a power struggle," the captain said.

"I think so," Blaisdell conceded. "But I'd rather not discuss our politics in front of a Betazoid."

"Then let us discuss Khortasi," Worf said. "You claimed to have spoken with him recently, yet he died over six weeks ago. How do you explain this?"

"Perhaps the man I spoke to lied about his identity," Blaisdell said with a shrug. "Do you expect me to discuss my government's business with outsiders?"

"I expect to uncover the truth," Worf said.

"You?" Blaisdell asked. He rose to his feet and stared down at Worf. "I think not. Captain Picard, do you have any *relevant* questions for me? If not, I'd like to oversee the repair of my ship."

"I have a certain curiosity," Picard said. "If the Romulans are a problem, why doesn't Hera ask the Federation for help?"

"We prefer to look after ourselves," Blaisdell said. "In any case, Hera is outside Federation territory, in a sparsely settled section of space. You'd have no reason to send us help."

"The Federation plans to colonize this region," Picard said. "Our presence in this region will grow. So will our interest in defending it."

"But not our interest in working with you," Blaisdell said. "If you are quite through, I'll leave now."

"By all means." Picard gestured at the door. "But once your ship is ready, you will not continue to Aldebaran."

"As you wish." Blaisdell gave Picard a sardonic nod and left the ready room.

Picard rubbed his chin in thought as he stared at the door. Blaisdell was rude, and frankly, the captain was glad to see him leave, but that very rudeness made him feel suspicious. "I wonder what he's really up to?" he asked.

"Nothing honorable," Worf said at once. "But we have all the time we need to investigate him. Commander La Forge is having trouble repairing the *Temenus*."

"That's quite convenient," Picard said in amusement. "Counselor Troi, what do you have to say?"

"Captain Blaisdell knows the exact motive behind the sabotage," Deanna said, "and it wasn't a move in a power struggle. I also had the impression that he was probing us for information, although I can't say if he learned anything. His mental control is impressive."

"I wish I knew what he wanted to learn," Picard said.

"Captain, there's something else," Deanna added. "I don't sense that Blaisdell is this abrasive by nature. I believe that what we just saw was an act put on for our benefit. He's at heart a sociable man, but he definitely does not want contact with us. When he spoke I had the feeling he was deliberately choosing simple words, as though he regards us as just barely able to understand him."

"Hera was founded by eugenicists," Worf noted.

"So he may regard himself as the superior product of selective breeding," Picard said in distaste. "It's amazing how that madness has persisted."

"That's not it, Captain," Deanna said. His words somehow touched off an intuitive insight into the Heran. "He's doing his best to behave as *we* would expect a eugenicist to behave—monumentally arrogant. He's difficult to read, but the act doesn't match his personality. He's actually embarrassed to behave this way."

"Clever," Worf rumbled. "This act would discourage any investigation."

"Indeed," Picard mused. "Because we already think we know what he is, we wouldn't pursue an investigation. Mr. Worf, the fact that he's hiding something from us strikes me as a cause for concern. See if you can find out what he's hiding." He stood up, signaling the end of the discussion.

Worf followed Deanna out of the ready room and onto the bridge. "Counselor," he said quietly, "I require your advice."

"Of course, Worf," Deanna said. She went to his post with him. "Are you still wondering about Dr. Kemal?"

Worf shook his head. "The problem is K'Sah. Have you met him?"

"No," Deanna said. "He's the Pa'uyk exchange officer, isn't he? I think he's only been on board for a week."

"And I do not know how he has survived that long," Worf said. "His behavior is unacceptable."

"Do you mean that he's rude and combative?" Deanna asked.

Worf grunted. "You've heard of him."

"He has quite a reputation." She managed not to laugh; the problem was obvious. Explaining it to Worf promised to be fun. "Where is he?"

"He is confined to his quarters," Worf said.

"Let's see him," Deanna said, and led Worf into the turbolift. "Deck eight?" she asked Worf.

"Deck eight, section three," he said, and the turbolift started down the shaft.

Deanna looked up at Worf. "I spoke with Dr. Kemal," she said. "Can you tell me anything about her?"

"Commander La Forge has developed an interest in her," he said. "He says that she has a delightful sense of"—he grimaced in distaste—"humor."

"And you disapprove?"

"Humor," Worf growled. Deanna had heard Worf claim there was nothing really wrong with the human sense of humor, but she knew Worf's idea of humor had different standards. To a Klingon, "die laughing" was not a mere figure of speech.

"I'll talk with Geordi when I get the chance," Deanna said as the turbolift stopped. "But there's something troubling Astrid, and I had hoped she might have said something to you."

Worf grunted as they left the elevator. "She broke one of K'Sah's hands by accident."

"I see," Deanna said, more to herself than to Worf. "That would upset most humans . . . but it doesn't explain the intensity of her feelings."

K'Sah's cabin was near the lift station, and as Deanna and Worf entered it Deanna noted that its decor was martial but not orderly. Several clumsy-looking swords and clubs hung on the walls. A pair of throwing knives jutted from a wooden target. Dirty, wrinkled uniforms were scattered here and there. A fetid stench had defeated the ship's air purifiers. For somebody who had been here only a week, Deanna reflected, K'Sah had generated a remarkable amount of chaos.

An egg-shaped mass that looked like a two-meter-wide lump of papier-mâché occupied the floor space that had once held a bed. Deanna sensed that K'Sah lay inside it, and then she let out a startled yelp as the Pa'uyk burst out of it as though attacking prey that had wandered too close to his lair. You've got to expect things like this from somebody who evolved from a trap-door spider, she reminded herself, but as he stood up, she sensed that he had enjoyed scaring her.

K'Sah snapped his jagged mandibles together as he looked at Deanna. "A Betazoid," he grumbled. "That's a step down from humans."

Deanna planted her hands on her hips as she glared at him. "If we didn't have laws about garbage disposal, you evolutionary backslider, I'd shove you out the nearest airlock," she said in mock sternness.

"Mouthy, aren't you?" K'Sah said. He flexed his four arms as if to show off the spikes protruding through the coarse fur. "Maybe I'll do something about you later."

Deanna snorted in derision. "I've got a better idea, you overstuffed moron. Let's find a cliff and play lemmings. You can go first."

"What is going on?" Worf demanded. "Counselor—"

"Is he always this rude?" K'Sah asked Deanna.

"Put a lid on it." Deanna turned to Worf, who was almost beside himself in confusion. He had never known the aristocratic Betazoid to speak rudely with anyone, no matter what the provocation. "I can tell you the problem, Worf," Deanna said, smiling despite herself. "Ensign K'Sah unconsciously expects everyone to act like a Pa'uyk, and what we call 'bad manners' are normal behavior among them."

"Then I am surprised that any Pa'uyk live to adulthood," Worf said.

"No, there's a good reason for the way they act." Deanna looked at K'Sah, who was backing into his lair. "We're sitting down, pinhead. Have you got a problem with that?"

K'Sah waved a hand. "I can disinfect the chairs later."

"You know about sanitation? I'm astounded." Deanna sat down and gestured for Worf to take a chair. "Pa'uyk aren't rude, Worf," she said. "They challenge one another with insults to prove their good intentions. It's a substitute for combat."

"This makes no sense," Worf said. "Insults lead to battle."

"Among most species, yes, they do," Deanna said. "But among Pa'uyk, 'rudeness' serves the same purpose as smiling does among humans. It's a gesture that helps make society run smoothly."

"Wait," K'Sah said in confusion. He was halfway into his lair, and its trapdoor rested on his head like a rumpled helmet. "You mean it's normal for humans to grin like idiots all the time?"

"And Betazoids," Deanna said sharply, "so watch it, you Romulan swamp-sucker. Ensign, most humanoids evolved from different types of tribal apes, and one of the things parallel evolution gave us in common is the need to feel like we belong to a group, a 'tribe.' We feel uncomfortable when we're on the outside; the smiling reassures us that we're still accepted."

"I see," K'Sah said. One of his shaggy forearms brushed at his faceted eyes, somehow giving the impression that he was thinking hard. "I always figured—that damned, eternal smiling makes you look like you're up to something."

"What has this to do with Pa'uyk?" Worf demanded.

"It's something they have in common with Klingons," Deanna said. "Both of your peoples are highly warlike and aggressive. Neither of you have the sort of social instincts that humans inherited from their evolutionary ancestors, so your people had to find other ways to make a society work—ways that use your instincts."

"How about that, Wart?" K'Sah asked. Despite his sneering tone Deanna could sense his interest. "We're brothers under the skin."

"You're more like distant cousins," Deanna said, sensing Worf's disgust with the comparison. "Extremely distant cousins, several times removed. Klingon society uses the concepts of honor and courage to denote appropriate times for combat. Worf, I'm sure you can think of circumstances in which you'd want to fight, but it would be dishonorable to do so."

"There is at least one such circumstance," Worf said, looking pointedly at K'Sah.

K'Sah snorted. "Maybe we can find time for something later on, you *toDSaH.*"

"And that's how Pa'uyk keep from fighting, Worf," Deanna said, while Worf growled at the Klingon obscenity. "They channel their aggression into less dangerous avenues, such as insults, threats and gambling. It's a form of diplomacy; when they're talking, they're not killing one another. It works quite well for them."

Worf growled as he mulled that over. "I cannot have one of my ensigns insulting everyone," he said.

"Of course not," Deanna said. She wondered if K'Sah had met the captain yet—no, almost certainly not. "But there are several things we can try here. Perhaps you and the security staff can accommodate yourselves to Ensign K'Sah's behavior and return his insults; make a game of it. The rest of the time, Ensign K'Sah, *you* could restrain your behavior—"

"What if I don't want to?" he asked.

"Then I will ask Dr. Kemal to arm wrestle with you," Worf said.

"Spend some time on the holodeck, dimwit," Deanna suggested. "Even a flea-brained mud-wader like you should be able to set up a program that lets you release your feelings."

K'Sah nodded dubiously. "Hijack a starship, knife a

few officers, eat a Klingon—" He scratched his carapace. "It can't hurt to try."

"And try to avoid people who don't understand Pa'uyk behavior," Deanna said, standing up. "By the way, Worf, the Pa'uyk attitude toward rules is that they're meant to be broken. Keep that in mind when you and K'Sah make your arrangements."

"Killjoy," K'Sah muttered as Deanna headed for the door. "Hey, Worf, what's this 'honor' thing she was babbling about?"

Deanna sighed as the door closed behind her. Oddly enough, K'Sah seemed genuinely interested in learning how Worf defined honor . . . but she wondered if the Pa'uyk would live long enough to hear the answer.

After he dealt with K'Sah, Worf went to his quarters and worked on the computer. It was late at night when he finished his investigation of the Herans. He had found nothing to either confirm or deny his suspicions, and the lack of evidence was in itself suspicious. An investigation could always find something.

What little he did have seemed disconnected. First, there were the contradictory readings on Dunbar. The sickbay instruments said he was a normal human, while Par'mit'kon's tricorder said he was impossibly healthy and strong. Barclay, a superb engineer despite his inherent nervousness, had inspected all the instruments involved and swore they were functioning as they should.

Second, there were the records on Hera. They made Hera sound like a planet settled by obsessed fools. Herans seldom left their world, discouraged visitors, and had no official contact with the rest of humanity. That near-total lack of outside contact made Worf suspect that they had a secret to keep, a notion that agreed with Deanna Troi's observations.

Third, there was their size. Dunbar and Blaisdell were both two meters tall and weighed over a hundred kilos. The radiation-charred bodies Dr. Crusher had removed from the *Temenus* suggested that the rest of the crew had been equally big. While such size was not unknown among humans—Kemal came to mind, and Riker was not much smaller—it was improbable that everyone in such a small group would be so large. It was as though the Herans had been mass-produced.

Or modified . . . Selective breeding was an inefficient, unreliable process; Khan Singh's creators had depended as much on luck as science for their results, and it seemed improbable that Hera's founders could have duplicated their fortunes. But there were other, better ways to redesign a species. Genetic engineering came to mind. Perhaps that had something to do with whatever secret the Herans were hiding.

The possibility bore investigation. The Klingon began a computer search for links between Hera and genetic research.

Central Security had delayed her execution, which could only mean that they had a reason to keep her alive. Marla Sukhoi could not imagine what that reason might be. She did not think she was of any further use to Central.

Marla lay on her cell's cot and wondered what would happen to her children. When she and her husband had decided to move against Unity and the *Temenus* they had quietly arranged for her brother and his wife to take care of them, so their physical welfare was no problem. But the loss of their parents would devastate them, and Central Security would always suspect them of disloyalty.

And she still did not know if they had destroyed the *Temenus*. All of their sacrifices might have been for nothing.

She tried to distract herself by reviewing her interrogation. The question about the originator file intrigued her. The implication had been that something in the file would change her attitude toward the originators, and by extension, toward the rest of the primals. All things considered, that was about as likely as changing her attitude toward breathing. Even if it were possible to ignore what the originators had done to Hera, no one could ignore the constant primal attacks, or their well-documented hatred of normal people such as herself.

And why shouldn't we hate the originators? Marla asked herself. The structure of her brain might keep her from becoming swamped by raw emotions, but she could still maintain a detached, intellectual hatred of their evil. The history books told the story well: how the genetic engineers had callously developed a race of expendable superhuman weapons, and then attempted to make additional, secret modifications to their handiwork, so that the new generation of Herans would be utterly loyal to their creators. Central Security had exposed the scientists before they could complete their plot, and the Modality had executed them for attempted treason. Bad enough to be a living weapon, Marla thought, but to be bred for slavery as well—

The lights went out and the buzz of the force fields ended. Suddenly alert, Marla sat up on her cot and listened. She heard the burr of a disrupter cutting through rock and metal. It swiftly grew louder.

One wall of her cell collapsed and there was light. As she backed away from the opening a foot shoved several blocks of rubble out of the way and two people entered the cell. "Marla Sukhoi?" one asked. He was young, perhaps twelve or thirteen years old. "Can you travel?"

"Yes," she said. Marla resisted the urge to ask questions. If she was not being rescued she would find out soon enough, and it would make no difference in her situation.

"Good," the boy's companion said. The man handed her a sonic stunner and went to the door. He drew something from a coat pocket and tossed it into the hallway, and eerie blue light crackled outside the door. Marla felt a tingling from the stun bombs. "Come on," the man said after the glow faded. "Sukhoi, stay between us."

"Where are we going?" Marla asked.

"To the tube station," the man said. "Do you know the way?"

She recalled the path she had taken, from the station to the interrogation room to this cell. "Yes. Let's go."

The lights were out all through the complex. Finding her way by memory was no problem, but at each corridor intersection and stairwell the man stopped to pitch another stun bomb. Their fringe effects grated on her nerves, and several times Marla and her rescuers stumbled over the unconscious bodies of security agents in the dark. Men and women called out orders and reports in the darkness around them.

There was light when the trio emerged into the tube station. The white glare came from the open door of a capsule, and it showed a pair of guards standing alongside its entrance. They reached for their weapons as Marla and her rescuers walked into the station. With their own weapons already drawn, Marla and her rescuers held the advantage. The two men tumbled to the floor and the trio climbed into the capsule.

The man chuckled. "Not bad for somebody who flunked basic aggression."

The boy looked defensive. "I passed it the second time."

"I was talking about me, nephew."

"Oh." The boy placed an electronic pad over the control unit in the capsule's front. After a moment the door slid shut and the capsule rushed into the tubeways. "They won't catch us now," he said. "We're masked from the rest of the transit system."

"Possibly." The man put his stunner into a jacket pocket and held out his hand. Marla shook it. He was red-haired and handsome, and old enough to be one of the firstborn, the first generation of gengineered Herans. "I'm Selig Thorn. That's my nephew Dallas."

Marla didn't recognize the names. "You're radicals?" she asked.

He nodded. "We've been called that."

"Did you know my husband?" She sat down on a

capsule seat. "Did he belong to your organization?" Lee had never mentioned belonging to any political organization, but after her experience with the interrogators she still felt disoriented.

"No," Selig told her. He sat down facing her. "We didn't learn about him until after Central arrested you. If it's any comfort, he destroyed the *Temenus*. At least it didn't make its last scheduled report."

"I see." Marla slumped in her seat. She had almost too much to think about now, but all that mattered was the success. There would be nothing to provoke the primals now; they would not come flooding down from the sky. Whatever else happened, her children would be safe.

Chapter Seven

BLAISDELL AND DUNBAR were in Engineering, watching Geordi La Forge as he tinkered with the reactor core. Both men had been harrying Geordi with sharp questions about the core's failure, and they'd come close to tripping him up. They obviously realized there was nothing wrong with the core. Astrid watched them from the opening of a crawlway, feeling guilty as she spied on them. The two men were a threat to the *Enterprise,* and she should tell someone everything she knew about Hera. Everyone assumed they were normal humans, and that assumption could get somebody killed. She *should* tell—

She looked at her hand, which had raised halfway to her comm badge. Tell, and she would get herself and her parents in trouble. Their lives wouldn't be worth a redshifted photon. She forced her hand down.

Blaisdell and Dunbar walked out of Engineering. Astrid slid back into the crawlway and emerged a few minutes later in a corridor. She queried the computer, which told her that the two men had gone to Ten-

Forward. Getting lunch, she thought. That seemed harmless enough.

Astrid went to the brig, where Ensign Kellog was on duty. Astrid had offered to upgrade the brig's security software, and Worf had jumped at the chance to improve his security tools—although the security-conscious Klingon had made her wait while he obtained permission for a non-Federation citizen to work in a classified area. Captain Picard had granted approval almost at once; he evidently trusted her to be honest . . . a thought that stirred her sense of guilt.

Astrid chatted with Kellog as she reorganized the programming. Not a bad job, she thought, but it had shortcomings that could have given a determined person a means of escape. She fixed them with an almost absentminded effort. Astrid was more interested in what Kellog had to say about Geordi La Forge. He seemed . . . nice, she thought. Easy to like; not at all what her parents had told her to expect in an old human. And he had seemed vaguely repelled by Riker's comments about the Khans and *homo arrogans*. She wished she could take the chance to know him better. Except that would mean lowering her guard, and if he found out what she was, he wouldn't want anything to do with her. Especially because she had been lying to him, and his friends, by concealing what she was.

Astrid finished her work, left the brig and rode the turbolift up to deck ten. She wanted to take another look at these two men, just to see what they were like. Aside from her parents, she had not seen another Heran since leaving her homeworld, and the need to see somebody like herself was like a hunger. With a little luck she could find an excuse to talk with them. The Herans couldn't get any more suspicious than they were now, and maybe it would turn out that they weren't up to something.

"Worf, we've got a problem," Riker's voice said over the turbolift intercom. "Report to your quarters."

"On my way." Worf had been going to Ten-Forward to

confront Blaisdell and Dunbar. Now he diverted the elevator to the turbolift station nearest his quarters. He hoped this "problem" would not delay him long. He was looking forward to the chance to face the Herans, and possibly fight them.

Worf walked into his quarters and reached for his phaser, a reflex touched off by the wrongness: Riker was not here. Worf's mind caught up with his reflexes and told him he had walked into a trap, and that was when something clamped on to his shoulder. As the door slid shut behind him the Klingon saw Dunbar standing beside the door frame, his face impassive as he held Worf by the shoulder. Worf snarled at the Heran and drew his phaser.

Worf barely saw what happened. As he raised his weapon Dunbar's free hand flicked out, plucked the phaser from his grip and dropped it. As Worf struggled Dunbar tightened his grip on the Klingon's shoulder and lifted him off the floor. Worf snarled and struggled to get free, but Dunbar's hand held him like a steel vise, and the man did not even flinch when Worf kicked him in the kneecap.

Dunbar raised his tricorder to Worf's face. Sensing that the device was a weapon, Worf grabbed the man by the wrist and tried to push his arm back. For all the good that did he might as well have tried to stop a planet in its rush through space. Lights winked on the tricorder as Dunbar held it against the Klingon's face.

Dunbar carried Worf across the room. "Damn it all," he muttered, and Worf heard regret in his voice. "If it matters, Klingon, I wish I didn't have to do this."

Worf was still holding Dunbar's wrist. Now his fingers grew numb and slid away from the man's arm. He felt hot and dizzy. When Dunbar dumped him on the floor it was all Worf could do to roll onto his side. His limbs would not answer when he tried to stand. He began to shiver and growl with fever. As though in a dream he saw the Heran take his wooden statuette of the Klingon hero

Kahless, break it and hold his tricorder to it. Then Worf knew nothing.

Astrid walked into Ten-Forward, saw Blaisdell sitting alone at his table, and stepped back into the corridor. She reviewed her glimpse of the lounge, confirming that Dunbar wasn't there. "Computer," she whispered, after the lounge door had slid shut behind her. "Where's Dunbar?"

"Vlad Dunbar is in Ten-Forward," the computer answered.

That obvious impossibility could mean only one thing. "Kemal to Kellog," she said as she hurried toward the nearest turbolift. "The Herans have tampered with the computer."

"You're sure?" Kellog answered.

"Yes. I'll explain later. Get someone down to Ten-Forward to watch Blaisdell. Get somebody else to look for Dunbar; he isn't in Ten-Forward, as the computer says. Kemal to Worf. Kemal to Worf."

There was no answer, and she felt an urgent certainty that Dunbar was connected to Worf's silence. But how was she supposed to find Dunbar? She couldn't search the entire ship, and she couldn't trust the computer—

Maybe she could. "Access medical computer," she said as she entered the turbolift. "Override code Kemal two, two, eight, nine. Locate Vlad Dunbar."

"Vlad Dunbar is in deck seven, section fifteen," the machine answered.

Deck seven, section fifteen, was a curving passage lined on both sides with doorways. Astrid saw no one here now. She queried the medical computer again, and it told her that Dunbar was in Worf's quarters.

She nodded absently at that. Dunbar must have been preparing to kill Worf. "Kemal to Worf," she said, and again received no answer. "Computer, locate Lieutenant Worf."

"Lieutenant Worf is in his quarters."

Astrid went to Worf's door. The sliding panel was supposed to be soundproof, but she could hear through it: several thumps, a muffled growl that had to be Worf, a wooden snap. "Open door," she said. "Override code Kemal two, two, eight, nine."

"Access denied," the computer said.

Arguing with the computer was useless. She kicked the center of the door, then kicked again, knocking it out of its guide slots. She grasped its exposed edge and pulled it free.

Dunbar was kneeling over Worf while he worked with a tricorder, and he looked up as Astrid forced her way into the room. Worf was alive, although unconscious; Astrid could hear his labored breathing and the thudding of his eight-chambered heart as he lay on the deck. A cracked wooden statue lay beside him. Dunbar saw her and reached for Worf's phaser. Astrid decided she would have to fight him, and at once she hurled herself at Dunbar.

Dunbar forgot about the phaser and sprang at her. She danced out of his way. Dunbar looked surprised as his first lunge missed her, but he spun around and charged her again. This time he slammed into her and they went sprawling on the carpet. Dunbar rose to his knees and sent a fist crashing into her side. Astrid grunted at the impact, but Dunbar's position had made it impossible for him to use his full strength and she was not seriously hurt. Astrid grabbed his wrist with both hands and held on, squeezing as hard as she could. She twisted the arm, forcing Dunbar down onto the floor.

Dunbar swung with his free arm, but instead of delivering another blow his hand clawed at the floor. Astrid saw him grasp the phaser. She twisted around on the floor, still clutching his wrist as she planted her feet against the side of his chest, while he set the weapon to its most powerful level and tried to aim at her. She kicked as hard as she could and felt his ribs snap under the impact. She kicked a second time and Dunbar went limp. Astrid held on to his wrist until the lack of a pulse assured her that she had killed him.

She crawled over to Worf, who had regained consciousness. His face was gray and sweaty. "It's all right," Astrid told him. "He's dead."

Worf answered with a rasping snarl. His eyes had an unfocused look. Astrid touched his forehead and realized he had a high fever. "Transporter room, medical emergency," she called, picking up his phaser. "Two to sickbay."

The transporter engulfed Astrid and Worf and put them in the sickbay. Astrid forced down the fear she felt at her presence *here* as she scooped up the man and put him on the nearest biobed. "He's sick," Astrid said as Dr. Crusher came out of her office. Her chest hurt from where Dunbar had hit her; she ignored the knifing pain.

Crusher ran a scanner over Worf, then blinked in amazement at the readings. "Where in hell did he get *vorag* fever?" she demanded.

"The Herans," Astrid said. Despite herself she took a step back from the doctor and her anger. She felt more afraid now than she had while fighting Dunbar. "Dunbar attacked him. I killed him," she added bleakly. The realization settled on her soul like a block of neutronium. She had killed, as efficiently and unthinkingly as any weapon.

Crusher ignored her. She produced a hypospray and injected Worf. "Thank God the transporter biofilters eliminated the virus. That's all that kept the infection from killing him. As it is, it's going to be touch and go." Worf snarled quietly as the doctor worked over him.

Astrid watched the man stir. She could understand why the Herans would want to kill Worf, but why had they used a biological weapon? After a startled second that thought made everything fall into place; the answer became so obvious she wondered how anyone could have missed it—and what better way was there to conquer the galaxy? "The Herans caused that epidemic," she said.

"Really?" Crusher asked as she worked on Worf. "Even assuming they could transport a virus aboard this ship, why would they want to make half the crew slightly ill for a few hours?"

"You haven't analyzed the genetic material in the virus, have you?" Astrid asked.

"No, I haven't had the time."

"I suggest that you analyze it, Doctor," Astrid said. "Then compare it with Heran DNA, normal human DNA, and DNA from people who had the fever."

Crusher looked up from Worf, who was beginning to stir. "What am I supposed to look for?"

"The virus was a genetic-engineering tool," Astrid said. "They were trying to give Heran genes to old—to normal humans, so we'd pass them on to your, uh, our offspring."

"What's so special about Heran genes?" Crusher asked.

"Run the tests, Doctor," Astrid said. She felt her nerve slipping. "You'll be surprised."

The conference began six hours after Picard learned of the killing. His command staff seemed unsettled as they took their seats in the conference room. Worf still glowered with anger and shame, which was to be expected; he had been no match for Dunbar in hand-to-hand combat. Riker, Deanna, Geordi and Crusher seemed distressed and bewildered in various degrees. Data looked perplexed, as though faced with a situation beyond his comprehension.

Picard called the meeting to order. "Dr. Crusher, is my crew in any immediate danger?" he asked.

"No, sir," she said. "The *vorag* spores and the virus have been eradicated. Lieutenant Worf is fit for duty, and the rest of the crew's physical health is excellent. But over four hundred people, half of the ship's human complement, had the plague. I expect psychological problems."

"We'll discuss that in due course," Picard said. "Mr. La Forge, what about the computer system?"

"It's been tampered with—by a genius," Geordi said. "I ran a diagnostic and I just barely found evidence of several programs. They erased themselves without a trace while I watched. At least the computer is clean now. And now we know why the sickbay instruments registered the Herans as normal humans, while Dr. Par'mit'kon got some wild readings on his tricorder. One of the items in Blaisdell's kit let him insert false data into Dr. Crusher's instruments, as long as he was within a few meters of them. He wasn't around to do that when Par'mit'kon checked Dunbar in Engineering."

"Very well," Picard said. "Mr. Worf, have you any idea of how the Herans introduced these diseases on to the *Enterprise?*"

The Klingon nodded. "Commander Data and I have examined Dunbar's 'tricorder.' It was more than a tricorder. The device destroyed itself, but not before we proved that it could construct microorganisms atom by atom—"

"Test-tube life?" Crusher asked. "No one has ever synthesized a living organism from the ground up."

"The evidence proves that the Herans can do so," Data said.

"It seems the Herans make very good use of their biological skills," Picard said. "Mr. Worf, their attempt to murder you implies that they believed you were about to expose a secret."

"It does," Worf agreed. "I was investigating Hera and its possible link to genetic engineering, and it is clear now that they were monitoring my computer activity. They must have decided to eliminate me before I could uncover their plans."

"Your death from *vorag* would have made us suspicious as hell," Riker said.

Worf shook his head. *"Vorag* spores are sometimes found in *khrolat* wood, and my statue of Kahless was made of *khrolat*. Dunbar broke the carving and poisoned its inner grain. My death would have seemed a bizarre accident."

"Why was he waiting in your room?" Riker wondered. "It seems like a perfect set-up without his presence."

"Vorag is not instantly fatal," Worf said. "I might have reached the sickbay before I could die. Dunbar—" Picard saw the shame on his face as he glowered at the tabletop. "I fought Dunbar to no avail. I was like a child in his grip."

"Thank you, Mr. Worf," Picard said. "It's vital that we know their abilities. You will find ways to fight them." He saw Worf straighten in his chair at the praise. "Did your computer search uncover anything about the Herans?"

The Klingon shook his head. "They appear to be nothing more than misguided cultists."

"Well, they're not," Crusher said. "I've run a few tests on the surviving Herans, and the results are startling. Their strength and stamina are incredible. Their immune systems are perfect. Their metabolism is highly efficient. Reflexes, bone strength, muscle tone—Worf, you needn't feel ashamed. They're more like fighting machines than people."

A sudden uneasiness swept over the captain.

"We should all bear in mind that her actions in this matter have been commendable," Picard said. "Doctor, can you verify her statement that this virus was a genetic-engineering tool?"

"Yes," she said. "Computer, display the viral RNA map."

Picard and the others turned their seats to look at the wall display. Crusher got up and walked over to it. "This shows the layout of the genetic material inside the virus.

The first point to note is that there is twice as much material here as is normal in a virus. The second point is the behavior of the virus in an infected body. Except under one circumstance, when the virus invades a cell it replicates itself like any other virus.

"The exception occurs when it infects the reproductive organs. Then this RNA generates over five hundred changes in the host's DNA, effectively rewriting certain portions of it. This guarantees that the host's offspring will be genetically identical to Herans, and this limitation to the reproductive system makes the changes harder to detect than a whole-body transformation." The display shifted, showing side-by-side comparisons of two DNA maps. Red lines highlighted differences between the two data sets.

"This plague is a diabolic means of conquest," Worf said. "Within a generation, one's enemies would *be* Herans—Commander?" Riker had muttered a word: *Venice.*

"Plague," Riker said, raising his voice. "This explains why *Temenus* was on its way to Aldebaran II. Considering all the traffic that goes through the Aldebaran shipyards, it's the perfect focal point to launch a plague, just like medieval Venice accidentally did with the Black Death."

"I agree," Crusher said. "Standard quarantine procedures wouldn't stop every case. Somebody could climb aboard a ship on Aldebaran, go to Earth or any of a hundred planets, take a shuttle down to the surface, and . . ." She let her voice trail off suggestively.

"But our quarantine procedures are good," Geordi said. "We wouldn't spread a plague. So why did the Herans infect us?"

"This may have been a last chance," Picard suggested. "Even before I told Blaisdell to return to Hera, it must have been obvious to him that we would expel him from Federation space."

"I don't buy that," Riker said. "Why didn't they just

go home, wait a few months, then try for Aldebaran again? Or Earth, for that matter?"

"That would have been a sound strategy," Worf said. "We can be glad they did not do this."

"At least we've contained this disease," Picard said. "Doctor, I take it that everyone who's had this disease has undergone a genetic change. I want you to investigate methods to reverse the damage. I expect a report in twenty-four hours."

Crusher hesitated, then nodded. "Yes, sir."

"Excellent," Picard said. Putting some spirit into that word seemed to take all his effort. To think that this minor ailment could create such a drastic change—he forced himself not to think about his own situation. "Counselor Troi, I think it's safe to assume that we have a major morale problem on our hands."

"We do," Deanna said. "Several hundred people have been assaulted on one of the most basic levels possible. It's still too soon for people to know how to react—"

"I can tell you how I'm reacting," Riker said, an edge in his voice.

"You're outraged," Deanna said. "But for most people on the *Enterprise,* this is just now sinking in. They're still stunned."

"It's more than that, Deanna," Crusher said. "We're being used, against our will, by people who admire the likes of Khan Singh. It's bad enough that they've changed several hundred people so that any future children of theirs will match Hera's version of 'perfection.' What's worse is that, as of now, we're only aware of the physical changes that will appear in such children."

"What might we expect, Doctor?" Picard asked.

"Certain personality factors are influenced by our genetic inheritance," the doctor said. "Suppose that these changes include factors that will push these potential children to act like Khan Singh? Jean-Luc, would you want to raise a child who was predestined to become a conqueror?"

"The question is what we do now," Riker said. "The

Herans have committed an act of war. We can't ignore that."

"Nor will we," Picard said. "But I don't intend to rush blindly into this, Number One. There are too many unknowns." Far too many unknowns, he thought as the meeting ended. And the meeting had gone badly. It had felt disorganized, and propelled more by anger and confusion than by determination to find answers. Picard suddenly understood how medieval humans must have felt when confronted by a bad omen.

In a way it was unfortunate that Kemal had not died while fighting Dunbar. Worf owed his life to her, but that did not change the dishonorable way in which she had concealed her identity. He found it awkward to be in her debt.

At least he was not in Blaisdell's debt, and the Heran had information that Worf needed. As soon as the conference had ended Worf went to the brig. The Heran was busy inspecting his cell's food replicator when Worf walked up to the force door. "I'm still not going to answer your questions," he said. He continued to study the replicator as though Worf's presence meant nothing to him.

"I already have many answers," Worf said. "I know that the virus was a genetic engineering tool."

Blaisdell's head snapped around. "Who betrayed us?"

"You did," Worf said. "You were foolish to unleash this plague on the *Enterprise.* Our scientists—"

"Primals could not have figured this out unaided," Blaisdell said.

"Did you expect us to ignore an epidemic on this ship?" Worf demanded. "Did you think there would be no investigation? Were we to consider your presence a coincidence?"

"Yes. You had no other evidence. Most peculiar." Blaisdell returned his attention to the replicator.

"Have you spread this plague to other planets?" Worf asked.

Blaisdell ignored the question. After a moment Worf went to the duty post, where Ensign Yamato stood watch. The Klingon pushed the sound-suppress button on the console, isolating Blaisdell. "Has the prisoner said anything?" Worf asked Yamato.

"No, sir," the ensign answered. "He's spent the time inspecting his cell."

Worf grunted. "Keep me informed of his activities."

"Yes, sir. Sir?" Yamato hesitated. "I've heard this rumor that Kemal is one of *them.*" He nodded toward the cell.

"Then you have also heard that she killed Dunbar," Worf said.

Yamato nodded. "I have, sir. I was just wondering if you wanted me to get a cell ready for her, too."

Worf glared at him. "Why do you believe that is necessary?"

The human wilted. "I just thought—"

"That is not your assignment," Worf said. He left the brig in a foul mood. Yamato's words did not sit well with him. Kemal had behaved dishonorably by hiding her nature, but that did not justify Yamato's suggestion— and Kemal's actions had somewhat redeemed her honor.

Worf took the turbolift to sickbay and went into Dr. Crusher's office. She sat behind her desk, skimming over a series of test results. "I wish to know about this epidemic," Worf said. "Have there been similar occurrences elsewhere?"

"I haven't had the time to check," Crusher said. "How soon do you need to know?"

"Now," Worf said. "Blaisdell is unresponsive to questioning. Information will give me leverage."

"Dr. Par'mit'kon can help you," Crusher said. "I have to go back to the physiology lab in a moment. We're running more tests on Kemal. We've got a lot to learn."

Worf grunted. "You held back information at the conference," he said, in what he hoped was not an accusing tone.

"I did," Crusher said. She leaned back in her chair and

rubbed her eyes. "Worf, you're not human. Maybe you can be objective about this, and God knows I need some objectivity—and some secrecy."

"If there is something about the Herans—" he began.

"It isn't them," Crusher said. "It's us. The captain told me to look for a cure for this . . . this situation, some way to return everyone to normal. I already have, and our genetic-engineering tools are too crude to reverse what's been done to us. There is no cure."

Chapter Eight

"WE'VE BEEN CAUGHT FLAT-FOOTED," Admiral Allen Trask said. Starfleet's senior intelligence officer possessed the classic lean and hungry look, and he sounded grim as he spoke to Picard. Behind him, the ready room's viewscreen showed the confusion in his office at Starbase 171 as aides called up computer data and sorted through secret, hard-copy files. "We've been working nonstop since we got your message yesterday. All our information on Hera says it's nothing more than a crackpot colony. Captain, if I didn't know your record I would suggest *you* are wrong."

"Yes." Picard tapped his fingers on his desk. "Do you have any information at all that's not in the general files?"

The admiral gestured to one of his aides, who handed him a data pad. "There have been a number of deaths and ship disappearances on and around Hera," he said after reading the display. "They've all been adequately explained—piracy, accidents, plasma storms, and so on. There was also some sort of crisis on Hera about twenty years ago. We don't know its nature, but we estimate that some two hundred Herans left the planet. The small number suggests they were government officials fleeing a purge. We didn't develop much interest in this because all of the refugees went to non-Federation planets."

"Including Zerkalo," Picard said.

"I know," the admiral said. "I'll send someone to Zerkalo to investigate the Kemals. Meanwhile, how soon can you deliver the Herans to us?"

"We can reach Starbase One-Seven-One in two days, Admiral," Picard said. "We can hand over Captain Blaisdell at that time."

"And the other one," Trask said. "We'll want Kemal for interrogation, too."

"Are you requesting that I transfer her, sir?" Picard asked.

"I'm telling you to arrest her." The admiral eyed him. "You're going to be difficult about this, aren't you?"

Picard weighed his words carefully. "I intend to obey the letter of the law, Admiral."

Trask sighed. "Picard, the Simon Tarses affair left us all with some bad memories, but we can't afford to let it distort our judgment."

Picard nodded gravely. "On what charge shall I arrest her, Admiral?"

"On deliberate falsification of identity."

"That is not sufficient grounds for an arrest, sir," Picard said. "You cannot prove criminal intent."

"I will. Arrest her. That's an order. Trask out." The Federation seal replaced his image.

An eager beaver, Picard mused, recalling a peculiar American idiom. Allen Trask had only recently been appointed to command of Starfleet Intelligence, in the wake of several debacles that had almost proven disastrous to the Federation. Starfleet Intelligence had failed to uncover the Romulan attempt to invade Vulcan and their involvement in the Klingon civil war, Ambassador T'Pel's true identity as a deep-cover Romulan spy, a Romulan assassination plot involving Geordi La

Forge's kidnaping and brainwashing, the Antidian attempt to disrupt the Pacifica conference, various Cardassian preparations to absorb disputed border areas—and my own capture by the Cardassians, Picard thought with a shudder. Starfleet Intelligence had been fooled by the Cardassians into sending Picard into a well-designed trap. The Cardassians had ruthlessly stripped him of his dignity, and then subjected him to hideous tortures in a meaningless effort to break him. The Cardassians had quite literally brought Picard to his limit before Starfleet had negotiated his release. He could easily imagine how Astrid felt, alone among hostile aliens and not knowing what fate to expect.

The realization of empathy produced a strange sensation. Picard had always held eugenics in contempt, yet Astrid Kemal had not asked to be what she was, and she had shown loyalty to the Federation. "Computer, display Dr. Kemal's personnel file," he ordered.

Picard selected the salient facts as data marched across the screen. Born on Zerkalo, age twenty-two-point-one years. No records were available from her home planet; as a matter of principle the anarchic Zerkalan government refused to divulge personal information. Brilliant academic record, doctoral degree at age nineteen, short but impressive record at the Daystrom Institute. Species, human, according to a routine physical exam—an exam given by an Andorian physician, whose records made it clear she was not overly familiar with human physiology. "Picard to Dr. Crusher," he called. "Can I see you in my ready room?"

Picard called the bridge and ordered the course changed to Starbase 171. The doctor appeared a few minutes later and seated herself at a gesture from Picard. "Doctor, does Astrid Kemal meet the legal definition of a human being?" Picard asked.

Beverly Crusher ran her fingers through her auburn hair. "Sir . . . I don't know how to answer that. Genetically she's almost identical to normal humans, but there are several differences."

Picard forced himself to remain patient. "I'm not asking for a simple yes or no. Can you make a case for her humanity?"

Crusher looked at him across the desk. "What exactly do you want, Jean-Luc?"

"I want to avoid an injustice," Picard said. "Now, what are these differences you mentioned? How significant are they?"

"Well, the physical differences aren't too important. There are slight changes in her muscle tissue and bone-cell structure that give her enormous strength. Her immune system is perfect, her metabolism is highly efficient, and we still don't know the limits of her endurance; we've put her through some strenuous tests that would exhaust even Worf, and she quite literally hasn't even worked up a sweat. Healing—she broke two ribs during her fight with Dunbar. By the time we noticed them, three hours later, they were almost fully healed.

"Then there are the differences in her central nervous system," Crusher continued. "You're aware of how computer enhancement can improve a video image. The Heran brain contains several neural sets which perform similar functions. The result is a remarkable increase in visual acuity. When I gave her a standard eye test and told her to read the bottom line on the chart she responded, and I quote, 'Chart Fifteen-A, Vance Optometrical Institute, copyright 2361.' Most people can't even *see* that line.

"Her senses of hearing, smell, touch and balance are equally enhanced. She's ambidextrous and has an almost Vulcan ability to disregard pain. Her reflexes are almost as good as Data's. She can follow two conversations at once. She had clear memories of conversations she heard when she was three months old. She can read at least ten thousand words per minute and do some sophisticated mathematical calculations in a matter of seconds. None of this has shown up on any of her medical exams."

Picard nodded. "It seems inevitable that she would have held back during an examination. But none of this is truly significant, Doctor."

"Well, *this* is," Crusher continued. "She's incapable of a panic reaction. You can startle her, but there's no increase in adrenaline levels. I've found that she has a neural network that acts as a . . . well, call it a damping circuit, a safety valve, to hold down any strong emotion. I don't know how that affects the rest of her emotional makeup."

"That doesn't disqualify her as a human being," Picard said. "We recognize healers, telepaths and metamorphs as human—"

"There's a difference," Crusher said. "I could go into a courtroom and swear up and down that she's human. No one will care. The fact that she's genetically engineered, and that she concealed this, will decide the issue."

"Perhaps," Picard said. "But no decision has been rendered yet. Until then we owe it to her to defend her. I'd like to see her now, if you can spare her from your tests."

"I can." Crusher stood up. "Jean-Luc, she fits the legal definition of a human being. An impartial court would back that up. But before you throw away your career to defend her, you'd better find out if *she* thinks she's human."

Worf was not due on the bridge for another hour, and his first stop as he went back on duty was at the security department. K'Sah was on duty with one of La Forge's technicians, and together they were examining the computer systems. La Forge swore that the system was clean, but the Herans had proven themselves too clever for Worf's comfort. He wanted to make sure they had no more tricks to play.

K'Sah looked up from the computer terminal. "Nothing so far, Lieutenant," he said. "Finding something here is harder than picking a pocket on a Starfleet uniform."

"Keep looking," Worf ordered. "Is Blaisdell still in his cell?"

"Yeah, and eating like a pig," K'Sah said. "Dunbar acts like he's dead, but I think he's up to something."

"He's dead, Lieutenant," the technician said in disgust. "We've looked at that body a dozen times."

K'Sah looked at her in suspicion. "Count on humans to stand up for one another."

She glared at K'Sah. "If you think any decent human will stand up for maniacs like—"

"Enough," Worf said. "Have you found anything?"

The woman shook her head. "Lieutenant, I've tried every test I know on the computer system. All I can say is, either there's nothing there or the Herans are too damned good for me."

Worf dismissed the technician, then glowered at K'Sah. "You were ordered to maintain good behavior. Explain yourself."

"It's the humans who need explaining, Lieutenant," he said. He looked at the door, which had slid shut after the technician had left. "Now I know why they smile all the time. They really are up to something!"

"What is it that you suspect?" Worf demanded.

"I'd think even a Klingon could see it," K'Sah said. "The humans have found a way to reconfigure their whole species. More brains, more muscle, the works. Give them twenty years to breed a generation of superhumans, and they'll try to conquer the galaxy. And the way they pretend they're upset over this—it's a nice little act, isn't it?"

Worf could think of only one answer to that. *"Plakh,"* he swore. The obscenity derived from an ancient term that meant "the absence of war," which until lately had been the nearest word the Klingons had to "peace." It left a foul and satisfying feel on Worf's tongue.

K'Sah rolled his eyes in disbelief. "Don't tell me you trust them!"

"I do," Worf said. "They would not act so dishonorably."

79

"There you go with that 'honor' noise again," K'Sah grumbled. "What makes you think humans have honor? What *is* honor, anyway?"

"At the moment," Worf grated, "honor is all that keeps you alive."

The Pa'uyk made a rude noise. "What good is staying alive if the humans are going to wipe us all out, Klingon? What makes you think you can trust them?"

"I know them," Worf said. "I was raised by them. Cease these insults *now!*"

"And they say Tellarites are touchy," K'Sah muttered, backing away from Worf. "Whatever happened to good old Klingon suspicion?"

Worf bared his teeth and growled. K'Sah kept backing away. The door opened behind him and he backed out of the room. The door seemed to snap shut at Worf's final growl.

The woman who entered Picard's ready room seemed in full possession of herself. "Dr. Crusher said you wanted to see me, sir," Astrid said.

Picard nodded. "Please sit down, Doctor. Are you aware of your legal position?"

"Yes, sir," she said. "Falsifying personal information is a crime."

"If you've falsified anything," Picard said.

"I was born on Hera, not Zerkalo," she said. "And I didn't tell anyone I'm genetically engineered. Add my lying to the fact that I've been working in classified areas, and that I'm not a Federation citizen, and you have excellent cause for suspicion."

"Quite," Picard said. "There will be an investigation, of course, and you are hereby restricted from access to the ship's computer and all areas normally off-limits to civilians. I hope this will be only a temporary inconvenience. For the present I have a larger problem to face. What information can you give me about Hera?"

"Not much, sir," she said. "There's what I remember,

and the things my parents told me. The trouble is, everything is eighteen years out of date."

"That could still be informative," Picard said. "I'm calling a meeting of my senior officers at thirteen hundred hours tomorrow. Would you share your knowledge with us?"

"Yes, sir."

"Very well," Picard said. "I want you to know that I appreciate your actions in this matter, both in stopping the Herans and in revealing yourself. That can't have been easy. You must be apprehensive about the consequences."

"I am," Astrid said, and hesitated. "But . . . it's a relief, in a way. We've got this saying back home, that after your house burns down you don't have to worry about the roof falling in. I've always been scared that people would find out what I am, but now I can stop waiting for the worst to happen."

"With any luck there will be no 'worst,'" Picard said. "Your actions persuade me that you are not a Heran agent. Mr. Worf's investigations of your activities on this ship absolve you of any involvement with Blaisdell or Dunbar. Now, if I know Dr. Crusher, she's put you through every test in the medical inventory in the past few hours."

"No, she hasn't," Astrid said. "Dr. Crusher didn't conduct any mental tests. She may have missed something important. My parents always told me we were designed for high intelligence," she added.

"I'll mention this to Dr. Crusher," Picard said. He pushed his chair back from his desk, bringing the interview to an end. "You must be looking forward to a rest."

"Yes, sir." Astrid got up and left.

I did not handle that well, Picard thought. He knew Astrid needed more reassurance than he had given her, although it was hard to judge what she felt. Astrid masked her feelings well, and even her admission about being scared had a conversational quality. Picard found himself comparing her to Simon Tarses, who had seemed so forlorn and hapless when he was exposed as part Romulan. He found it hard to accept her detachment. No doubt her calm was a product of her genetically engineered nature, but it seemed arrogant, as though anything mere humans could do to her was trivial.

That's the plague thinking, Picard told himself. He realized he was upset by what had happened to him, and he would have to guard against its effects on his thinking.

The situation was bad enough. The human complement of the crew was disturbed by what had been done to them, and Deanna Troi was already hard at work helping them cope. The plague's victims had been hit hard. Any children they had would be . . . changed, Picard thought. Not fully their children, in a sense. The physical changes were trivial, and might be seen as beneficial—but what of the mental changes? How would these children act when they grew up? Would they become power hungry creatures like Khan Singh, or would something in them make them subservient to any would-be tyrant?

There was no way to know. The future seemed fraught with menace.

Chapter Nine

THERE WAS ONE SILVER LINING to the crisis, Geordi thought: It would let him hang on to the *Temenus* a while longer. *Enterprise* had a brilliant design, of course, but the things he'd seen aboard the Heran courier had already suggested several improvements in the systems. He wasn't sure yet, but he believed he might find a way to boost the *Enterprise*'s top speed by at least half a warp factor. Geordi couldn't wait for the chance to start tinkering.

Studying the *Temenus* wasn't easy. "I could swear this warp damper is pure iron," Geordi told Reg Barclay as he scanned part of the drive. "And I don't see how it can work with just one element in it."

"It m-must be the crystal structure," Barclay said.

"It can't be that," Geordi said. "Iron crystal structures are pretty well known, and none of them are suitable for warp damping."

"M-maybe the Herans found a new structure," he said. Suddenly his words poured out in a torrent. "Or, or a new way to grow crystalline structures? What if they assembled different crystal forms, one over the other? The layer interactions could give the overall structure an enhanced damping ability."

"Could be," Geordi said. He adjusted his tricorder and took a new reading. "I'm picking up some major quantum amplitude changes, but I can't get a good enough reading on a tricorder. Let's take this back to Engineering and see what we can find." Geordi started to detach the damper from the warp drive's housing.

"If you don't mind I want to stay here," Barclay said. "I want to, to take another look at the nav sensors."

"Sure." Geordi smiled despite himself. Barclay was a bundle of apprehensions. "Still nervous about riding the transporter?"

"No, I'm over that," Barclay said. "It's just, just that going back to the ship, the plague and everything—"

"We've got the virus cleaned out of everything," Geordi said.

"It isn't the plague that scares me," Barclay said. "It's just that, it, it's—" He squeezed his eyes shut as though concentrating on how to force the words out. "It's the crew. People act different. Wrong. Like the plague did something to their minds and they didn't notice. And it isn't just the people who had the plague, it's everybody. Being on the ship is like spending a night in a haunted house, all day long."

"I hadn't noticed," Geordi said. "I guess I've been too busy being scared myself."

That clearly startled Barclay. "Scared? You?"

Geordi nodded. "Yeah, me." He unconsciously fingered his VISOR. "Dunbar made no bones about hating people like me, even when I was fixing his ship. When you mix arrogance like that with the sort of intelligence the Herans have, and their technology—" He shivered despite himself. "It gives me a bad feeling, like somebody painted a phaser target on my back."

"Well, the, the Herans won't be a problem anymore," Barclay said. "I mean, we've got a handle on the situation, the plague I mean, and what can they do against Starfleet? They, they tried something foolish, but they're going to have to come to their senses now."

Geordi sighed. It was a hell of a thing, he thought, when Reg Barclay was less uptight than you were. "I guess we've both got our fears," he said, and disconnected the damper. "I'll take this back to Engineering myself."

Geordi signaled the *Enterprise* and was beamed into a transporter room. He nodded to the transporter technician on his way out. The woman seemed only half-aware of his presence, as if she were a zombie going through the motions of her job. As Geordi stepped into the corridor he remembered what Barclay had said about haunted houses.

"Geordi?"

Geordi froze at the sound of Astrid's voice. He wanted to ignore her, but he was an officer and Starfleet demanded a certain sense of propriety. He turned around and looked at her. "What is it?" he asked, his voice rougher than he had intended.

She walked up to him. "I hear you're working on the *Temenus.* I'm not busy. Maybe I can help."

"I don't need any help," Geordi said. The last thing he wanted was a Heran hovering around him.

"You could use me," she said. "That ship was designed for use by Herans. You may have missed some things."

"I haven't," Geordi said. "I know what I'm doing, *Doctor.*" He turned away and headed for the nearest turbolift.

Astrid followed him. "Have you found the weapons yet?"

"There aren't any." Anger made his throat tighten. Anger—and fear, he admitted. He was the sort of person the Herans would eliminate in their conquest. An ominous phrase from ancient mythology floated into his mind: *You have been weighed and found wanting.*

"There are weapons," she insisted. "They're hidden as something else, but they *are* there. I'd check the shield systems first."

"You would? Fine," Geordi said. "You check them. Engineering," he said as he stepped into the turbolift. The door slid shut on her.

Geordi waited for his anger to subside while the lift slid toward Engineering. He couldn't believe her gall. First she had pretended she was human, and now she was acting like nothing had happened. He had every right to be angry.

So why did he feel like such a heel?

Enterprise was twenty hours away from Starbase 171 when Worf noted activity in the long-range sensors. "Picking up a ship," he announced to the bridge crew. "Bearing zero-three-eight, mark zero two, approaching at warp factor eight. Configuration——it is an Aeolus-class scout. It will rendezvous in ten minutes."

"Hail them," Riker ordered.

"Belay that," Picard said, standing up. A ship on that bearing must have come from Starbase 171. He felt no surprise that Admiral Trask had jumped the gun. "Number One, you have the bridge. I'll be in transporter room three."

Picard left the bridge for transporter room three. When he entered the room he found it occupied by a transporter technician and Astrid Kemal, who stood by the platform with a duffel bag slung over her shoulder. The transporter technician was studiously ignoring her. "Dr. Kemal?" Picard asked. "Where are you going?"

"I just got a message from the *Marconi,*" she said. "I'm under arrest."

"No, you are not," Picard said. "This arrest has no legal basis."

"That won't stop them," she said. "There's nothing I can do."

For all her calm demeanor Picard heard the despair behind her words. He had known that brand of hopelessness while a prisoner of the Cardassians, and it roused his sense of—not anger, but of combativeness. "Doctor, you must not surrender to an injustice," Picard said in a quiet, insistent voice. "You will survive only by standing up for your rights . . . and by knowing that you are not alone."

For a moment she seemed at a loss for words. "Thank you," she said at last.

Picard nodded as the intercom signaled. "Captain, we've just rendezvoused with the *Marconi*," Riker's voice said. "There's a message for you."

"Down here, Number One," Picard said. He smiled grimly. "Admiral Trask, this is Captain Picard."

"You don't sound surprised to hear me," Trask's voice answered.

"I've been expecting you, sir," Picard answered. That was a slight exaggeration, he reflected, but one that might keep the admiral off-balance.

"I see," Trask said. "Do you have what I ordered?"

"Have your transporter room stand by," Picard said. He looked to the technician. "Beam Captain Blaisdell from his cell to the *Marconi*'s brig."

"Aye, sir." The technician worked her control console. Blaisdell appeared briefly on the transporter pad, but he did not fully materialize before he vanished.

Trask spoke again after a few seconds. "Where's the other prisoner?" he demanded.

"There is no other prisoner, sir," Picard said. "Admiral, may I beam over and explain the situation?"

"No Captain, you may not," Trask said. "I'm going over there."

"Yes, sir," Picard said. "Picard to bridge. Number One, Admiral Trask is transporting over. Raise the shields after he arrives, and do not lower them except on my order."

"Yes, sir," Riker answered.

A few seconds later the admiral materialized on the transporter stage. "Welcome aboard, Admiral," Picard said, holding the irony from his voice.

Trask ignored him and looked at Astrid. "Dr. Kemal? You're under arrest. Come with me."

Picard held up a hand, stopping her. "On what charge—"

"Let's skip the dancing, Picard," Trask said. He touched his comm badge. "Mr. Chen, lock on and beam us over."

Nothing happened, and Picard cleared his throat. "Our shields are up. Admiral, I suggest we discuss this in private."

Trask's lips had compressed into a thin, angry line. "Very well," he said. "We'll use your ready room—while it still *is* your ready room, Captain."

"Certainly." Picard turned to Astrid. "If you'll excuse us, Doctor?"

Picard and Trask left the transporter room. They walked past several people on their way to the turbolift, all of whom shied away from the senior officers as though they were carrying a new plague. Picard wondered if his own anger was as obvious as Trask's. He forced his feelings down, burying them in his professionalism.

Trask turned on Picard as soon as the ready-room door had slid shut behind them. "Are you bucking for a court-martial, Picard?"

"No, Admiral." Picard waited until the admiral had taken a seat before he sat down behind his desk. "I might ask you the same question. You have no legal grounds on which to arrest Dr. Kemal. Certainly Starfleet lacks the authority for an arbitrary arrest."

"I have my own authority," Trask said.

Picard nodded. "In that case you could be charged with false arrest, as well as with ordering a subordinate officer to participate in a felony. Those charges are themselves legal grounds for an arrest."

The admiral stared at Picard. "I honestly think you'd arrest me," he said slowly.

"I would, Admiral," Picard said. "But there's no cause for either of us to go to extremes. If all you require from

Dr. Kemal is information, you'll find she's willing to answer your questions."

Trask glowered at Picard. "You don't understand the situation. We can't allow a possible enemy agent to run loose—"

"So you propose to arrest her without a proper charge and hold her indefinitely without a trial." Picard settled back in his seat. "Admiral, the Federation is not a twentieth-century police state. We cannot suspend our principles for vague reasons of 'national security' or 'law and order.'"

"Don't lecture me!" Trask snapped.

"I'm merely stating my position," Picard said.

"You're also verging on insubordination." The admiral drummed his fingers on Picard's desktop. "Kemal's a known liar. Can I trust her to tell the truth now?"

"Yes, sir," Picard said. "She was lying to protect herself, not to aid Hera."

"And you trust her," Trask said. "Why?"

"I've no reason to distrust her," Picard said. "She's been cooperative, and I cannot convince myself that her actions are anything but those of an honest, if frightened, individual."

"Maybe," Trask said grudgingly. "I won't arrest her— now. Maybe she'll slip up and reveal something, if she thinks we trust her. But if she steps out of line by a micron I'll have her in the brig."

The intercom signaled before Picard could respond. "Bridge to captain," Worf said. "We have a message for Admiral Trask."

"In here, Mr. Worf." Picard turned his computer screen to face the admiral, then stood up. "If you'll excuse me, Admiral?"

"Stick around." He gestured for Picard to stand behind his chair, then touched the screen's activator. "Trask here."

Vice President Chandra appeared on the screen. "Admiral Trask," the Federation's second-in-command said in a neutral voice. The dark, delicate old woman wore a sari, and she spent a moment adjusting it, as if to impress the admiral with his relative unimportance. "You were due to report a half hour ago."

"My apologies, Mrs. Vice President," Trask said. "We've just rendezvoused with the *Enterprise* and taken Blaisdell into custody. We'll interrogate him at Starbase One-Seven-One."

"What about the other Heran?" she asked.

"Sir, I don't believe it's necessary to arrest her—"

"You don't?" Chandra demanded. "Admiral, questions are already being asked about your competence. Your intelligence service has let us down—again. Can you prove that Kemal isn't a Heran agent? Are you going to compound your errors?"

Trask appeared to count to ten before he replied. "Mrs. Vice President, it is my judgment that it would be an error to arrest Kemal just now. She's more useful where she is."

"And you think she can be trusted?" Chandra asked.

"No," Trask said, "but Kemal is the one who exposed the Heran actions, and I don't know how cooperative she'd be in the brig. Besides," he added shrewdly, "she isn't going anywhere."

"So be it," Chandra said curtly. Her image vanished.

Picard let his breath out. He was impressed by the admiral's ability to make a quick decision—and by what he had seen. It was past time to apply some diplomatic tact to the situation. "I wasn't aware that you were under such intense pressure, Admiral."

"It goes with the job, Captain." Trask leaned back in his seat and closed his eyes for a moment, as though consulting some inner oracle. When he opened his eyes again he looked straight at Picard. "I've managed to get us off on the wrong foot."

"I've been somewhat less than diplomatic myself, Admiral," Picard said. "But we share the same problem—the well-being of the Federation."

"That we do," Trask said, and sat up in his chair. "Do you play chess?"

"Not very often," Picard said.

"I'm a grand master," Trask said. "In fact, I was getting ready to leave for the Moscow Tournament when this crisis brewed up. The chance to beat T'Chel of Vulcan again—well, I'll get her next year. Chess is a very good game for an intelligence agent, especially one who runs an intelligence bureau."

Picard nodded. "I can see how the game would teach one to develop his strategies."

"And to keep his options open," Trask said. "I forgot that when I tried to arrest Kemal. You were right to stop me; aside from violating her rights, it might have cost us the chance to learn something about Hera—if she's one of their agents."

"'If,'" Picard repeated.

"I hope she isn't," Trask said. "But she might be an agent with a very effective cover. Or, even if she's innocent, Hera might have maneuvered her into this position as a diversion. It wouldn't be the first time some spymaster sacrificed an innocent pawn."

Picard nodded in agreement and wondered what piece he represented on Trask's personal chessboard, and what position he occupied.

The capsule had stopped at a maintenance station. Marla had followed Selig Thorn and his nephew Dallas up an access ladder, to emerge in the heart of a pine forest. The irregular placement of the trees and the mixed nature of the secondary vegetation suggested this was a natural forest, seeded by the first settlers centuries ago and left to run wild. That told Marla she was in the Dryad Hills forest. She had ridden the capsule for less than thirty minutes, and the only other woodlands that close to the Modality complex were industrial forests, where robot-tended trees grew in geometrical rows.

Knowing where she was did not put Marla at ease. The

Dryad Mountains were a popular vacation area, and this was no time to be spotted by a patriotic camper. "Where are we going?" she asked Selig as they walked away from the station. Her whisper seemed abnormally loud in the cold, damp air.

"To my home," Selig said, and pointed up the slope. "It's on the other side of this hill, in Tethys. There's no trail, so we aren't likely to run into anyone."

"Let's move," Dallas said uneasily. "I don't want to wait around and find out if they're following us."

The walk over the hill was long and slow. Marla did not like walking by starlight; the light was not bright enough to let her see clearly, and she had to be careful of every step on the uneven ground. Once she thought she heard breathing in the distance, and she spent a bad moment before she realized it was only the sound of her own breath echoing off a rock ledge. The sound faded as she and the others drew away from the granite block.

It was still night when they entered Tethys. Several early risers were up and about, but no one seemed to notice the new arrivals walking down the main street. "Don't worry," Selig told Marla in a quiet voice. He had guessed at her nervousness, if he did not share it. "No one will report you. The Modality may have power, but it has no authority here."

"I see," Marla said.

"No, you don't," he said in sympathy. "Not yet. Unless you know why we rescued you."

"I don't," she admitted. "You can't be that desperate for recruits."

Selig chuckled. "We're not. We have tens of thousands of people who want to change the government; we no longer need numbers. We're doing this for the same reason you sabotaged the *Temenus.*"

Marla thought that over as she followed Selig and Dallas into a domed house. After the night's damp chill it was good to enter a warm and well-lit building. A tawny cat greeted them as they came in, rubbing against Selig's lower legs and purring loudly. "Koshka, this is

Marla," Selig told the animal. "She'll be staying with us for a while."

Marla knelt down and stroked the cat as it greeted her. She felt its presence in her mind as it probed her and decided she was a friend. After a moment the animal followed Dallas out of the room, and Marla sat down while Dallas fed the cat. "You said you rescued me for the same reason Lee and I attacked the *Temenus*," Marla said to Selig. "I don't see the connection."

Selig produced glasses of mulled wine from the replicator. He gave one to her and sat facing her. "Why did you and Lee try to stop Unity?"

"Well . . ." Marla shrugged helplessly and drank some of the heated wine. Its warmth felt good. "Somebody had to."

"But why you?" Selig persisted. "You took a great risk."

Marla nodded. "It didn't look like anyone else could stop Unity," she said. "And . . . look, we had a chance to stop it, and we couldn't just stand aside. That . . ." Marla shook her head. The explanation seemed as obvious as gravity, and as hard to define, "That would have been wrong."

"That's why we got you out of jail," Dallas said from the next room. "We knew you were there, we knew Central Security planned to execute you, and we knew how to get you out. Not doing this would have been wrong."

"We think that's why Central let us know they had you," Selig said. "They must have hoped to catch us when we made our move."

"Bait in a trap," Marla said. "I wondered why they kept me alive. But how do you know I'm not their agent?"

"We don't," Selig said. "But sometimes you have to take a chance."

Marla nodded slowly; Lee had understood that. "Thank you for getting me out of there."

"You're welcome," Selig said. He finished his wine.

His cat padded into the room, licking its lips as it rubbed back and forth against his leg. When Selig scratched it between the ears it sat down and thumped its tail against the floor. "You'll have to lay low; we can't have Central picking you up again. Dallas is our sensor expert. He'll tell you how to duck the surveillance 'bots, after you've had breakfast and a good morning's sleep. And Koshka is our empathic expert—which is another reason I trust you. He's quite good at spotting hostile people." The cat's purr deepened at the praise.

"I see." She felt weary, both physically and mentally. Even so there was a matter which could not wait. "What do I have to do to join your organization?"

"You joined when you decided to sabotage the *Temenus*," Selig said. "Rest now. You can make your decisions later."

Chapter Ten

DEANNA TROI AUTOMATICALLY took the measure of the command staff's feelings as they entered the conference room and took their seats. Geordi seemed worse than unhappy. Worf's anger still smoldered. Beverly Crusher was merely harried, and Data, as unreadable as ever. Will Riker was concentrating on the present; perhaps that was the only way he could avoid sinking into despair. The captain and Admiral Trask entered together, and sat down at the head of the table. Deanna sensed a professional alertness from the admiral, a sensation that gave her the impression of a master chess player contemplating a difficult game.

Astrid Kemal entered the room last. Deanna found it difficult to gauge her emotions. She felt frightened, ashamed and depressed, but each time those emotions intensified something happened to moderate them. Beverly Crusher had mentioned some oddities in Astrid's neural structure, and now it was obvious that the doctor had underestimated their importance.

"Our first order of business is to understand the

Herans," Picard began. "Dr. Kemal has volunteered to enlighten us on Heran history. Doctor?"

"Why are you doing this?" Riker asked.

Astrid faced him. "I'm a citizen of Zerkalo. The Herans are a threat to my world—"

"Only to its human population," Riker said. Deanna sensed how his professionalism struggled to control his anger. "You've been less than honest with us before. Why should we trust you now?"

Astrid hesitated. "Commander, why don't you hear what I have to say, and then decide if I'm sincere?"

"I'm willing to accept your words at face value," Picard told her. "If you'll begin, Dr. Kemal?"

"Yes, sir." She folded her hands and placed them on the conference table. "First of all, everything in the computer is true, as far as it goes. The first colonists landed in 2073, and they were unmodified humans. They believed in eugenics, and before they left Earth they screened themselves for genetic damage—"

"That must have limited their numbers," Crusher said.

"It did," Astrid said. Deanna was surprised by the sudden rise in Astrid's fear, although she gave no outward sign of it. "There were lots of mutations from both pollutants and fallout from the Eugenics Wars, and they needed several years to find enough suitable people. The first colonists only numbered two thousand, but they calculated that was enough to create a stable gene pool—"

"It wasn't," Crusher said. "They'd have had severe inbreeding and genetic drift after a few generations. And I doubt they weeded out all of the mutations. Twenty-first century medical technology wasn't sophisticated enough for that."

"They didn't know that," Astrid said. Her fear had grown so strong that it made Deanna uncomfortable, and this time it did not fade out. Deanna realized that Astrid felt threatened by the doctor . . . physically threatened. "The original colonists had this mystical belief that they were creating the conditions in which a superior race could evolve. They thought that a pristine gene pool and an unpolluted environment would allow the forces of evolution to work unimpeded—"

"Evolution doesn't work that way," Crusher said impatiently. "It's a blind process of adaptation, not a directed force."

"I said this was a mystical belief." Astrid faced Picard as though trying to ignore the doctor. Deanna sensed how Astrid felt trapped in the conference room. "After two centuries, inbreeding and latent mutations had caught up with them. The average life span dropped to forty years, most pregnancies miscarried, and half the population carried one or more lethal genetic diseases. A century ago the colonists admitted they were doing something wrong and began a crash effort to develop genetic engineering. They succeeded and were able to cure their health problems.

"Ideas change over time, and by now the founders' dogmas had turned into a concept of manifest destiny," Astrid continued. "Even though their doctrines had failed, the old humans still believed they could become a superior race. Genetic engineering gave them the tools to accomplish this, and even before they had cured all their diseases they began to design an improved human being. The originators—the genetic engineers who directed the project—planned to stick to the basic human type while pushing its limits as far as possible."

"That's reasonable," Deanna said. "Everyone wants their children to be as much like them as possible."

"That also makes it harder to tell Herans from human beings," Riker said. "That's the perfect disguise for an enemy agent—or a weapon."

"I agree," Astrid said. "And we were designed to be weapons." Deanna sensed how that statement troubled Astrid more than admitting she had lied. Her knuckles had turned white as she clenched her hands together atop the conference table.

Admiral Trask cleared his throat. "We were discussing Hera," he said. Deanna sensed that he was suspicious of

Astrid, as befitted an intelligence agent, but the sharpness of his voice was a deliberate ploy. He hoped to goad the suspected Heran spy into revealing something. "Kemal, we know there was some sort of crisis there about twenty years ago."

"I'll get to that, Admiral," Astrid said. "The geneticists made a final design, encoded all of the changes into a virus, and unleashed it. This was some seventy years ago. After 2300 every child born on Hera was like me. But the virus was crude and it had an unexpected side effect. The old humans who were exposed to it found their health was suffering. The virus had changed the DNA in every cell nucleus in their bodies, and that degradation accelerated the aging process."

"Are we at risk?" Riker asked Crusher.

"I'll set up some tests," Crusher said, "but I don't think so. We've undergone a more limited transformation here."

"Maybe," Riker said. " 'Old humans.' Is that supposed to be polite?"

"Yes, sir," Astrid said. "There's this term, 'primals,' that means—"

"I can guess," Riker said curtly. "Crude. Barbaric."

Deanna decided to get the conversation back on course. "Dying young and ill must have devastated your ancestors," she said.

"It had that effect on some of them, Counselor," Astrid said, "but it made the others more fanatical. They wanted to see Hera fulfill its 'destiny' in their lifetimes. The Modality—the Heran government—started pushing for a war of conquest against humanity.

"That provoked the crisis. The old humans had indoctrinated their children with a belief in manifest destiny and Heran superiority. Some of the children grew up believing that, but others had their own ideas. My parents told me that three factions that opposed conquest sprang up, for different reasons."

"What were their reasons?" Deanna asked, sensing that Astrid felt reluctant to talk. She was not keeping a secret, however; her hesitation made Deanna think of a

Victorian matron trying to discuss a gross indelicacy. "I can sense that they aren't your opinions."

Astrid still hesitated. "Well . . ."

"Talk," Trask snapped, clearly thinking she might be hiding a secret. "And don't tell us that it's too complicated for mere primals to understand."

"All right." Astrid's face darkened in embarrassment. "Some people saw no reason to attack anyone who hadn't harmed them, but they were a minority. A second group held that a war of conquest would be suicidal; Hera didn't have the means to win. And the third faction . . . the majority . . . said that old humans weren't worth conquering."

Only Astrid's embarrassment kept Deanna from laughing. She was half human herself and she might have taken offense, but this casual dismissal of the human race was too deliciously funny. The shock that radiated around the conference table only made it funnier. Only the captain seemed to take her comment with any humor. There was a faint smile on his lips, the first Deanna had seen since the plague broke out.

Worf recovered first. "We Klingons thought humans were worth conquering," he said.

"Thank you, Mr. Worf," Picard said, while Deanna fought down a new urge to laugh. Picard's smile was no longer quite so faint. "It's good to know that somebody still appreciates us. Doctor, I gather that the pro-war faction lost out in the crisis."

"Eventually they did," Astrid said. "The few remaining old humans tried to put them in power, but there weren't enough fanatics to keep them on top. In the end they ordered an invasion of the Federation's colonies near the Neutral Zone, but that backfired before it even got going and started a civil war. That's when my parents ran off; they didn't want to get caught in the crossfire. They—"

"Is this relevant?" Trask asked. "If it isn't, we need to stick to more immediate concerns. I need to find out if you Herans have any more surprises in store for us."

"Count on it," Geordi said. Deanna sensed that Astrid's presence evoked a sense of shame in the engineer, and he could not look at her. "The *Temenus* is unarmed, but it isn't defenseless. Its shields are as good as ours, and they've got a structure which lets them reflect a phaser beam back at its source. Plus, there's a modulated interference effect which interacts with a tractor beam to neutralize its pull."

"These are mere defensive weapons," Worf rumbled.

"And they make me wonder how much effort the Herans have put into *offensive* weapons," Geordi said.

Astrid nodded. "Hera has been fighting various aliens for over a century, as well as old-human pirates. To survive, their tactics and weapons have to be excellent—"

"That's obvious," Trask said. "I'd like to discuss this with your tactical staff, Picard—without a Heran present." He gave Astrid a pointed look.

Astrid stood up and left the conference room. The admiral looked at Geordi and cleared his throat. "There's something you didn't want to say in front of Kemal, isn't there?"

Geordi nodded. "I've been all over that ship," he said. *"Temenus* is better than anything we have."

"And that disturbs you," Deanna said. She didn't need her empathic sense to realize that.

"It intimidates me," Geordi answered. "From what I've seen on the *Temenus,* I'd say that technologically the Herans are fifty to a hundred years ahead of us. Fighting them could put us in the same position as the Aztecs. They outnumbered the Spanish conquistadores a thousand to one, but their bows and arrows couldn't defeat men with guns, horses and armor."

"They can't be that far ahead of us," Riker said.

"They are," Geordi said flatly. "The design of that ship is more than a work of genius; it's the end product of a very sophisticated technology. And when I think about how easily Blaisdell and Dunbar learned to use our engineering equipment, and subvert our computer system—well, I wonder if we can even begin to understand how advanced they are."

Picard nodded. "When I spoke with Dr. Kemal yesterday she raised the matter of Heran intelligence, and suggested that Dr. Crusher conduct a full intelligence test on her."

"I'll arrange that," Crusher said.

"I'd like you to wait a few days," Deanna said.

"We can't afford a delay," Trask said. He paused, cleared his throat again and went on, "Understanding the enemy's mental abilities is vital. Doctor, run those tests now."

"I won't allow that," Deanna said. "Astrid is in no condition to undergo any tests and yes, Admiral, I have the authority to veto any testing," she added, sensing his objection.

"What is the problem, Counselor?" Picard asked. "Dr. Kemal seems to be taking events quite well."

"'Well'?" Riker echoed. "She looks like the cat that ate the canary."

"Maybe so," Deanna said. "But despite appearances she's upset and frightened. What's more, she's absolutely terrified of you, Beverly."

"I find that hard to believe," Crusher said, although the comment disturbed her. For all her anger over the plague, Deanna knew that the doctor felt no need to hurt Astrid. There was nothing vengeful in her. "Her designers made some significant changes in her brain. One thing they gave her is a—well, call it a neural circuit which deflects and neutralizes certain strong emotional impulses."

"That 'circuit' can be overloaded," Deanna said. "Every time you spoke to her I thought her heart would stop. It isn't a rational fear; it's as though you embody some childhood bogeyman. Add that to everything else that has happened, and I'm certain Astrid is close to her breaking point."

"All right, Counselor," Trask said in a rough voice. "Calm her down and do it fast. We still need her cooperation."

"Do we?" Riker asked. "Can we trust her?"

"She's driven by a very powerful sense of guilt," Deanna said. "She's trying to make amends for lying to us. That's why she's answered our questions as truthfully as possible, even when she felt ashamed of what she said."

"That still doesn't tell me if we can trust her," Trask said. "There are too many unknowns . . . in . . . her—" Trask stopped and was suddenly wracked by coughs.

Deanna sensed Crusher's alarm. The doctor rose from her seat, went to the admiral and ran a medical tricorder over him. "My God," she said in flat disbelief. "Admiral, you've got the plague. Transporter room, medical emergency, two to beam to sickbay." They vanished.

Deanna gaped at the space where the two people had been. "I thought the ship was clean," she said.

"It is," Geordi said in bewilderment. "I supervised the decontamination myself. I know we didn't miss anything."

"Then there is a second source of contamination," Data said.

"But where?" Deanna asked. Baffled looks were her only answer.

"Will, wait."

Riker had left the conference room alone after the meeting broke up. He walked quickly, as if trying to outrun an impending disaster, and now Deanna hurried to catch up with him. He thought she looked unhappy. "We need to talk," she told him.

"About what?" Riker asked.

"About what this plague is doing to you," she said. "I don't have much time before my next appointment, but I'll cancel it for you."

With a sigh he stopped his quick walk and faced her. "There's not much to say, Deanna. I'm angry. The

Herans are using me as breeding stock, to perpetuate their own species, and I feel—I don't know. Used. Maybe I'll get over it in time . . ."

"Not if you don't talk about it," Deanna said. "What role do you think Astrid has played in all this?"

He shrugged. "I haven't thought about that."

"I know, Will," Deanna said. "And if you haven't thought about that, then why do you feel such animosity toward her?"

Riker began to protest, then checked himself. "I'm uncomfortable with what she is," he said. "You heard her. She thinks she's superior to everyone else, that she has the right to inherit the galaxy. She thinks this plague is the best thing that could happen to us primals."

"Is that what she thinks?" Deanna raised an eyebrow in aristocratic surprise. "Why, Will Riker, I had no idea you were a telepath."

Her teasing irritated him. "You wanted to know what I think, didn't you?"

"And now *you* know what you think," she responded. "That isn't like you."

"This is realism, Deanna," he said.

"No, realism is what I sense in her, and what you trust in me." Deanna looked up at him. "Will, at times I think we're like two planets in orbit around one another. Sometimes we move apart and sometimes we move closer together. Now it's as though you're in an escape orbit. You're moving in a direction that will take you away from me forever."

"What do you want from me?" he asked.

"Get to know Astrid," Deanna said. "Talk to her for a while. Otherwise you'll never get over this; you'll just make it a part of you."

Riker sighed. "I never could say no to you."

"And don't think I wouldn't take advantage of that." Deanna smiled at him, then walked away.

Riker stood in the corridor for a long moment, then asked the computer for Astrid's location. The response sent him to Ten-Forward. The lounge was full, and he saw Astrid standing at the bar. Despite the crowd there was an empty space on either side of her; people were avoiding her. Guinan was handing Astrid a glass of orange juice when Riker stepped up to the bar next to her. Guinan nodded to Riker. "What'll it be?" she asked.

"The usual." Riker looked at Astrid. "What brings you here?"

Astrid shrugged. "This is a good place to be."

"To see how the "old humans" act?" Riker asked as Guinan filled a glass in front of him.

Astrid shook her head. "I'm just tired of lying and hiding. Besides, maybe they should see how the enemy acts."

"I thought you claim to be on our side," Riker said.

"Maybe I don't know which side I'm on," Astrid said. She looked at him. "Never mind what I say. Do I act like I'm on your side? If I did, Worf wouldn't have nearly died, and maybe this plague wouldn't have happened."

Riker felt puzzled. "What are you trying to say?"

"That only a damned fool would trust me."

"Riker, you shouldn't try to meet women in bars," Guinan said easily. "You don't have the knack. Here." She had been mixing a drink while they spoke. Now she pushed the glass in front of Astrid and took away her orange juice.

Astrid looked uncertain. "I don't drink, Guinan."

"I know, and I think I know why," the hostess said. "You've been afraid that you would relax too much and tell people about yourself. It's a bit late to worry about that, isn't it?"

Astrid regarded the drink with obvious ambivalence. It was large, and Riker estimated it held a liter of fluid. "If I lose control—" she began.

"Don't worry," Guinan said. "I had a drunk in here the other day who was a lot nastier than you could ever be, and I handled him without any trouble."

"Well . . ." Astrid shrugged, picked up the drink and sipped it. "Nice," she said. "What's it called?"

"It's a roofraiser," Guinan said. "Hurry up; if you

don't drink it within a few minutes of mixing it, it loses its flavor."

"Okay." Astrid started drinking in earnest.

Riker sipped his drink. "Who was the drunk?" he asked Guinan.

Guinan smiled. "K'Sah. He tried picking a fight before I pulled my pulse-rifle on him. Then he was a good little spider."

"That sounds like K'Sah," Riker said. He'd heard Worf grumble about the exchange officer, and a few other people had passed on some unlikely stories about his lack of manners. "Guinan, is it just me, or does everyone have a problem with K'Sah?" he asked.

"I don't know," Guinan said. "Here's the funny thing, Riker. I think he *liked* being held at gunpoint. Either it was a great act, or he's crazy."

"It's neither," Astrid said. Half of her drink had vanished. She blinked hard, several times, as though she and her eyes had a difference of opinion over focusing. "I heard a bit about Pa'uyk. Nastiness is their version of good manners. You know, like the way we think Klingons act rude? The poor guy thinks all our smiling and politeness is a trick, like all that stumbling I did."

"That was an act?" Riker asked. It didn't surprise him.

Astrid nodded. "My folks told me it would help keep you old humans from getting suspicious. Whoever heard of a monster tripping over her own feet? I mean, can you imagine Khan Singh taking a pratfall?"

"No," Riker said. He remembered a picture of Khan Singh in a history book, and he had to smile at the image of the proud, cruel-faced man sprawling on the floor. But the smile faded at once. He was not going to let her manipulate him, even though, dammit, there was something about her that made him *want* to like and trust her.

Guinan picked up the conversation as Riker sipped his drink. "I guess you really were scared of people finding out about you."

Astrid nodded. "When I was a kid Mom and Dad always said if anyone found out I'd be lucky if they only killed me. Told me the old humans would put me in a zoo or carve me up in a lab." She laughed nervously. "Were wrong. Yesterday I walked out of that lab."

"Why would they tell you things like that?" Riker asked. "We don't use people as lab animals."

Astrid looked him over. "Where were you when I was five?" she asked at last.

Riker didn't want to think about the implications of her words. He might never like her, he told himself, or trust her, but that was no excuse for rudeness. "I'm sorry I've been rough on you," he said.

She nodded in acceptance of his apology. "This can't be easy for you, either."

"It isn't," Riker admitted. "Combat and away team missions are one thing. At least there you expect danger. But this? It isn't even an act of war." He told himself to stop talking before he said the wrong thing to her.

"Treating you like something in a zoo," Astrid said. "The Klingons would say *jay' lulonqu' batlh.*"

"They would," Riker agreed: They have abandoned honor. "An eloquent people, the Klingons."

"Yes." Astrid looked around the lounge, then rested an elbow on the bar and leaned closer to Riker. "Maybe you can tell me. Why're they so scared of us?"

"Which 'they'?" Riker asked. "The crew?"

"Old humans," she said. "Even before the plague I'd hear things about superhuman monsters. It can't be just because of Khan Singh, I mean, come on, four hundred years is a long time to carry a grudge. So what have you people got against us?"

Riker shook his head, not knowing how to answer. Guinan answered for him. "Look at human history," she told Astrid. "Europeans almost exterminated the Amerinds and Australian aborigines. They also killed every last Khan. Deep down, humans have always feared that somebody would do the same thing to them."

"That isn't it!" Riker protested.

Guinan smiled at him. "That's how it looks to *this* nonhuman. If you've got a better answer, I'm listening."

"Maybe we just don't like the idea of somebody replacing us," Riker said, "which is what the Herans have in mind."

"A week ago you didn't even know about us," Astrid said. "Take you, for instance. You're the one who was talking about *homo arrogans*. So why do you think Herans are the worst thing since . . ." Her voice trailed off, and then her face brightened. "Oh, that's right. You're from Alaska."

The *non sequitur* puzzled Riker. "What's that got to do with anything?" he asked.

"Uh . . . nothing. Just that, uh, you big, strong frontiersmen don't like the idea that there's something bigger 'n' stronger than you. Meaning no offense." She held out her empty glass to Guinan. "Could I have another, please?"

Riker was about to press her on the change of subject when the lounge door opened and Dr. Par'mit'kon walked in. Most humans found his fishlike face unreadable, but Riker had learned how to decipher his expressions. The physician was in a grim mood. He walked up to one of the human diners and spoke to her. Riker couldn't hear his words, but the woman's olive face turned an ashen color. Par'mit'kon scanned her and gave her an injection. "Something's wrong," Guinan said.

"Yeah." Astrid seemed to listen while Par'mit'kon spoke with another human. "There's a second outbreak of plague," she said. "The viral protein coat has changed and the old vaccine won't work now. They're reimmunizing everyone." Astrid shook her head. "Ought to leave now."

"There's no reason for that," Guinan said.

"Folks will feel bad enough without me around," Astrid said. "I'll go."

Guinan watched her walk out. "They don't make monsters like they used to," she commented dryly.

"Meaning what?" Riker asked.

"Meaning that for somebody who's supposed to be an

arrogant, cold-blooded killing machine, she's awfully meek. Not only that, she obviously feels guilty over what she did . . . or didn't do. When was the last time you saw a monster with a conscience?"

"Maybe she's putting on a good act," Riker said. Synthehol lowered a drinker's inhibitions in much the same way as alcohol would, but synthehol's effects could be consciously dismissed by the drinker. Kemal might have been talking freely because she was drunk, or she might have been feigning intoxication.

Guinan smiled at him. "Riker, I was getting people drunk when your ancestors were telling one another that 'aeroplanes' were a wild idea that would never work. You saw the genuine article there. If I were you, I'd wonder what makes her act that way."

"So you think it *is* an act?" Riker asked.

Guinan picked up a cloth and began to wipe down the bar. "Listen to me," she said patiently. "There's something very civilized about her, and if you know anything about history, you know that civilized people make the most dangerous warriors."

"Staying ahead of Central Security isn't too hard," Dallas Thorn told Marla. The boy had spent much of the day showing her how to defeat Central Security's surveillance techniques with null fields and probability multipliers, and Marla now carried a packet of defense chips in her pocket. "Central doesn't have our motivation. Sometimes they're so careless you'd think they were a bunch of primals."

"'Old humans,' not 'primals,'" Selig said as he entered the workshop. He sat down with them. "'Primal' is a Modality buzzword. Don't let them do your thinking for you, nephew."

"I don't," he said. "It's just that I hear the word so much, it gets to be second nature."

"We all have to look out for that," Selig said.

Marla felt puzzled. "What's the big deal?" she asked. The two terms seemed interchangeable.

" 'Primal' makes the old humans sound stupid," Selig explained, "which they aren't—*they* made *us*. We can't hide from them forever, and when we have to come out into the open we'll have to deal with them. Insulting them and telling ourselves they're backward won't make that any easier."

"If we can deal with them," Dallas said.

"We're supposed to be smarter than they are," Selig said. "We'll find a way. And don't forget that the Modality wants us to think of them as primals. That's why they use the word in the schools and newsnets. It helps justify their plans if we think of the old humans as something inferior."

Marla nodded in understanding. She had never thought about the subject before, but now the implications seemed obvious. "Thinking of them as 'old humans' reminds you that they were here first," she said. "And that they've got a lot of experience."

"Yeah, great experience," Dallas muttered. He got up and walked out of the workshop.

Marla kept silent until she heard him leave the house. "I said something wrong, didn't I?"

"In a way," Selig told her. "His parents were at the Delphi outpost when it was destroyed."

"Oh." Hera had established a base in the Tau Delphi system five years ago; Tau Delphi III was a class M planet, and the ideal site for Hera's first colony. A group of weapon smugglers from inside the Federation had simultaneously decided that the world made an ideal pirate base, and when they found the colony they ruthlessly wiped out the pioneers after they had surrendered. The few survivors reported that the old humans had killed the settlers because of what they were. The Modality had chosen to ignore the massacre; retaliation would have accomplished nothing, and it might have drawn attention to Hera. "So Dallas resents old humans," Marla said.

"He does," Selig said. His cat slinked into the workshop and rubbed against his knee. Almost absently Selig scratched the tawny animal between its ears. "How do you explain what they did? How can anyone be smart enough to handle a starship, and have everything they could want, and still go around killing people and breaking their own laws?"

"I can't explain that," Marla said. "I can't even explain some of the things the Modality does."

"They want power," Selig said. "That's the basic flaw in the Modality. Its founders set it up so that only the 'best' people could join it, and the idiots defined 'best' in their own terms. Ruthless, power hungry—" Selig stopped and took a calming breath. "It's hard to be objective about this."

"I know," Marla said. His anger reminded her of something that had happened during her captivity. "Selig, the Senior was there during my interrogation. Ulyanov asked me if I knew something about a secret file. He called it the 'originator file.' Have you ever heard of it?"

"No, but that proves nothing," Selig said. "The Modality has a lot of secrets. Exactly what was said?"

Marla thought. "Very little. Ulyanov said, 'Yes, but I wonder why the Sukhois have such a high opinion of the primals.' Then he asked me, 'Have you seen the originator file?' I answered, 'The what? I don't know what that is.' Then he said, 'Do you? Tell me what you think about the originators.' I said, 'Evil, murdering—' and I choked up. Ulyanov said, 'She hasn't seen the files.' The way he said it made it sound as though something in the files would change my mind about the old humans. He was also concerned that what I had heard about this originator file might turn people against the Modality."

"Odd," Selig said.

"Maybe I misunderstood him," Marla said doubtfully. "I was heavily drugged at the time."

"Perhaps," Selig said. He hoisted the cat onto his lap and idly scratched its ears. For a moment Marla watched the animal luxuriate in the attention. She envied the cat;

it knew nothing about conspiracies and lost families. It looked up and made a rowling noise to Selig. "But Koshka doesn't think there's anything wrong with your memory."

"Could he be wrong?" Marla asked, a question which drew an affronted look from the animal. "I can't imagine anything that would make me stop hating the originators."

"Neither can I," Selig said. Then he added in wonder, "But it seems the Modality can."

Chapter Eleven

"I'VE IDENTIFIED THE SOURCE of the new infection," Beverly Crusher said to Picard and Admiral Trask. She sat down behind her office desk. "It's Paul Sibio, one of my orderlies. He was one of the first people to catch the original plague."

"Wasn't he properly treated?" the admiral demanded.

"Treated and cured, Admiral," Beverly said. "But he started showing symptoms about the same time you beamed over. They were mild and he thought the problem was only overwork, but when I checked him his body was saturated with the new virus. We've treated him and he's no longer contagious. We've immunized everyone against this new virus, and there were only seventeen cases, so we're all right for the moment.

"But we *will* have more epidemics," she continued. "The plague carries a bit of programming that I missed. This extra program is inserted into a few random cells around the body, along with the rest of the viral genetic material. Some time after the original infection ends it comes to life and causes the contaminated cells to start

112

producing a new virus. This virus contains the same genetic information as the original, but it constructs a new protein coat, one which the immune system and our immunization shots don't recognize. Every victim of the plague can become a new source of infection days, months, even years after the original infection."

Picard looked at the data on the screen. "This would explain why Blaisdell infected the *Enterprise,*" he said. "We thought we had eliminated the plague. Instead we could have spread it across the Federation, contaminating dozens of colonies. It's our good fortune that we made no planetfalls before we uncovered the plague, and that we had Dr. Kemal's help here. Blaisdell couldn't have expected that."

"Bless his arrogant little heart," Admiral Trask said. He rubbed at his eyes. Picard doubted the man had slept last night. "This is a good way to saturate a population with the plague."

Beverly nodded. "Someone might escape the first round, or have a natural immunity to one form, but eventually they would catch it. I'm looking at means to combat this, but until I find an answer I'm ordering the *Enterprise* be quarantined. Nonhumans can come and go, because they can't carry these viruses—"

"What about Blaisdell?" Picard asked. "Could he have infected the *Marconi* after we beamed him aboard?"

"No, sir," Beverly said. "Herans can't carry diseases; their immune system is perfect. But until we can eliminate the disease we don't dare have any contact with the rest of the human race. That could be permanent," she concluded.

"Understood," Picard said, and looked closely at the doctor. There were bags under her eyes, artfully hidden by makeup. "Beverly, did you get any sleep last night?"

"I caught a nap this morning," she said. "Don't worry about me, Captain. I know my limits."

"This ship and your patients won't be served if you push yourself to those limits," Picard said. "Consider what overwork did for Mr. Sibio's judgment. Get a good night's sleep. Captain's orders," he said with the ghost of a smile.

The intercom signaled then. "Bridge to Captain Picard," Riker said. "Sir, we're receiving a distress signal from Deep-Space Seven."

"On my way," Picard answered. Trask strode out of the room with him, and the two men reached the bridge a moment later, where Riker relinquished the command chair to Picard. "Report, Number One," Picard said as he sat down.

"It was an automated distress signal," Riker said. "All it gave were the bare facts—three cloaked ships appeared and opened fire on the station's outer defenses. The ships appeared at bearing twelve-mark-thirty-two."

"Right on a line with Hera," Trask said, in a voice which said he was only half guessing.

Data swiftly ended any need for guesses. "Receiving a new message from Deep-Space Seven," he reported.

"On screen," Picard ordered.

An Andorian in the uniform of a Starfleet captain appeared on the main viewscreen. "This is Deep-Space Seven," he said in the whispery voice common to his people. "Captain Tharev broadcasting to all ships in our sector. We have been attacked by unknown ships. They have retreated, but we expect further attacks. All ships in sector should beware of possible attacks. All ships in sector, please respond."

"This is the *Enterprise*," Picard said. "Captain Tharev, what is your status?"

The blue-skinned man checked the console in front of him. "We have lost our defense capabilities," he said. "I am surprised that we have no casualties. This was a very precise attack, but we cannot resist another such attack. Can you come to our assistance?"

Picard glanced at the tactical display. "Not in less than five days."

The cuplike antennae atop Tharev's head writhed as he nodded. "I understand, Captain."

"Can you identify the attackers?" Trask asked.

Tharev nodded again. "Their configuration is unknown, but we have definite sensor scans." He gestured to someone off-screen, and Picard saw information appear on Data's console. "Their power was remarkable."

As Picard read the data he realized that was an understatement. Then he looked at the sector chart. "The *Belfast*, *Discovery* and *Cutty Sark* are all within twelve hours of you," he told Tharev.

"We await them," Tharev said. "Deep-Space Seven out." The Andorian vanished from the screen.

Trask was on his feet. "Data, let's see the information on the attackers."

"Yes, sir." The android's hands moved and a starfield image filled the main viewscreen. As data reeled across the bottom of the screen, a graceful white shape flickered into visibility. Phaser bursts snapped from its needle nose with a rapidity that exceeded that of any weapon in the Federation's arsenal. Then it vanished again, ahead of a phaser barrage from the station's defenses.

Data assimilated the image and information without any of the dismay Picard felt. "This is an automated ship," he said. "Sensors detected no life on board. Shields are equivalent to that of a Galaxy-class starship. The cloaking system was absolutely undetectable by the defense sensors. The energy-utilization curve matches that of the *Temenus*."

"It even looks like the *Temenus*," Riker observed. "What is this? A show of force?"

"It's only a robot ship," Trask said. "It won't be much of a problem."

"Automated war machines do lack the versatility of organic minds," Data agreed. "But given the capabilities which this ship has demonstrated, it may present a considerable challenge if it applies hit-and-tun tactics." The comm system signaled and he turned to Picard. "Captain, you have a message from Starfleet Command."

"Let's have it," Picard said.

Admiral Huang, Starfleet's Chief of Staff, appeared on the screen. He was a small Chinese man, and only his iron gray hair suggested his true age. "Captain Picard," he said. "How much progress have you made in your investigation of the Heran situation?"

"That's difficult to assess, Admiral," Picard said. "We've found that the Herans and their technology are more impressive than we expected. We've also discovered that this plague is more sophisticated than we thought. Anyone who has had the disease can produce a new form of the virus long after being cured. In effect, I have a ship full of Typhoid Marys."

"I see." Picard thought that Huang looked distracted. "One more problem . . . I'll require transmission of all your data on the Herans within the hour, Jean-Luc. I know you haven't had time to prepare full reports, but I cannot wait. The situation is degenerating."

Trask nodded. "We've just heard about the attack on Deep-Space Seven. The ships came from Hera, no question about it."

"We know, Allen," Huang said. "We received a declaration of war from Hera, ten minutes after the attack began. They denounce the Federation for numerous alleged attacks against Hera and promise to conquer us if we do not surrender at once. Conquer or surrender, they promise to expose the entire human race to this genetic plague. And they seem to think we'll enjoy that. The arrogance of this 'Modality' astonishes me.

"There is more," Huang continued. "There have been other attacks against Federation ships at several scattered points. There have been no injuries, but the Herans have disabled their warp drives and left them drifting. A few hours ago our long-range sensors detected three ships, similar to the *Temenus,* as they left Hera on divergent courses—for Federation space. Our analysis suggests that they will make a further effort to spread this plague."

Trask nodded somberly. "I concur. Can we intercept them?"

"That's problematic at best," Huang said. "Not that it matters. Starfleet Command is now organizing a task force, one Galaxy-class starship, four heavy cruisers, eight destroyers and sixteen troop transports, under the command of Admiral Hoskins. It will reach Hera in ten days. If the Herans won't negotiate a peace, we have to be ready."

"What about the diplomatic option, Admiral?" Picard asked.

"We've tried contacting the Herans," Huang said. "Their only response to our subspace hails is to repeat their demand for our surrender. But we should continue the effort. Jean-Luc, take the *Enterprise* to Hera and see if you can accomplish anything. But proceed with caution. You are not to place your ship at unnecessary risk. Huang out." The transmission ended.

Worf growled quietly. "These attacks are a diversion," he said.

"They look halfhearted," Riker agreed. "But what were they diverting?"

"Our defenses," the Klingon said. "Now we must send ships to defend Deep-Space Seven against further attacks, and to aid the crippled ships. This will leave fewer ships available to intercept other Heran craft. A sound move," he said in grudging admiration.

"It's time for a move of our own," Picard said. "Mr. Data, hand the *Temenus* over to the *Marconi*. Then set a course for Hera, warp factor eight."

"That's a bit fast, sir," Riker said.

Picard nodded. "We'll require nine days to reach Hera, Number One. That puts us just one day ahead of that task force. That won't leave us much time, but it will have to do."

"I'm not convinced that we should resist this war, Picard," Trask said. "The more I learn about the Herans, the more dangerous they seem. Defeating them may be our only choice for survival."

"No," Picard said stonily, as the *Enterprise*'s engines

came to life and she turned for Hera. "We *will* find another choice."

"If the Herans give us a choice," Trask said. It was an admiral's prerogative to have the last word, and he exercised that right by leaving the bridge before Picard could reply.

A moment later Picard gave control of the bridge to Riker and went to find Astrid. The computer located her in Ten-Forward, and when Picard entered the lounge he found her sitting at a table at the front of the lounge, where she looked out the observation window. To his irritation Picard noted that no one sat at the tables near her, despite the large number of people in the lounge. "May I join you, Doctor?" he asked.

"Of course, sir." She kept staring out the window. "We're going to Hera aren't we?"

"I suppose it's an obvious move," Picard said.

Astrid looked at him as though reading his mind. "Something new has happened," she stated.

Picard nodded. "Hera has just declared war on the Federation and demanded our surrender. There have been several attacks. The *Enterprise* has orders to negotiate a peace settlement, if possible. I'll need your advice on how to proceed."

She nodded. "I can tell you one thing that might help. There's an active resistance to the Modality on Hera. It knows about the plans for this plague; that's why it sabotaged the *Temenus*."

"You're certain?" Picard asked.

"Quite. It's the only explanation that fits the facts."

"I see," Picard said. "Blaisdell claimed that the sabotage was the result of a power struggle among Hera's leaders."

"He lied," Astrid said. "He played to your preconceptions. The only information you have on Hera implies that Herans are like Khan Singh—conceited, arrogant and egotistical. You'd expect people like that to be stupid enough to fight among themselves, and to be ruthless about it. He was trying to get you to underestimate us and dismiss us as fools."

"Counselor Troi has said much the same thing," Picard told her. He found himself trusting what she said. There was something almost contagious about her air of self-assurance. "Have you any idea of how extensive this resistance might be?"

Astrid shook her head. "There have always been Herans opposed to war and conquest, but I don't know how much things have changed in the past eighteen years. I know their first interest will be in Hera, so I wouldn't count on them being friendly to the Federation."

"Nonetheless, one may hope they are," Picard said. He looked up as Guinan approached the table with a tray. "Guinan," he said in greeting.

She nodded pleasantly. "Mind if I join you?"

"Not at all." The three identical goblets on her tray told Picard that she had planned to sit with him and Astrid. "Your company is always welcome."

"Especially when the place seems so empty." She handed out the glasses and looked around the lounge as she sat down. The tables near them remained empty. Well, Picard thought, at least people are seeing that I will not shun Astrid; they would have to draw their own conclusions from that. Sometimes leadership was a quiet, subtle thing.

Astrid was clearly aware of the way people were behaving—or not behaving—around her. "It's their business," she said.

Guinan shrugged. "Maybe so, but I hope you don't go in for getting even. It could be awkward."

"I've given up acting awkward," Astrid said, and inspected her glass. "Is this another roofraiser?"

"No, it's wine. Real wine," she added, and smiled at Picard. "I want to see if our resident vintner can identify it. How about it, Captain?"

Picard took a sip, and during the next hour he found

himself discussing wines with the two women. His family owned a sizable vineyard in France and produced a well-regarded vintage, which made him something of an expert on the subject of wines; he finally identified Guinan's offering as a recent Falernian. Astrid seemed intrigued by the talk, and she clearly regretted its end when Picard had to leave. That had to be loneliness, Picard thought. Her position could not have been an easy one.

In theory the *Enterprise* could maintain warp eight indefinitely, but as a practical matter Geordi disliked prolonged flight at that speed. Warp eight pushed everything to the limit and accelerated the wear and tear on the ship's systems. It also meant he had to stay in Engineering and maintain a closer watch on a lot of different functions. He didn't mind the extra work, however, and he was in no mood to stir around the ship.

"Something wrong, Commander?"

"Huh?" Geordi looked behind him and saw Gakor. The Tellarite's pink, snoutlike face showed curiosity. "No, everything's fine. Why?"

"Well, you've checked that panel five times in the past hour, and I wondered if you'd spotted a problem."

Geordi shook his head. "It's just things," he said vaguely.

"You mean it's that plague," Gakor said. "I don't see why you humans are so upset. The Herans are doing you a favor."

"You think so?" Geordi was too dispirited to feel angry. He knew that Gakor was only looking for an argument; it was a Tellarite custom to argue over every imaginable topic, to see if anything new or interesting could be uncovered by a discussion. "Look, how would you feel if somebody decided to 'improve' your people without your permission?"

"It depends on the improvements," Gakor said. "Give my children higher intelligence, great strength, perfect health, sharpened senses . . ." He squinted myopically at

Geordi. "I'd roll in the mud with that any day, Commander."

Geordi almost smiled. Gakor knew that his people resembled Terrestrial pigs—a point he liked to work into his jokes. "And suppose they grew up to be like Dunbar and Blaisdell?" Geordi asked.

"Or Kemal?" he countered. "That's personality. A lot of that depends on how the kids are raised. I'd say Kemal was raised right."

"Maybe," Geordi said. His level of self-irritation reached the critical level. "Keep an eye on things. I have to take care of something." He left Engineering and went to Deanna's office.

He found the Betazoid empath taking a short break between patients. She sprawled on one of the office's chairs with her eyes shut as the computer played Vulcan lyrette music for her. Geordi found the tones and rhythm too alien for enjoyment. "I've been listening to human problems all day," Deanna explained. Her eyes remained closed, which did not offend Geordi. He knew that her empathic sense meant more to her than mere sight. "I need something unhuman."

"Oh." Geordi sat down. He hoped his problems weren't adding to her burden. "Have you had the chance to see Dr. Kemal yet?"

"Why?" Deanna said. "Do you think Astrid has some special problem I should know about?"

"Aside from being the only Heran on the ship—" Geordi stopped and shook his head. He wasn't fooling Deanna any more than he was fooling himself. "I really hurt her feelings. Maybe I should work this out by myself, Deanna."

"Tell me what happened," Deanna said. "At the conference the other day I noticed that your feelings about her were very confused. I'd really like to hear about this, Geordi."

"Well, the day after the plague broke out she looked me up and offered to help me analyze the *Temenus*. I just saw red when she started talking to me, and I was rude as hell. The thing is, the day before I'd been joking with her in Ten-Forward. She must have expected a lot better from me."

"And you don't know what to do about it," Deanna said.

"No," Geordi said. "I don't. I . . . guess I've been hiding out in Engineering, so I could avoid thinking about this."

"Then you'd better stop hiding from her," Deanna said. She opened her eyes and stood up. "Well, I have another visitor in a few minutes. Thanks for telling me all this, Geordi."

"What's to thank?" he asked. "You have enough trouble without my problems."

"Yes, but you're the first person who's come in here feeling sorry for somebody other than himself." Deanna stretched her arms over her head as though basking in the sun. "I was beginning to forget people could feel that way."

Chapter Twelve

A WARRIOR'S HONOR demanded that he offer formal
thanks to one who had saved his life, and Worf had
postponed that duty long enough. He went to Astrid's
quarters and signaled, and stepped in when the door slid
open. Astrid was seated on her bed, and she stood up for
him. *"Nuqneh?"* she asked in Klingon: What do you
want?

Worf gave her a formal nod. "I have come to thank you
for saving my life. I owe you a debt of honor."

"You owe me nothing, Lieutenant" she said. "Had I
spoken when honor required, you would not have been
in danger."

"I know," he said. Her dishonorable silence had kept
him from thanking her . . . or was it dishonorable? "Did
you keep silent only for yourself?" he asked.

She shook her head. "I was protecting my parents as
well."

"That is honorable," Worf said. "My debt stands."

Astrid spread her hands. "I accept this. Will you
accept my hospitality in return?"

"I shall." Worf sat down. "I have found this duty less than easy," he admitted.

Astrid bowed her head in agreement. "You must feel like Kavargh," she said.

"There is a certain dilemma," he said. Kavargh was the hero of one of his favorite operas: a warrior who owed a debt of honor to a disgraced and treacherous noble. The dilemma was not entirely unwelcome; it gave him a unique sense of his Klingon heritage, something he did not always feel while surrounded by humans.

The intercom signaled. "Lieutenant Worf, report to the conference room. Dr. Kemal, the captain requests your presence in the conference room."

Worf scowled as they left Astrid's quarters. "I am curious," Worf said. "Would you think it is possible for a Klingon to defeat a Heran in close combat?" His defeat at Dunbar's hands still rankled.

She looked thoughtful as they entered a turbolift. "It would be difficult," she said after a moment, "but any Heran you fought would think he could defeat you, so he might be overconfident. And Dunbar put all his strength into a direct attack, like a wild *targ*. You will also remember that I broke K'Sah's hand. That happened because he startled me; we can be surprised," she said as the lift stopped.

Worf scowled as they stepped out of the turbolift. Her response amounted to a tactful no—and it held another form of denial. "You sound eager to find weakness in yourself."

"My parents told me I was designed as a weapon," she said. "I do not want to think of myself as a killing tool."

"You should not deny what you are," Worf said as they walked into the conference room. Picard and the rest of the command staff sat at the table, along with Admiral Trask. Distantly, he heard the blunt-toothed babble of human speech. He ignored it.

"I am not pleased by what I am," Astrid said as she sat down next to Worf. "I want to know that my soul is my own, not—"

"Lieutenant," Admiral Trask said in the human tongue. "Mind letting the rest of us in on the conversation?"

Worf tried not to look ruffled. "We were discussing philosophy, Admiral."

"Oh, really?" The admiral looked at Astrid. "Let's continue the discussion. What sort of 'philosophy' lets a Heran work for the Federation?"

"It's what I wanted to do, sir," she said. "You work with the very best people—"

"Including primals who might put you in a zoo, or chop you up as a lab specimen?" Trask leaned forward. "I talked to Guinan. She said that you had some interesting comments. If you're so scared of humans, why did you take a job where you'd be surrounded by them? Sooner or later we were bound to find out about you."

"Maybe something inside me wanted people to find out," Astrid said. "Try living a lie; it's like burying a piece of yourself every day. You have fear where other people have trust. You can't have friends, because you can't let anyone know the real you. It's no way to live."

"But you're still scared of us," Trask said. "Why?"

Astrid folded her hands on the tabletop. "When I was a girl my parents always warned me that old humans were crazy and violent, and if you found out what we were we'd be lucky if you only killed us. After we moved to Zerkalo they taught me to do things like trip over my feet so I wouldn't attract attention. They were always afraid I'd do something that would alarm the old humans—they never had a second child because they said raising me was risky enough."

"'Crazy and violent,'" Picard repeated. "What gave them that impression of non-Herans?"

"Sir, it's a common attitude on Hera," Astrid said. "The old-human colonists wanted to conquer the galaxy, which is a crazy idea by itself. The originators *made* us to be weapons, and they destroyed their own health in the process. They tested hundreds of designs before they came up with us, and these 'designs' were *children;* when they didn't work out, they were euthanized. Murdered, in the same labs where they were created.

"And there were incidents on and around Hera involving old humans. A month before my family left Hera, a survey team in the Delta Medea system was almost wiped out by some old-human smugglers. The survivors said they'd been cooperating until the smugglers figured out what they were, and then the prospectors bombarded them from space. Then there was a case where another old-human pirate crew blackmailed the Modality. They wanted a hundred tons of dilithium every year, in exchange for not telling anyone what we are."

"None of that could have left a favorable impression of what you call 'old humans,'" Deanna observed.

"Counselor, it all left a frightening impression of old humans," Astrid said. "We—"

"Which brings me to another point," Trask said. Worf watched him lean forward and jab a long finger onto the tabletop. "If Herans are so damned scared of us, why didn't these monsters just exterminate us? They could have arranged that a lot more easily than this genetic-engineering bug, and it would have been safer for them."

"They need us alive," Riker suggested. "If humanity died off overnight it would destabilize this entire quadrant. You'd literally have a half-dozen empires—Gorn, Romulans, Orion pirates, Ferengi, Cardassians, even the Klingons—fighting over what was left of Federation space. Hera could be destroyed in the chaos. We protect them just by existing."

"I can think of a simpler explanation," Picard said. "The Herans shrink from extermination for the same reasons we would. They are not murderers."

Admiral Trask frowned at him. "But they are our enemies."

"No, sir," Picard said. "I recognize them as adversaries, but not as enemies."

Trask grunted. "That's a noble sentiment, Picard. The Herans may carve it on humanity's tombstone—dammit, what is it?" The intercom was demanding his attention.

"Bridge," a woman's voice said. "We have a message for Admiral Trask from Zerkalo."

"Put it on the screen," Trask said.

A battered young human in the uniform of a Starfleet security lieutenant appeared on the room's viewscreen. Worf thought he looked defeated, both physically and mentally. "Admiral Trask," the man said in obvious relief. "You have to get us out of this mess."

"What 'mess'?" Trask asked. "Report, Lieutenant."

"The Zerkalan police, sir." The man seemed to shake himself before he made his report. "Pursuant to our orders, Commander Zawara and I came to Zerkalo and attempted to locate the two suspects. The local authorities gave us permission to question them, and we thought—sir, Commander Zawara did everything by the book, but when we entered the Kemals' home they overpowered us and expelled us. We were retrieved by a medical team who reported us to the Zerkalan police. We're charged with . . ." he hesitated, ". . . trespass, forcible entry, assault, possession of weapons and use of weapons."

Worf heard the admiral grind his teeth; his flat human molars made an unpleasant gritting sound. "Where's Zawara" he demanded.

"He's still in the hospital," the man said. "Sir, can they do this?"

"They can," Astrid said. "Lieutenant, what's your name?"

He blinked in surprise. "My name? Hans McDowell."

She nodded. "Were my parents hurt, Hans McDowell?"

"Your parents?" McDowell looked dismayed. "Uh, Ivan Kemal burned his hand when he grabbed Commander Zawara's phaser. The power cell ruptured when he crushed it. I managed to stun Lenore Kemal, but my shot was ineffective and she tossed me through a window before I could fire a second burst."

"I see." Astrid ran a hand over her eyes. "When you have permission to question somebody on Zerkalo, it means you wait for them to show up at the police station. If they feel like cooperating. Going to their home is illegal, unless you have evidence of criminal intent on their part. And weapons? Even our police don't carry anything stronger than sonic stunners."

"We didn't know about that," McDowell said.

"Somebody should have told you," Astrid said. Her fingers drummed lightly on the tabletop. "There are some people who don't want us to join the Federation. Maybe the right person kept quiet to stir up an incident. I'll talk to a few people and see if I can straighten this out. Don't let yourself worry, Hans McDowell."

Riker looked suspicious as the connection broke. "You're going to help? Why?"

Astrid looked puzzled. "Shouldn't I? They were set up and I want to see my planet join the Federation. It's in our best interest. Operator, connect me with Judge Selemanaban."

"Judge Selemanaban is unavailable," a masculine computer voice replied.

"Can you get President Stoneroots?"

"One moment."

Worf felt surprised. "This is your planetary president? This seems informal."

"That's how we do things," Astrid said. "The government is just a part-time thing for us. Besides, Sto's known me since I was four."

Worf saw a new scene appear on the conference room's screen: a cluttered workshop. A massive Derevo tree stood in the center of it, its roots planted inside a mobile hydroponics tub that soaked them in nutrients. It turned an eyestalk toward the phone, then pulled several tentacles from a disassembled robot and waved them at the phone. Astrid smiled and returned the gestures. The

Derevo's tub floated it across the workshop to a bench, where Stoneroots touched its tentacles to a voder pad on its workbench. "Okay, 'trid," the pad said. Its voice was rich and resonant, with what Worf thought of as a standard Federation accent. "We'll talk mouth-style for your friends. I guess you heard the news."

"I heard some of it, Sto. Are my folks okay?"

"They're fine," it said, giving her a speculative look with several bobbing eyestalks. "When we asked these Federation cops why they were here, they gave us this wild story about genetic plagues and secret agents, and you and your folks being genetically engineered."

"We are," Astrid said bleakly.

Stoneroots waggled a tentacle at her. "I always thought you were too pretty to be just human."

"Th-thanks," Astrid said. Worf watched her knuckles turn white as she clasped her hands together. "Sto, are my folks having any problems?"

The Derevo waved a tentacle in dismissal. "Aside from these cops everything's been peaceful."

"Good," Astrid said. "I was scared I'd get them in trouble."

"Over what?" Worf thought Stoneroots seemed genuinely perplexed. "It would've been polite if they'd mentioned this, but that's their business. Say, you aren't having any trouble, are you?"

"Nothing I can't handle," she said. "Sto, what are you going to do to those cops? What happened was a misunderstanding. Somebody didn't brief them on our procedures. You can't blame them for that."

"I can't, but other people can," Stoneroots said. "Don't worry, all we'll do is deport them, after we—"

Trask looked shocked. "'Deport' my agents?" he said to Stoneroots. "Who do you think you are?"

"Well, they tell me I'm the president of this open-air loony bin." Several of Stoneroots's eyestalks peered out of the screen. "Are you that admiral these cops talked about?"

"I'm Admiral Allen Trask," he said.

The tree seemed to nod. "Keep yourself available. We're going to extradite you for a trial."

"You can't do that!" Trask said.

"Guess again," Stoneroots said. "We really object to having our citizens abused. A lot of people are worked up about this." The eyestalks swiveled toward Astrid. "Are you sure you're all right?"

"I've had a few problems," she said, "but Captain Picard's helping me. I'm all right."

"I see." It hesitated as though certain she was hiding the truth. "Call me if there's anything you need, 'trid."

Trask turned to Picard after the connection broke. "Zerkalans seem to be your sort of people, Picard," he said.

"I find much to admire in President Stoneroots's attitude," Picard replied.

"Dammit." Astrid slowly bent over the tabletop as if caught in the grip of a massive gravitational field. She hid her face against one arm, and her shoulders shook as she pounded a fist against the table. The blows punctuated her words. "Dammit—dammit—they told me—had to be careful—dammit, this didn't have to *happen!*" Her fist smashed the tabletop. Half-meter-long cracks radiated through the composite material.

Worf saw that her hand was bleeding. Crusher got up and went to Astrid. When the doctor reached for her hand Astrid pulled away, and for a brief moment Worf saw the animal fright on her face. It faded, however, and Astrid put out her hand. "You've broken the fifth metacarpal bone," Crusher said after she had examined the injury. "Go to sickbay. You might feel more comfortable with Dr. Par'mit'kon," she added.

"Thank you." Astrid stood up and spoke in a level voice, as though the pain did not touch her. "Doctor, you were supposed to run some more tests on me."

"Counselor Troi wanted to wait," Beverly said. "She says you were upset the last time I tested you."

"I was." Astrid paused, an introspective look on her face. "I can handle it now."

Deanna looked dubious. "I don't think it's a good idea yet, Astrid."

"Counselor, I want to do this," she said. "There are a lot of things my parents never told me about myself. Maybe they didn't know themselves. I need to find out, to know what I am."

"We'll talk about this after your hand has healed," Deanna said. Astrid nodded and left the conference room.

"She does not behave like a weapon," Worf said, looking at the cracked and dished-in tabletop. He knew the material's strength, and it surprised him that Astrid had suffered only a minor injury. "Her instinct is not to attack what she fears."

"Lucky me," Crusher said uneasily as she returned to her seat. "Counselor, I take it we just saw an emotional overload."

"We did," Deanna said. "She's managed to control her fear before now, but it was just too much when she discovered that all her hiding and lying were unnecessary."

"On Zerkalo, maybe," Geordi muttered. Worf wondered at the shame in his voice, but said nothing; the plague had disturbed all of the ship's humans in different ways. "I wonder if her 'designers' understood what they were doing."

"What do you mean?" Riker asked.

"Well, like Worf said, she doesn't act like a weapon," the engineer said. "Maybe her emotional differences would serve a purpose in combat, but I'm not sure these designers thought about the effects they'd have on people when they weren't fighting."

"I have to agree with that," Deanna said. "In my time with her I've noticed several oddities about her emotional makeup."

"What are they, Counselor?" Picard asked.

"First of all, she has a strong tendency to feel guilt when she does something she considers wrong," Deanna said. "It's been raised to an almost pathological level. On the surface that seems like a good idea. A Heran soldier would probably rather die than disobey an order or run away from combat."

Worf growled thoughtfully. Guilt was not a Klingon emotion, although he suspected it was similar to a sense of dishonor. "Dunbar apologized to me when he attempted to kill me," he said. "Was that guilty behavior?"

"Yes," Deanna said. "Normal humans don't enjoy taking life, even when necessary. It produces guilt, which could make a soldier hesitant about going to war, or starting one. Astrid feels guilty about killing Dunbar, even though she knows it was the only way to save her life—and yours, Worf. It's a very strange emotion to build into would-be conquerors."

"That didn't stop the Herans from attacking us," Trask said. "What else have you found?"

"She's not very aggressive," Deanna said. "Herans have a genetic predisposition toward extreme aggression, but they're taught to control it at an early age in 'aggression classes.' She took the first of these classes before she left Hera, and her parents continued this training after they reached Zerkalo. Astrid says that these classes are unpopular because the necessity of taking them reminds the Herans that they were designed as weapons."

"And you believe that?" Trask asked.

"*She* believes that," Deanna replied. "And it fits what I know of her and the other Herans. Aggression can be a useful trait, but too much of it can disrupt a society."

Worf grunted; that observation ran counter to every Klingon's experience in daily life. "Soldiers should be aggressive," he said.

"That's true," Picard noted. "But off the battlefield, aggression can be a dangerous trait in a soldier."

"Khan Singh had a lot of aggression in him," Riker said. "What else can you tell us?"

"Most humanoids have an instinctive need to belong to a peer group," Deanna said. "A tribe, a family, a society. Again, this sense has been amplified in Astrid. It produces a powerful sense of loyalty, which is a useful emotion in a soldier, but it's closely related to empathy. Astrid finds it easy to empathize with her enemies, which is not a soldierly trait."

"Perhaps somebody sabotaged the designers' plans," Worf said.

"That is improbable," Data said. "Sabotage in a genetic-engineering project would not result in a healthy, functional entity. The results we have observed in Dr. Kemal would require a large amount of careful planning."

"Then maybe the designers outsmarted themselves," Trask suggested. "But there's no question that these self-appointed superhumans are willing to attack us, no matter how unhappy they feel about fighting."

"There is another matter," Worf said. "We know little of Herans beyond what Dr. Kemal has told us."

"I know," Trask said. "Even if she's totally honest, we can't assume she's a typical Heran. We have to guard against thinking that just because she seems like a decent kid, the others are like that." Worf nodded in approval of the admiral's sentiment; for a human, Trask had a lively sense of suspicion.

"Bridge to captain," a man's voice said over the intercom. "Sir, we have a transmission from Starfleet Command."

"Pipe it down here," Picard said.

Admiral Huang appeared on the screen. Worf thought he looked unhappy, which in a Starfleet admiral suggested the pleasant prospect of trouble. "Captain Picard, if you can negotiate with the Herans, the Federation Council wants you to obtain a cessation of hostilities and an assurance that these assaults will end. But if you can't deal with them, you are to scout their system and deliver a tactical report to Admiral Hoskins."

"And then we'll crush them," Trask said.

"No, Allen," Huang said. "We'll blockade their planet and neutralize their military forces. There is one bright spot," he continued. "The Klingon Empire is sending a fleet to aid us in our operations against Hera. Huang out."

"He didn't say when the Klingons would join the party," Riker observed as the admiral's image winked out.

"They will coordinate their attack," Worf assured him. "Captain, I suggest that I contact the Klingon force and make certain they understand the situation."

"Make it so," Picard said.

Worf got up to leave. He did not share Picard's dismay at the thought of war. He wanted to avenge the dishonor of his defeat at Dunbar's hands, if the Herans were capable of giving honorable combat. Whatever they were, they had a very peculiar notion of how to fight a war.

Chapter Thirteen

"I DON'T RECALL seeing you in here before, Commander," Slava ibn Abdalla said. The ship's senior botanist deftly snipped the thorns from one of the roses he had cut for Geordi. Ibn Abdalla cultivated the arboretum as a hobby, and he somehow managed to make plants from a score of incompatible ecologies flourish. The air was a riot of clashing odors: sweet, spicy and musty, along with several scents that could only have pleased a thoroughly nonhuman nose. "I guess engineering doesn't leave you much free time."

"Well, it leaves me enough time to put my foot in my mouth," he said. He watched as ibn Abdalla wrapped the rose stems in translucent plastic. "I hope this does the trick."

"Roses are a good way to begin an apology," ibn Abdalla said. He gave Geordi a quizzical look. "Although I doubt you could have hurt a woman's feelings badly enough to need a dozen long-stemmed roses. You don't seem the type."

"I'm a man of many talents," Geordi said as he took the roses. "Thanks, Lieutenant."

Geordi left the arboretum and asked the computer for Astrid's location. She was in one of the observation galleries on deck ten. He felt nervous, but he reminded himself he had put this off too long out of embarrassment.

The observation gallery was a section of corridor along the outer hull, set with large windows. Geordi found Astrid looking at the starfield off the ship's port side. Astrid was the only person in the gallery, and she looked at Geordi as he walked up to her and held out the flowers. "I'm sorry for the way I acted," he said awkwardly. He felt himself floundering, unsure of what to say next.

"Thank you," Astrid said as she took the roses. Geordi thought she looked pleased. "How have you been?"

"All right," Geordi said. He wished he wasn't so nervous; it had been a long time since he had felt this uncomfortable around a woman. He told himself that it was not because she was genetically engineered. "I've been kind of busy . . . you know."

"Same here," she said. She sat down on the window's sill, bringing herself down to his eye level. Geordi found that he liked that. "I've been taking psychological tests, recording what I remember about Hera—things like that. Intelligence ought to be able to deduce something from that."

Geordi nodded. "I want to thank you for that advice about the *Temenus*. I should have given you credit at the conference, and I wish I'd had enough sense to have you look at *Temenus* with me," he added.

"I don't think there was much else to find," she said. "The Herans wouldn't have put much secret equipment on it. There was too much risk of a ship like that being captured. Probably—"

A sharp, piercing whistle interrupted her. "Hi, monster!" somebody shouted from the far end of the gallery.

Geordi looked and saw a tall, massive spider-creature shamble toward him on four legs.

"K'Sah," Astrid said in quiet resignation. "Geordi, do you know anything about K'Sah?"

Geordi nodded. "Worf warned me about him, but Counselor Troi tells me he's been learning to mind his manners," he added.

"Good." Astrid looked at K'Sah as he stepped up to her. "What can we do for you?"

"It's what I can do for you," K'Sah said. "Worf told me to keep an eye on you, so here I am . . . you know, the old Starfleet obey-your-orders bit. Say," he added, as if seized by a pleasant idea, "you've known old wrinkle-head quite a while, haven't you, La Forge?"

"I've know *Lieutenant Worf* ever since they commissioned the *Enterprise*," Geordi said. He thought about tacking on a Pa'uyk-style insult, then decided against it. K'Sah was trying to accommodate himself to a human-style sense of decorum; it might confuse him if a human suddenly spoke like a Pa'uyk. "How are you getting along with him?" Geordi asked.

"Weird." K'Sah turned his faceted eyes on Geordi. The engineer suddenly understood how some people felt when confronted by his VISOR; there was no way to read any emotion into the Pa'uyk's gaze. "Uh, I don't mean Worf, or you, okay?" K'Sah went on. "Or Kemal, I guess. I just mean—" His mandibles snapped open and shut several times. "Things are simple back home. When you want to do business, you talk a good fight, so no one thinks you're hiding what you feel. When you don't tell some creep how you can suck the juices out of his squishy, soft-shelled body—uh, nothing personal, it's not your fault you evolved without chitin—it means you're probably planning to fight.

"But you people make no sense!" he continued. "You'll be polite and smile, and you won't fight, or you'll turn around and vaporize the person you were being nice to. Or you'll threaten someone, then make friends with them. Or maybe kick them out the airlock. So who knows what to expect from you?"

"Give it time," Astrid said. Geordi could understand the sympathetic look she gave the arachnid. Like her, he was alone amid incomprehensible, possibly dangerous beings. "There are rules—"

"That's exactly what I mean!" K'Sah said in exasperation. He slammed a pair of fists against the observation window. "Everything here has rules, and one rule is that the rules change every time you think you've sunk your pincers into them. And Worf—*he* should make sense, only he doesn't. Ask him why he acts the way he does, and he says something about honor, whatever that is. Any idea what he means by 'honor'?"

Geordi shrugged. "'Honor' is what makes Worf do what's right, even when he'd be better off doing something else."

K'Sah seemed irked. "It sounds like those wrinkles on his scalp go all the way down to his brain. What's 'honorable,' and what isn't? How do Klingons tell the difference?"

"Look at it this way," Astrid said. "Honor keeps you from doing something you could get away with doing, and if you have to ask yourself if you can get away with it, it isn't honorable."

"That's another rule, isn't it?" K'Sah sounded bleak. "The explanations aren't allowed to make sense."

"Give it time," Geordi said, echoing Astrid. "Look, the next time you use the holodeck, ask the computer to set you up with a simulation of Kahless the Unforgettable. He's the Klingon who came up with their concept of honor."

K'Sah seemed to eye Geordi in astonishment. "And people say you never have any good ideas. I'll try that." He sauntered away.

Geordi watched K'Sah leave the observation gallery. "So much for him obeying Worf's orders," he said.

"I don't need a bodyguard," Astrid said. "But why do

you suppose he kept asking those questions about Klingon honor?"

"He's probably looking for new ways to annoy Worf," Geordi said. He sat down on the windowsill next to her. "How have you been? Really?"

"Okay," she said. "People have calmed down. Anyway, you've probably got some questions about the *Temenus.*"

"Well . . ." he began. A couple of crewmembers, humans, walked into the gallery. Astrid couldn't have seen them from where she sat, but they spotted her, stopped and turned around. The hostility on their faces made Geordi realize how lonely she must be. "I'd rather hear about Zerkalo. Why don't we talk about it in Ten-Forward?"

She looked dazed. "I'd like that."

The Dixon Hill mystery novels had been written in the twentieth century, and they had been lost in the chaos that had followed the Eugenics Wars. From time to time, librarians stumbled across a "new" Hill novel, misfiled amid other books or hidden in an obscure archive, and downloaded it into the Federation publication network. Picard had flagged the ship's computer to notify him whenever a Hill novel appeared in the net.

Picard was about to bed down for the night when the computer informed him that *The Final Account* was available. Smiling in anticipation, Picard went to the replicator. *"The Final Account,* hardcover format," he said. "Leather binding and rag-cloth paper."

A book appeared in the replicator, but not the Dixon Hill novel that Picard had requested. Instead the book bore a large red title: *Francis Bacon: The True Bard of Avon.*

Picard was not amused. Over the centuries, many people had tried to claim that the plays associated with William Shakespeare had been written by someone else. The mere thought of this angered him.

"Computer," he said, and repeated his request for the Dixon Hill novel. Another copy of *The True Bard of Avon* appeared.

"Computer," Picard said, "where did this book come from?"

"It is a gift from Lieutenant Worf," the machine answered.

Picard sighed. Worf would never play a joke on anyone; the Klingon viewed humor as a curse. "Picard to Worf. I'd like to see you in my quarters."

Worf appeared moments later. He scowled as Picard handed him the book. "Yes, sir?" he said, looking with distaste at the large volume.

"The computer claims it is a gift from you," Picard said.

"That is not true," Worf protested. "Shakespeare had the soul of a Klingon. I would never . . ."

"I didn't suspect you of anything," Picard said. "It would appear we are both the victims of a rather infantile joke. I would ignore this if it did not involve tampering with the computer."

"I will investigate, sir," Worf said. He glowered at the book as though wishing it had a throat to rip out.

"Very good," Picard said. He smiled as Worf left the room, and wondered if he or Worf had been the intended butt of this joke.

It was ship's evening and Riker had the bridge. Everything was quiet, which suited him. He was in no mood for trouble. The only break in the routine of reports was a coded message for Admiral Trask, and that only added to the evening's reassuring feel of normality. Private messages were just one more part of the routine.

Riker was halfway through his watch when Deanna came in. She looked upset. "Are you all right, Counselor?" Riker asked.

"No." She sat down next to Riker. "I just had this nightmare. I was watching the *Enterprise,* and I was very frightened—of *us*. I . . . in this dream I felt like I was Astrid Kemal, but she's awake, so I wasn't picking up one of her nightmares."

Riker barely hesitated. "Yellow alert, captain to the bridge. Mr. Data, I want a full sensor scan for Heran ships. Find whoever's watching us."

"Aye, sir." Data had been sitting at the navigator's position. He went to the science officer's station and searched the space around the *Enterprise.*

Riker stared at the bridge's main viewer. The screen showed nothing but the starfield ahead of the ship. Riker hoped that something would show up, to give him the chance to give the Herans a taste of their own medicine.

Very carefully, Deanna touched his wrist. "How did you get along with Astrid in Ten-Forward?"

Riker let out a sigh. Deanna, either through her question or her touch, had drained the anger from him. "Not as well as I should have," he said. "She didn't stay in Ten-Forward long, and I haven't had the time to look her up again. Deanna—"

"I know," she said. "This isn't the time or the place. We'll talk later."

Data spoke. "Commander, there is heavy interference, but I have fragmentary readings on two ships at bearing thirty-eight-mark-zero two, range approximately one billion kilometers—odd," the android said, as his hands moved over the control panel before him. "I now read only one ship."

Deanna got up and joined him at the science station. "Could it be a sensor ghost?" she asked.

"That is probable," Data said. "The one positive sensor contact is generating unusual interference patterns. I can barely detect it."

"But we have one solid contact," Riker noted. "Helm, come to that bearing and pursue," he ordered.

"Aye, sir," the helmsman said. *Enterprise* hummed with power as she entered a slow turn.

Data remained at the science officer's station and made a further report as Worf, Picard and Admiral

Trask entered the bridge. Worf took over his station while Picard and Trask seated themselves. "I now have partial readings on a ship similar to the *Temenus*. It is heavily shielded and changing course to evade us. It has a crew of three."

"A picket ship," Trask suggested, reading the tactical information on a viewer. "A sentry. Its position places it almost directly between Hera and the Federation."

"And it knows we're here," Picard said. "Mr. Worf, hail that ship."

"Aye, sir." Worf touched a spot on his control panel, then touched it again. "No response, sir."

"Apparently they have nothing to say," Picard said.

"It's running *away* from the Heran system," Riker said, reading the data on the main viewer. "Almost as though it's trying to distract us."

"I agree," Picard said. "Resume course for Hera. Let's see how it responds."

Enterprise turned slowly and the ship was only halfway through the maneuver when Data spoke again. "The Heran ship is turning to bearing two-twelve-seven, mark six two," he said. "Accelerating to warp nine-point-nine-five."

"Intercept course," Worf reported. "It is charging phasers."

"Red alert," Picard ordered. "Time to intercept?" he added as the general alarm sounded.

"Fifty-seven seconds," Worf said. "They are firing torpedoes—correction, one torpedo."

"Only one?" Riker asked uneasily. He couldn't shake the feeling that the Heran ship was as dangerous as it was arrogant, and that its torpedo would outclass its Federation equivalent.

"One is enough," Picard said. "Helm, steer evasive. Mr. Worf, return fire with photon torpedoes, tight spread."

"Aye, sir." Seconds later Riker heard the torpedo tubes discharge their first volley.

The Heran torpedo struck as the tubes were reloading.

The bridge seemed to shudder with unusual force at the explosion. "Impact on forward shield," Worf reported. "Down fifty percent."

"They've got something new," Trask said. Riker nodded in agreement. One torpedo shouldn't do that much damage.

Seconds later the *Enterprise*'s torpedoes found their target and the Heran ship was lost in the glare of annihilating antimatter. "Their forward shield is down only fifteen percent," Worf reported as the glare cleared. Riker and Picard traded a surprised look at the small ship's power.

The tubes fired again as the Heran ship pressed its attack. Unlike the *Enterprise* it made no evasive turns, accepting a second torpedo hit as it closed the range between itself and the Federation vessel. "They want to get within phaser range," Riker said to Picard, recalling Geordi's analysis of the *Temenus*'s shields. The *Enterprise* would be unable to use her torpedoes at that short a range; the detonations would endanger her as much as they did the enemy. Phasers could be equally dangerous.

Picard saw that as well. "Helm, tie into the weapons station," he said. "I want the tightest possible turn as we fire phasers. Slow to warp three."

"Do you think we can dodge a reflected beam?" Trask asked.

"Perhaps, Admiral," Picard said as the tubes launched a third round. "A phaser beam's speed isn't infinite. We'll have a chance."

A torpedo hit rocked the *Enterprise*'s starboard side, and then the Heran ship was within phaser range. Its phaser beams laced into the saucer-shaped primary hull, and the bridge lights dimmed as the computer rerouted power to the shields. *Enterprise* returned the fire, and its shots seemed to glance off the enemy ship as harmlessly as flashlight beams striking a mirror. The shields reflected the energies back toward their source, but the *Enterprise*'s tight maneuvers spoiled their aim. Even so, Riker realized that the near misses were just barely that.

Alarms sounded as a shield burned out. *Enterprise* continued to pump energy into the Heran ship, and for all its courage the attacker was no match for the *Enterprise*'s phasers. In an instant its shields overloaded and collapsed, and its metal skin peeled away like foil as sequential explosions rippled through its hull. Then the reactor detonated, and the main viewscreen dimmed against the flood of light.

Riker let out his breath. "Indeed, Number One," Picard said dryly. "Secure from red alert. Report damages and casualties, and resume course for Hera."

"Aye, sir." Riker looked at the main viewer, where glowing fragments of the Heran ship still tumbled against the stars. "If they all fight like this . . ." He shook his head as his voice trailed off.

Underground meetings are by necessity secret, and Marla had a bad scare when Alistair Molyneux materialized in Selig Thorn's doorway that night. "Don't worry," Selig told Marla, seeing how startled she was. "Director Molyneux recruited me into the resistance."

Molyneux was the last person Marla would have suspected of radical leanings. He was in charge of Hera's military defenses. "You?" she blurted.

Molyneux's grin made him look even more boyish than normal. "Me and half of my staff," he said as he sat down with the other people in the front room.

Marla shook her head. "Now I know how to destroy the Modality. Tell them and give them all heart failure."

"I wish that could work," Molyneux said above the chuckles in the room. "I'd try it, because we've run out of time."

That brought silence. "Unity," Nanda Yee said. She looked unsurprised, as though she had always expected the worst. "The old humans have already found out about the plague?"

"Yes," Molyneux said. "Everything has gone wrong. The *Temenus*'s crew was rescued by a Federation starship. Blaisdell repaid his rescuers by infecting them with the Unity virus. We've intercepted subspace messages which prove that the old humans know what was done to them, and they know what we are. Just as bad, the Modality sent a trio of high-warp robot cruisers to raid human space. They stopped short of murdering anyone during the raids, but they did considerable damage to a station and at least a dozen starships. The Modality followed this with a declaration of war."

"Why?" Marla asked in shock.

"To provoke the old humans, of course," Dallas said.

"Or to provoke Hera," Molyneux said. "The Modality has released a false version of events, making it sound as though we're the victims of old-human aggression. The idea is to make us fight first and think later. In any case the Federation has reacted exactly as we feared, and as I'm sure the Modality hoped. They've dispatched an invasion force which will arrive in six days, now. A few hours ago the Modality sent all five of our primary combat ships to intercept the attack force.

"There's more. A short while ago they launched three couriers—*Heraclidae*, *Arcadia* and *Pelasgus*—with orders to infect Earth and two other old-human worlds with Unity if Hera is attacked. In addition, the Modality has activated its ground defense plan. Among other things, they're going to issue programs to allow household replicators to make weapons."

The realization that Lee's sacrifice had been for nothing had numbed Marla, but now she shared the dismay that hung in the room. "Are they stupid?" John Yakovlev demanded, in the worst insult one Heran could apply to another. "Do they think everyone's going to fight to the death to defend the Modality?"

Molyneux shook his head. "They think that if everyone is armed, the Federation will think twice about invading us."

"That's probably right," Dallas said acidly. "Instead they'll stand back and fry us from orbit."

"I agree," a young woman said. She had introduced herself to Marla as Serai Tsu-Chang, a historian specializing in old-human societies and psychologies. "The old humans will fight to win, no matter what the cost. They won't care how many of their enemies they kill. That's their traditional approach to war-making."

"And they devastated whole planets during the Klingon Wars," Molyneux said. Marla thought he looked weary. "I know our military position better than anyone else. We can't keep the old humans from destroying us."

"Why not?" someone asked. "They outnumber us, but we can make better weapons, and we were designed to be weapons ourselves. And they're not much better than savages. Why not turn against them?"

"Khan Singh thought that way," Tsu-Chang said. "So did an old human named Custer."

"And any war against the old humans would be one of annihilation," Molyneux said. "Even if we could win, I took this job to defend Hera, not to become a butcher. Our best option is to surrender before the old humans invade, and hope to negotiate a peace before we're wiped out. It's a gamble, but the alternative is certain destruction."

"There's one thing wrong with that plan," Selig said. "The Modality will never surrender."

"Can we overthrow them before the Federation attacks?" Yee asked. "We could form a provisional government and surrender."

Selig shook his head. "We don't have the resources for a direct assault."

"Can we make it impossible to fight?" Marla asked. When the others looked at her she continued, "If we can keep the Modality from handing out weapons, we'll knock out a big part of their plan. And if there's some way to immobilize Combat Operations and Central Security, it won't matter what orders they give."

"My group has studied something that might work here," Yee said. "We've developed a fractal worm program. It infiltrates and disables a computer system, and when it senses it's being erased by the safeguards, it reproduces itself—with enough changes so the system has to develop a new approach to erase it again. It will keep a system disabled for at least a week."

"That should be long enough to force a surrender," Molyneux said. Dallas got up and walked out then. Marla gestured to Selig to wait, then followed the boy outside.

There was a small grove of fruit trees behind the Thorn house, and Marla followed Dallas into them. When she caught up with him he was sitting under a tree with Selig's cat. "Terrific," the boy said as he scratched the cat's head. "Surrender to the primals and *trust* them."

Marla sat down with him. "Can you think of a better alternative?" She watched him shake his head in the starlight. "Neither can I."

"Nor I," Molyneux said as he came out of the house. He sighed. "I'm a hell of a defense director. My first real war, and I'm looking for a way to surrender before it starts."

"Your job isn't to fight," Marla said as he walked over and sat down with them. "It's to defend Hera. You can't defend it by letting it be destroyed."

"It still galls me," he said, and shook his head. "It means trusting the primals to be reasonable, which is chancy. Damn the Modality for getting us into this mess."

"Why did they do it, anyway?" Dallas asked. "You're one of them. You should know."

"They claim it's for the best," Molyneux said. "We'll raise the old humans to our level, which will do them good. And when the changes take effect in another generation, that'll spell an end to the attacks, and to the danger of our being discovered as something different. We'll look like just one more planet afflicted by this unknown process."

"Sometimes I think the Modality just wants power," Marla suggested.

"I agree," Molyneux said. "If Unity had worked, we would have conquered the human race without it even knowing, and the senior leadership thinks it's inevitable that any Heran would follow the best leaders around."

"Who just happen to be them," Marla said.

Molyneux nodded. "The Modality believes its own doctrines. Now all they're doing is compounding their mistakes. If they can't conquer the galaxy with brains, they'll do it like savages."

"They act like they all flunked basic aggression," Dallas said. "Or did they decide not to control it?"

"I don't know," Molyneux said. "Me, I have my aggression buried so deep I hardly even feel it. Most people do. But maybe you need to let it come to the surface to rule a planet and deal with the old humans." He shook his head. "Anyway, Marla, Selig told me that you heard something about an 'originator file' during your interrogation."

"I didn't hear much," Marla said. "Just enough to convince me that they think the file could change our attitudes about the originators. Don't you know anything about it?"

Molyneux shook his head. "I know it exists. But what it contains—well, people have disappeared just for having heard about it. The question is, what's so important about changing our attitude? The Senior acts like it's a threat to the Modality. If—"

The cat growled. "Trouble," Dallas murmured. "Where is it, Koshka?"

The cat growled again and rose to its feet, aiming its body toward the west. Marla heard the hum of a high-speed transport in the air. The hum's decreasing pitch told her it was slowing rapidly.

Light glared and the Thorn house exploded. Through the tree trunks Marla saw phaser beams slice down from the sky and pick off people who ran out of the burning structure. Marla held still, not daring to breathe.

Molyneux pulled a cloth from a pocket and unfolded it on the ground. "Stunner," he whispered, and a handgun appeared atop the pocket replicator. He gave the weapon to Dallas, then armed himself and Marla. "Koshka, are there any more assault carriers out there?" The cat shook its head.

Marla waited. The carrier landed between the house and the grove, and a half-dozen Central Security operatives climbed out. They circled the house as it burned, scanning it and applying quantum modulators to the flames, strengthening the chemical bonds in wood and other materials until they became too strong to break and release their energy. "Okay, they're all dead," a man said a moment after the fire went out. "Where are you going, Amalthea?"

"I heard something in those trees," a woman answered. Marla heard her walking toward the grove. At once Koshka got up and padded toward the ruined house, growling quietly.

"You heard a cat," the man said in annoyance. "Come on. We have to get back to base." The Central Security agents returned to their vehicle, and a moment later it accelerated into the night sky. Marla started breathing again.

Dallas clipped his stunner to his belt. "They wiped us out," he said numbly. Marla could only nod. By destroying the resistance's leaders now, they had neutralized the resistance at a crucial moment. There would be nothing to interfere with the Modality's plans.

Molyneux had reached the same conclusion. "They've won."

"No," Marla said, surprising herself. She had not come so far only to see everything lost. "Do you have any other contacts with the resistance?"

"I know some people in South Mytilene," Molyneux said. "Assuming that CS hasn't wiped them out, too."

"They wouldn't bother taking out more than the top leaders," Marla said as she stood up. "That would be pointless. We'd better get moving."

"In a minute," Dallas said. He stood up and stared at the wreckage where his uncle had just died.

Chapter Fourteen

"I CAN TELL YOU what they hit us with, but I can't tell you how they did it," Geordi told the people gathered around the conference table. Picard thought that the young engineer seemed bewildered. The rest of the command staff and Admiral Trask listened intently to him. Only Astrid, who sat next to Geordi, appeared calm. "That torpedo wasn't armed with antimatter. Its warhead was a quantum black hole, with a mass of approximately ten tons. A black hole that small isn't stable; it evaporates through quantum tunneling, losing mass one particle at a time until its blackbody temperature rises exponentially and—"

"I think we're all familiar with elementary physics," Admiral Trask said.

"Then you know that when a quantum black hole dies, it instantaneously releases all of its remaining mass as energy," Geordi said. "The end result is the same as a matter-antimatter reaction—a burst of high-energy gamma rays. But our photon torpedoes only carry ten kilograms of antimatter. This is a lot more potent."

"Quantum black holes are rare," Riker said. "Does this mean the Herans can make them?"

"Yes, but don't ask me how," Geordi said. "And don't ask me how they can make them explode when they choose. It's theoretically impossible—which means they have better theories than we do. This is what I was afraid of. They're so advanced that they could be a match for the entire Federation."

"We were a match for that ship," Trask said.

"Just barely," Worf said. "The enemy vessel was no more than a scoutship, yet it was almost as heavily armed as the *Enterprise*. A more powerful ship could prove—challenging."

"And we're likely to face bigger ships when we reach Hera," Picard noted. He felt grimly amused by Worf's tone. "Their home planet won't be defenseless."

"I concur," Trask said. "We have to fight but, dammit, going to war is always a gamble, and I don't know the odds on this bet."

"Does this mean you're willing to negotiate with Hera?" Picard asked him.

"No." He looked grim. "It means I got a coded message from Starbase One-Seven-One before the attack. Blaisdell tried to escape. He was being transferred from the *Marconi* when he got loose, killed two guards and stole a runabout. The *Marconi* chased him down, and when he wouldn't surrender they destroyed him. Blaisdell almost made it, too. Somehow he coaxed warp nine from that runabout. The *Marconi* damaged its warp drive during the pursuit."

"So you would rather not fight people who are that determined," Deanna Troi said.

"That's right, Counselor," Trask said. "People who'll fight to the death are dangerous. I just hope this isn't the shape of things to come."

"As do I," Picard said. He turned to Astrid. "Doctor, when we spoke in Ten-Forward you mentioned the likelihood of a Heran resistance movement. We may hope that they are more amenable to peace than the Heran government. Have you any thoughts on them?"

"Beyond the fact that somebody sabotaged the *Temenus?*" She nodded calmly. "If they're like me, they're scared. If they know about the Modality's actions, they're going to be unhappy with it. Not only has the Modality endangered Hera, but—*attacking* people—Captain, we'll fight when we're attacked, we'll defend ourselves, but the idea of starting a war—it . . . it . . ."

"It makes you sick," Geordi said.

"I guess that's the word," she said. "I don't know what it feels like to be sick, but what I feel now is horrible."

"But you aren't in this resistance," Trask said. "You don't know what they're thinking—*if* this underground exists."

Astrid shook her head. "It exists. Hera has always been divided into factions. You're right, I can't know what they're thinking, but I know what they *feel.* Give them a chance for peace and they'll take it."

"How?" Riker asked. "From what you say, they're convinced we're a bunch of genocidal maniacs. What would make them think otherwise?"

"Maybe we should show them that we *want* them to survive," Geordi suggested. "They know things we'll want to know. They have to know we'd lose all that if we wiped them out."

"They're bound to have a cure for what they did to us," Crusher said. "That would be more important."

"It sounds terrific," Trask said in a sour voice. "We tell them to disarm, let us occupy Hera, and hand over all their secrets, in exchange for which we graciously allow them to continue breathing. Suppose they don't buy it?"

"Then we'll have a problem," Picard said. "But it could form the basis for negotiation."

The intercom signaled for attention. "Go ahead," Picard answered.

Ensign Rager spoke. "Captain, we have a message for Dr. Kemal from Zerkalo."

Picard nodded to her. "Go ahead," Astrid said.

President Stoneroots appeared on the conference room's viewscreen. "Hi, 'trid," it said through its computer translator. "Why didn't you tell me they tried to arrest you?" It held up a tentacle. "I know, I know. You didn't want anyone to worry. So, what's going on?"

Astrid sighed. "It's pretty much a dead issue now," she said. "Captain Picard talked them out of arresting me."

"No, he didn't," Stoneroots said. "I just called Ambassador Bakhra on Earth. She says there's a warrant for your arrest and she can't get it rescinded, even though it hasn't any legal basis. Is that admiral still around?"

"I'm here," Trask said.

Stoneroots eyed him coldly. "We now give you the same message we gave to your Federation. If you don't stop mistreating one of our citizens, Zerkalo will end its negotiations to join the Federation. And if anything happens to her, Allen clan-Trask, we shall hold you personally accountable."

Trask glowered at him. "If you're threatening me—"

"We are," Stoneroots said. "And we keep our threats. We have already filed extradition papers on you, and we are holding your agents as material witnesses. If you want to face some extra charges at your trial, then keep acting the way you have. All." Its image winked out.

"Sto means it, Admiral," Astrid said. "When a Derevo starts talking in the plural, it—"

"I've studied Derevo customs," Trask said. "But if that oversized fruit tree thinks it's going to be easy to extradite a member of Starfleet, it's wrong. And if Zerkalo wants to walk out on us, let them. The Federation doesn't need them."

"No more than we 'need' any other planet," Picard said. "And this withdrawal could have unpleasant repercussions on other worlds. The Bajorans in particular are quite sensitive to any perceived bullying."

"If the Zerkalans follow through," Trask said. "They'd lose a lot by withdrawing, especially when it comes to commerce."

"Sto doesn't bluff," Astrid told him. "And if you think it said that just because it's my friend, you're dead wrong. We Zerkalans put a lot of value on individual rights."

"I take President Stoneroots's promises seriously," Picard said, "but I am confident that we can resolve your problem without further inconvenience to you, or aggravation to your world. Dr. Kemal, have you any suggestions on how to negotiate with the Herans?"

"Be straightforward with them, sir," Astrid said. "If they want a way out of this mess, they'll take it."

"If," Riker said. "Captain, they've gone too far to back down. They'll fight, and they'll have something up their sleeves."

The Heran attack had burned out a shield generator, and the crawl space still reeked of ozone and scorched metal. Geordi spent an awkward half hour on his back as he struggled to remove a damaged control unit and clean the blackened contacts in its receptacle. Finally he was able to slide the replacement into position. His test equipment assured him that it was working properly, which was a relief. His task would have been a lot harder if the deflector grid itself had been damaged. "La Forge to bridge," he reported. "You should have full function on the starboard shields now."

"I do not," Worf answered crossly. "The computer is displaying an error message."

"I'll come up and check it," Geordi said. He wormed his way out of the crawl space and headed for the bridge.

Captain Picard was not on duty, and as Geordi entered the bridge he saw Will Riker seated in the command chair. Geordi went to Worf's station and ran a diagnostic on the shield controls. As he had half expected, the new control unit was not quite identical to the old one, and the minor differences in its circuits generated confusion in the computer. Geordi adjusted the programming while he thought unkind thoughts about manufacturers who changed the design of "standard" units.

Riker walked over to Geordi and Worf as he finished. "I understand you saw Kemal yesterday," he said quietly.

Geordi nodded, although the question made him uneasy. Will Riker was one of his best friends, and Geordi didn't want the man's dislike of Astrid to put them at odds. "Astrid and I had dinner in Ten-Forward," he said.

"Did you have any problems?" Riker asked. "Deanna tells me that a few people are still grumbling about her. I want to nip any trouble in the bud."

"There wasn't any trouble," Geordi said. "We had a long, quiet dinner, and went for a walk in the arboretum."

Riker nodded. "Have you found out anything about that practical joke?"

Geordi was glad to change the subject. "No, and I don't think I will. There's no evidence of tampering in the computer."

"Evidence will exist," Worf rumbled. "Someone has assaulted my honor, and I shall have vengeance."

Geordi nodded. To a Klingon, honor was all-important. A dishonored Klingon could become an outcast, so distrusted that few Klingons would willingly deal with him or his family. By making Worf appear to have offended the captain, someone had placed his good name in jeopardy. "This narrows your list of suspects," Geordi said. "You're not just looking for a computer expert. You're looking for somebody who either doesn't care how important your honor is, or who *wants* to see you dishonored."

"It might be K'Sah," Riker suggested. "He seems to have it in for you, Worf."

Worf growled in agreement, then shook his head. "Unfortunately, there is evidence that K'Sah is not guilty."

Geordi nodded. "The duty log shows that he was on the bridge when the captain got that book, and he wasn't using the computer."

"He could have set up a delayed program," Riker suggested.

Geordi shook his head. "A trick like this had to be done in real time; I could find the trace from a booby-trap program like that. Besides, K'Sah isn't a cyberneticist."

Worf growled. "K'Sah is a—" An alarm flashed on the tactical display, interrupting him. "Someone is transmitting a subspace message," he said. "It is not authorized."

"Yeah." Geordi glanced at the readouts, then began working the controls. "They aren't sending from any of the usual comm stations. And I can't get a fix—damn." The transmission ended.

"Nothing?" Riker asked.

"Nothing on our end," Geordi said. "The signal was aimed at two-oh-eight-mark-twelve, but sensors indicate nothing at that bearing. What—I don't believe this. Commander, I recorded that transmission, and it just erased itself."

"Somehow I'm not surprised," Riker said grimly. "Bridge to captain."

"Go ahead, Number One," Picard answered.

"Captain, somebody on this ship just sent a coded subspace message. We can't identify either the source or a destination."

"Understood," Picard said. "Number One, Mr. La Forge, Mr. Worf, meet me in the conference room. I'll notify Admiral Trask."

"Aye, sir." Riker nodded to the other. "Let's go."

Captain Picard and Admiral Trask were already in the conference room when they arrived, along with Data and Astrid. Geordi sat down next to her. "Let's hear about this message," Trask said.

"There's not much to tell, Admiral," Geordi said. "It was a low-power transmission with limited range. It was routed through the computer system, and there was no way to identify the point of origin on this ship. It didn't seem to be aimed *at* anything, either. What's more, the message contained some sort of self-destruct program. The recording erased itself so thoroughly that I couldn't recover it."

"It sounds like we're dealing with a computer specialist here," Trask said. He looked at Astrid. "What were you doing fifteen minutes ago?"

"I was in my quarters. Alone."

"You can't deny that you could have done it," Trask said.

"I can't," she said. "My access to the computers has been restricted, but that couldn't stop me. Just the same—"

"—you didn't do it," Trask said sourly.

She nodded. "I didn't do it."

"So why don't I believe you?" Trask asked.

"Admiral, I believe her," Geordi said. He touched his VISOR. "I can sometimes see changes in people when they lie—increases in skin temperature, shifts in body-electric fields, other things. I don't see those signs in her. I think she's telling the truth."

Trask snorted. "You're forgetting something, La Forge. Her entire physiology has been modified. What works for a normal human won't work for a Heran. Lie to him, Kemal. How long have you been spying for the Cardassian Empire?"

Astrid hesitated, as though needing to shift mental gears before she could lie. "Ever since you recruited me, Admiral."

"Damn," Geordi muttered. His VISOR hadn't revealed the barest flicker in her physiological responses. "That still doesn't prove anything, Admiral. As for this computer problem, it isn't the first incident we've had lately."

"I know. Picard told me about his little 'gift,'" Trask

said. He faced Astrid. "Kemal, we're at war with Hera. Someone has been playing games with the computer. We've been attacked by a Heran ship. Now someone transmits a coded message, contents and destination unknown, and we just happen to have a Heran computer expert on board this ship."

"That's circumstantial evidence, Admiral," Picard said.

"Yes, and if this were peacetime I'd be laughed out of court," Trask said. "But this isn't peacetime and giving her the benefit of the doubt could cost us this war, not to mention the lives of everyone on this ship."

"Perhaps Counselor Troi would be best qualified to determine whether Dr. Kemal is telling the truth," Data suggested.

Trask shook his head. "I'd like to think that she could give us an easy answer, but I don't know how reliable her talents would be when the brain she'd be sensing has been modified. Worf, take her to the brig." Worf glowered at the table for a moment, then stood and nodded at Astrid.

Geordi watched in helpless frustration as they left the conference room. "I don't buy it," he said. "She killed Dunbar and she's been cooperating all along. Why would she turn around and send a message to Hera?"

"Because she could still be a Heran agent," Trask said. "The best liars are the ones who tell the truth—but not the whole truth. Her parents claim to be refugees, but this wouldn't be the first time that undercover agents have pretended to be refugees, or that they recruited their child into the family business. Why do you think we got so worked up about Simon Tarses?"

Riker nodded thoughtfully. "You're suggesting that Kemal represents a Heran faction that doesn't believe in spreading this plague, but that still wants to conquer us."

"I am," Trask said. "That's the funny thing about master races. They need inferiors to prove they're superior, and to do their dirty work for them. They wouldn't want to make us their equals. And her presence here might not be a coincidence. We're opening up Hera's sector for colonization. They'd want an agent on this ship to monitor us, and she pulled a lot of strings to get onto this ship."

Picard smiled slightly. "A rather large number of people have 'pulled strings' to join my crew, Admiral."

"Suppose I prove she didn't send that message?" Geordi asked.

"That is improbable," Data said. "It would imply that someone else made the transmission. There is no reason to suspect a second Heran agent aboard the *Enterprise.*"

"Herans aren't exactly inconspicuous," Geordi agreed reluctantly. "But maybe Blaisdell and Dunbar left a few surprises for us."

Picard nodded. "It is possible that we didn't uncover all of the programs they put in the computer. See what you can find, Mr. La Forge."

"It's a waste of time," Trask said.

"Perhaps," Picard said affably. "Admiral, might we have a word in private?" He glanced at his subordinates. Geordi, Data and Riker got up and left the conference room.

Riker stopped Geordi as soon as they were in the corridor. "Geordi—"

"What?" he said. "If you're going to tell me I'm wasting my time—"

"Take it easy," Riker said. "I think you're right about her. Trask's logic is as flimsy as a Cardassian apology . . . and that transmission was too clumsy to be hers. If she'd done it, she could have sent it without our knowing."

"This has disturbing implications," Data said. "If Dr. Kemal did not send the message, who did? And why?"

"That's what we'd damned well better find out," Riker said.

Picard looked at Trask for a long moment after the others had left the room. He felt a well-controlled anger at the admiral's actions. "Admiral, I demand to know why you arrested Dr. Kemal."

"You demand?" Trask touched his collar insignia. "In case you've forgotten, captains don't demand things from admirals. It works the other way."

"I'm aware of protocol, Admiral," Picard said. "I'm also aware that the law must be obeyed even in time of war—perhaps most especially then, when the temptation to break it is greatest. This arrest is questionable."

"No one's going to question it," Trask said. He drummed his fingers on the tabletop. "I've got reasonable cause to arrest her—more than reasonable. Better safe than sorry."

"Better for whom, Admiral?" Picard studied the man as he remained silent. He could see the admiral's true motive easily enough. Starfleet Intelligence had been shaken by its repeated failures to uncover alien threats, and Trask's predecessor, Admiral Henry, had been forced to resign in disgrace. An arrest now would make Trask appear to be on top of the situation. Inaction, on the other hand, could be read as proof of incompetence. "It appears all I can say now is that I shall log my protest of this action."

"You do that," Trask said. "And I hope you're right, Picard, because if I'm right, I've allowed a Heran agent the free run of your ship until now. Which may mean none of us will live long enough to take the stand at my court-martial."

The intercom signaled. "Bridge to captain," Ensign Rager called. "Sir, we're picking up activity on the long-range sensors. The readings are unsteady, but they're at bearing three-ten-eight, mark eleven three."

"Sounds like another Heran ship," Trask said.

"Indeed," Picard said. "I'm on my way, Ensign."

The sensor readings had improved by the time Picard and Trask reached the bridge, and the main viewer showed a precise array of five small white ships. "They're approaching us at warp nine-point-eight," Rager reported as Picard took his seat. "Their shields are up and their weapons are armed. Interception in one minute."

Picard read the tactical display as Worf and Riker entered the bridge. Each ship was better armed than the picket vessel that had attacked the *Enterprise;* their individual firepower surpassed that of the Galaxy-class starship. "Readings indicate five Herans per vessel," Worf said. "Each ship is heavily automated. They would be highly vulnerable to casualties. Recommend we go to red alert."

"Belay that," Picard said. The *Enterprise* could neither outfight nor outrun this squadron. A belligerent display now might provoke the Herans into destroying the Federation ship. "Hail them, Mr. Worf."

An image appeared on the main viewer: a spacecraft cockpit, with five massive people wedged in among control consoles. All wore silvery pressure suits with open helmets. "This is Captain Jean-Luc Picard of the Federation starship *Enterprise,*" Picard said. "With whom am I speaking?"

"Captain Jane Nkoma, Heran frigate *Comet.*" The dark woman seemed as calm as Astrid Kemal. "Surrender."

"She comes right to the point," Riker observed dryly.

Picard nodded. "Captain Nkoma, I have orders to negotiate a peace settlement with your world before hostilities break out in the Heran system."

"Hostilities broke out a long time ago," Nkoma said. "We've lost hundreds of lives in old-human attacks."

The dark, red-haired man at Nkoma's right side glanced at a computer display, then leaned closer to her. "Picard," he said in a half-audible whisper, ". . . primarily a diplomat . . . never engaged in any deceptions . . . hardly even acts like a primal."

Nkoma looked at the man. "Anything else?"

He nodded once. "He's never attacked anyone first . . . known to refrain from making counterattacks while under fire."

"And his ship isn't on combat alert now. Most peculiar." Nkoma's gaze seemed to turn inward for a moment. "Proceed, Captain," she said at last. "You under-

stand we still have to stop that task force. Nkoma out."
Her image on the screen was replaced by the five Heran
ships against the starfield. The small frigates veered away
from the *Enterprise*.

"Funny thing, Picard," Trask said. "Somebody makes
a secret transmission, and a few minutes later we're
intercepted by Heran warships. I suppose it's just a
coincidence?"

"I believe it is," Picard said, returning his gaze. He
stood up. "If you will excuse me, Admiral, I have to
contact Starfleet Command—after I make a log entry."

"We're too late," Joseph Doving said. He pushed a
chair toward Marla and seated himself on the living
room's hearth. Molyneux tossed a log into the fire, then
sat down between Marla and Dallas. "The Modality
distributed its weapons programs right after the raids,
and they've been flooding the comm net with horror
stories about that invasion fleet. Everyone will be ready
to fight by the time the old humans land."

"We had plans to counteract their propaganda," Molyneux said. "We could still implement them, if enough
people have survived. How long will it take to reorganize
the resistance?"

"At least another day," Doving said. "The damage—
computer, display flowchart sigma."

A holograph appeared in the air, a seemingly amor-
phous tangle of red, green and yellow lines. "That's the
best information we have on what's left of the organization," Doving said. "They hit us just hard enough to
paralyze us for a few days."

"Just long enough to keep us from interfering," Molyneux said. "We'll have to go with what we've got. Can we
manage to take control of *one* territorial zone?"

"Possibly," Doving said. He got up and pointed into
one green area of the holograph. "The Macedonian
Plains are our best bet. We lost our primary leadership
there, but the battle crippled Central Security's zonal

force. There's a chance it could work. What have you got in mind?"

"Setting up a parallel government, independent of the Modality," Molyneux said. "The Federation only deals with recognized governments. Maybe we can keep them from destroying part of the planet."

"We need something else," Marla said. "Something to make dealing with us worth their while. If you were an old human and you'd had the Unity virus, what's the one thing you'd want?"

"A cure," Molyneux said. "Assuming there is such a thing. I doubt the Modality would bother developing one."

"It could be done," Dallas said. He idly scratched his cat's ears. "You could replace the modified DNA in a pri—in an old human, with DNA from their unmodified cell nuclei. You'd only need a good biocomp and a viral synthesizer, and a genetic library." Koshka growled in reaction to his distaste for that idea. Marla shared the feeling. It seemed criminal to replace healthy genes with sick ones, even if the old humans would regard it as a restoration of normality.

"That could work," Doving said. "We could lift the data from the Modality's labs and replicate the instruments. But how do we contact the old humans and convince them to trust us?"

"One thing at a time," Marla said. "First we need those plans."

Chapter Fifteen

WORD CAME THROUGH the next morning that the Heran squadron had intercepted Admiral Hoskins's task force. The first reports spoke of a skirmish, which developed into a series of feints and strikes. There were no casualties on either side, but each clash slowed the task force. It looked like the Herans wanted to buy time.

Geordi had paid little attention to the combat reports. "Let's try another pathway interrogation," he told his engineering team. He ran his hands over the engineering computer console. "But this time, let's reconfigure to watch for address label changes."

"Commander, we, we already tried that," Reg Barclay said. "We didn't find anything."

"It won't hurt to try again—" Geordi stopped and looked at the people around him. Barclay was wilting in exhaustion, while Gakor was fighting down a yawn. The technician at the computer display was sagging in her chair. "No, you're right, Reg. Let's call it a night."

"Where I come from, we call this 'morning,'" Gakor grumbled. The all-night session hadn't sat well with the

Tellarite, although he'd contributed his share of ideas to the work. Despite that, the computer had stubbornly refused to reveal any evidence of tampering or to yield any proof that Astrid could not have sent the coded transmission. There was not even a record that Captain Picard had received a certain offensive book.

Barclay hung back as the others left Engineering. "I, I don't think we're going to find anything, Commander," he said. "Whoever did this wouldn't leave anything in the computer. They must work with an independent unit, like a p-portable computer, something they plug into the system. We, we *could* set up a monitor program, to watch for a modem link with an outside unit."

Geordi nodded. That was probably their best bet, but it would take time to produce results, and meanwhile Astrid would languish in the brig. "Okay," he said, and shook his head. "But I can't get over the idea that we're missing something."

Barclay nodded wearily and left. Geordi started for his quarters, then changed his mind and rode the turbolift to the brig. K'Sah, who was on duty at the security console, idly toyed with his phaser as Geordi went to Astrid's cell, where she sat on the bunk. "Hi," Geordi said. "How are you doing?"

"All right," Astrid said, standing up. "You look tired."

"It's been a long night," he admitted. "I wish I could give you some good news, but I can't. We haven't found anything in the computer."

"Thanks for trying," she said. "I guess you checked the reset registers and shadow-RAM?"

"Yeah, and the archiving functions, too," Geordi said. "Even the power-use records don't show any untoward activity. All we can do is keep an eye on the comm system and wait for our friend to send another message."

"That's what I was thinking." She sighed. "I half wish I *had* sent it, just so I'd know how it was done."

"If it helps, Will Riker doesn't think you did it," Geordi told her. "That's despite the fact he doesn't trust you. And Captain Picard is pushing Trask to let you go."

"Maybe he shouldn't," she said. Astrid sat down on the bunk and gazed at the floor. "Maybe I did make that transmission."

That startled Geordi. "What's that supposed to mean?"

"It means maybe the designers added something to my mind," she said, "something to make me loyal to Hera. Some extra neural circuit, some compulsion. I don't remember doing it, but I keep thinking I could have been sleepwalking, or I could have been in a trance—I *don't know.*" She hit her fist on her knee.

"Then why did you kill Dunbar?" Geordi asked. "Why did you turn in Blaisdell, or volunteer for all those tests, or try to get those two officers out of jail on Zerkalo?"

"I don't know," Astrid repeated. "I thought I was trying to prove that Hera doesn't control me, but maybe it's because I was engineered to be loyal to whoever's in charge of me. Maybe I'm nothing but a weapon that has to follow a leader. Maybe—Geordi, you can't understand this. You weren't *designed*. You don't know what it's like to wonder if everything you feel is *you,* or if it was built into you because some maniac thought it would make you into a better weapon."

"No, I understand," Geordi said, hearing the resentment in her voice. When her head jerked up in disbelief he went on, "I've always been scared of people like you. It's stupid and I'm ashamed I thought that way. I never really asked myself *why* I was scared."

"Why?" Astrid asked.

"I wish I knew," Geordi said. He rested a hand against the hard metal of the cell's door frame, as if to steady himself. Talking about this to a genetically engineered superhuman did not come easy. "Maybe it's the things we hear when we're kids. You go to school and you learn about Hitler and the Khans and Kodos the Executioner—all the monsters who wanted to improve the race. You find it in historical plays and novels and jokes, too. I guess it sinks in and pops up when you don't need it. Like now." Yet he shook his head, feeling that he was no closer to an answer than before. "I know, it wasn't built into me, and I can get rid of it. But it's still as if somebody didn't give me a say in what I'd want to think."

"I never thought of it that way," Astrid said, and sighed. "I don't really understand old humans. When I was a kid I spent most of my time around Kalars. They aren't the same as you."

"They can't be that different from us," Geordi said.

"They are," she said. "They're less aggressive, but they have less curiosity, too. Maybe that's why none of them noticed I was a bit odd for an old human. And other things—Geordi, what do you know about getting even?" she asked.

"You mean, like revenge?"

"I'm not sure what I mean," she said. "Guinan said something to me the other day about 'getting even,' and I've been trying to figure out what it means."

"Oh." Geordi rubbed his chin. It figured that she wouldn't understand something like that. "Getting even . . . It's revenge, but it has this humorous connotation to it, too."

Astrid thought it over. "I don't get it," she admitted. "How can revenge be funny? I always thought it was serious."

This could be tougher than explaining a joke to Data, Geordi thought. "Well, revenge is serious if you're Hamlet, or a Klingon, but not all things call for transwarp retaliation. If somebody does something mildly unpleasant to you, or deliberately annoying, you get even by doing something similar to him. Usually the best technique for getting even is the sort of practical joke that upsets your victim without injuring him."

"It sounds like a Kalar justice rite." Astrid smiled weakly. "Geordi? What would Trask do if he knew I'd helped Worf rewrite the brig's security software? Maybe he'd get upset if he thought I'd given myself a way to break out."

"That would just get you in more trouble," Geordi said.

Astrid squeezed her eyes shut. "Geordi, Geordi, never tell a Zerkalan there's a way to get into more trouble. It's like waving money in front of a Ferengi."

"It isn't worth it," Geordi said. For a moment he was afraid she would call Trask and tell him. "Besides, it doesn't have the right feel for getting even. Look, they tell me living well is the best revenge. Just imagine how bad he's going to look when we prove you're innocent—and you *are* innocent."

The intercom signaled. "Crusher to La Forge. Geordi, I need you in sickbay right away."

"On my way." He paused. "Astrid, I'll be back the first chance I get."

As Geordi left the brig he saw that K'Sah was no longer at his post. Puzzled, he consulted the computer, which told him that K'Sah was in the corridor outside the detention area. Geordi stepped outside and looked around, but the Pa'uyk was nowhere to be seen. Geordi repeated his question to the computer.

"I'm here," K'Sah answered. Geordi looked for the source of his voice and saw that the spider-being had removed the grille from a ceiling vent and climbed into it. "One thing I like about this ship is it has lots and lots and lots of comfortable little lairs."

Geordi looked up at K'Sah. Only his head jutted from the opening, as though he were about to spring on his prey. "Aren't you supposed to be on duty, Ensign?"

"Why bother? Kemal isn't going anywhere. Besides . . ." His serrated mandibles twitched nervously. "I feel safer here."

" 'Safer'?" Geordi repeated. "Why's that?"

K'Sah's twitching increased. "Because of *that!* This politeness crud is driving me nuts! Back home, the only time anyone acts like what *you* call polite, it means they're ready to kill you. And you people *always* act that way!"

"I see," Geordi said. "Would it make you feel any

better if I told you that looking at you makes me glad I'm blind? I'll bet you climbed into that vent just to stink up the air system."

"This ship needs something decent to cover up that salty human stench of yours." The Pa'uyk climbed out of the vent and dropped to the corridor deck, making a perfect landing on its four feet. He headed for the detention area door, while Geordi left for sickbay.

Sickbay was busy when Geordi walked through its door. Half of the staff was at work, and three people occupied biobeds. One of them was Reg Barclay, who idly kicked his feet as he sat on his bed's edge. Geordi's VISOR showed him that Barclay's temperature was up, and his body-electric fields were oddly subdued. Another epidemic, Geordi thought. "Reg, are you all right?" he asked.

Barclay looked at him and let out a string of powerful, wracking sneezes that almost lifted him from the bed before they ended. "I'm fine," he said lazily. "Doc Par'mit'kon had to give me a sedative. Know something funny? All my imaginary fears, and I can't handle one real fear. You'd think I'd be immune by now."

Beverly walked up to Geordi and scanned him. "This is your lucky day, Geordi," she said, and injected his arm. "We've had another plague outbreak, but you weren't infected."

"This time," Geordi said. "Have you got a minute?"

"A short one," she said. "We're getting ready to immunize everyone again. What is it?"

"I was talking with Astrid when you called. Is there any way you can tell if she has something in her mind that could make her do things she's unaware of doing?"

"No," Beverly said. "I'd have to map out her entire neural structure, synapse by synapse, and run a dynamics analysis. That sort of project would take weeks to complete. Why? Do you think she's been doing things in a fugue state?"

"No, but she thinks she might have," Geordi said. "It scares her. I was hoping there's a way to disprove that."

"There's no direct way," Beverly said. "But indirectly—we're monitoring her while she's in the brig; that's a standard precaution against suicide attempts. If she slips into a fugue state, or something similar, we'll know. I'll let you know," she added.

"Thanks." Rubbing the injected spot on his arm—he hoped these immunizations wouldn't get to be a regular thing—Geordi returned to his quarters, had a sketchy dinner and went to bed. He knew he wouldn't get much sleep; he was on-duty again in six hours, and he was too wound up to doze off as he normally did.

Geordi got even less sleep than he had hoped for; he woke up after a dream in which he had been a cat burglar robbing an ancient combination safe. It had been a safe in his own office, and it had been packed with diamonds. A strange dream, he thought. Even if he'd had a safe in his office, why would he keep diamonds in it? There was nothing valuable about diamonds. You could replicate a ton of them in a minute, and their simple crystalline structure held no data. Information was the only valuable thing in the galaxy; everyone learned that in grade school.

He rolled over in bed and tried to go back to sleep.

"We lost." Marla didn't recognize the voice; it wasn't Doving. That, and the scratchy sound of the voice-only transmission, told her how badly the Macedonian Plains revolt had gone. Halfway around the world from its origin, the voice echoed flatly from the dome's walls. "CS beamed in forces from all over Hera, jumped them all over the place. They've got something new."

Marla nodded absently. "The Hephaestos Institute was testing a new transporter system. It must work."

Molyneux didn't seem to hear that. "What are our losses?"

"Almost total. If it helps, we accounted for over half of CS's troops. Delta three-eight out."

The carrier signal's low hum replaced the voice. "All

we did was to weaken Hera and make it easier for the old humans to beat us," Dallas said.

"They could do that anyway," Molyneux told him. "And we're not going to win this one by fighting. Unless you want to kill off all the old humans?"

"No," Dallas said, but only after a long pause that filled Marla with unease. "So how are we going to win?"

"By staying alive," Molyneux told him.

within vocal range from another. The sperm throat lies just behind us," Deltin said.

"Let's speak no more about it," Kinnear replied.

"And to prevent using it with the Catrkallan, we'll equip them to hunt out traces of harmony.

"Well, in this event, the enterprise being so fixed Miklu with intent. Now the beginning is a most complex affair," answered Bip.

Chapter Sixteen

"I HOPE THIS IS IMPORTANT, Doctor," Trask said, as Beverly Crusher entered Picard's ready room. Despite the orders Picard had given her, he thought she still looked overworked; it was clear she had taken only the bare minimum of rest in the past nine days. "We're only twelve hours away from Hera. The tactical situation—"

"That's what I want to discuss," Beverly said. She sat down and handed a data pad to Picard. "Captain, I've been monitoring Dr. Kemal for almost five days now. These are the latest biomonitor readings on her. They say that she's slightly fatigued, but otherwise in excellent health."

"How is this relevant, Doctor?" Trask asked impatiently.

"Admiral, she hasn't slept or eaten since she was locked up. She drinks a half-liter of water when she gets thirsty, which is about once a day. A normal human who tried that would be half-dead."

Picard nodded. "And you're saying that the crews of the Heran squadron are capable of the same effort."

172

"If anything, they're probably in better condition than Dr. Kemal," Beverly said. "On the other hand, you can imagine the shape Admiral Hoskins's crews are in."

"Readily," Picard said. "They may not be too weary to fight, but fatigue will handicap them. It's one more reason to avert this battle. We'll only take heavier casualties than we might otherwise expect."

"I think this would make the Herans more determined to fight us now," Trask said. "A truce would just give our people time to rest up. They won't throw away their edge."

"They may be more interested in survival than in an 'edge,' Admiral," Beverly said. "The more I study Dr. Kemal, the less certain I feel about the Herans. I can take any one point about them and say, yes, I'd want this in a conqueror. But when I put everything together, it doesn't add up to 'conqueror.'"

"Despite everything we've seen?" Trask asked.

"Or because of it," Beverly countered. "For example, all three of the Herans I've studied have unusually high serotonin levels, and almost twice as many serotonin receptor sites in their brains as we do."

"Proving what?" Trask asked.

"Just this," Beverly said. "Serotonin and its receptors are linked with some well-established types of positive social behavior, specifically, self-assurance and a lack of aggression. The Herans have that in abundance."

"Self-confidence is just another form of arrogance," Trask said. "And it's the prime ingredient of charisma. We respond to people with large amounts of self-confidence. We find it easier to follow them. That's what made the Khans so dangerous."

"You're missing my point, Admiral," Beverly said. "A healthy form of self-confidence means that a person is too secure to feel an irrational fear of strangers. These people don't need to fight. When they're threatened or attacked, they have to make a conscious decision to fight back. And this isn't a matter of social customs, or training, or environment; it's entirely genetic."

Trask frowned. "Doctor, you sound pretty sympathetic with the Herans."

"Maybe I am," she said. "Dr. Kemal is a very likable young woman, and the way she acts . . . well, what if they really are superior?" She held up a hand before Trask could comment. "I know, superiority is an outdated concept. But the more I study the Herans, well, there's a lot we don't understand about them."

"I understand that they attacked us," Trask said. "That's pretty basic."

"You're correct when you say we don't understand them, Doctor," Picard said. "Can you find what it takes to provoke an aggressive response from a Heran?"

"I'll see what I can find from my records," Beverly said. "But I can't conduct any experiments with Astrid while she's locked up—"

"Are you concerned about her feelings?" Trask asked.

"Of course," Beverly said. "She's my patient, and she's had it drummed into her since childhood that 'primals' would love to experiment on her. You saw how she reacted when I tried to examine her hand." The doctor looked melancholy. "I've never frightened anyone in my life. I'm not about to terrorize her."

"She's an enemy alien," Trask said, "not—"

"Experimenting on enemy prisoners is a war crime," Beverly said, standing up. "Any way you look at it, Admiral, I will *not* use her as a guinea pig. If you'll excuse me?"

Trask watched her go. "Computer, get Counselor Troi in here."

"Is something wrong, Admiral?" Picard asked.

"That's what I'd like to know," Trask said. "I can understand why Stoneroots would sympathize with her, but I don't expect that sort of disloyalty in human beings."

Picard frowned. "I think President Stoneroots's attitude—"

"—is easily explained," Trask interrupted. "It used to be nothing but a robot repair technician. Good at what it did, but not outstanding. Then, eighteen years ago, it began to file a string of patents for modifications to household robots—brilliant modifications, and the sort of modifications you'd want if you were raising a child in a world with an inferior technology, which is how Herans view us."

"'Eighteen years,'" Picard repeated. "That would be—"

"—right after the Kemals arrived on Zerkalo," Trask said. "Those patents made Stoneroots a wealthy vegetable, which financed its political career. It's obvious that the Kemals fed it information on Heran technology, so it's in their debt. That may have been their true motive in giving it Heran secrets."

"So you've investigated President Stoneroots," Picard said in distaste.

"Of course. There's something strange about the way it's acting here. *Nobody* threatens to ruin important diplomatic negotiations over one person."

"Nobody but a Zerkalan," Picard said. "I've studied their world, Admiral. Their 'anarchy' is in fact a highly structured system which places great emphasis on individual rights and personal responsibility toward others; they keep their government weak because they believe that governments become more interested in their own power than in the well-being of individuals. Your actions seem almost designed to provoke the Zerkalans."

"It can't be helped." He looked annoyed. "A lot of things can't be helped. This conflict—the more I learn about Herans, the more respect I find for them. I almost wish we could bring them into the Federation."

"'Almost,' Admiral?" Picard asked.

"They're too dangerous," Trask said. "I don't mean just their strength, or their intelligence. The real threat is their belief in their own superiority, which seems to have been designed into them. They'll never admit that they're wrong, or that they have to coexist with us; they can't. Take them in, and they'll destroy us from the inside."

Picard looked at the admiral for a moment. He had the uneasy feeling that Trask was sounding him out, to see how the captain might respond to a possible course of action. "Then how do you propose to handle them?"

"'Handle them'? I don't know yet. The way things look now, they may be a threat for generations to come." Trask looked around as Deanna Troi walked into the ready room. "Counselor, how does this ship's crew feel about Kemal?"

"There are a lot of mixed feelings about her, Admiral," Deanna said. She looked stern, which told Picard that Trask had forced her to interrupt a counseling session. "The hostility is fading. There's some confusion, but nobody blames her for anything Hera has done."

"How about sympathy?" Trask asked.

"That's also present," Deanna said. "She's a charming young woman in a bad position and, frankly, your actions are making her look like a martyr."

"I see," Trask said grimly. "What's the attitude toward Hera itself?"

"There's anger, but it's turned into a very bewildered anger," Deanna said. "People want justice, but they also want to know why the Herans made this attack. There are enough odd stories about the Herans to make people wonder if the situation is as clear-cut as it seemed at first."

"And you approve," Trask said. He looked to the captain. "Picard, there's a lot of unwarranted sympathy on this ship for somebody who is almost certainly a Heran agent. What are you going to do to improve morals?"

"I see no need for an improvement, Admiral," Picard said. "If we must fight, my crew will fight to the best of its ability. They will not let their sympathy for one innocent woman"—he spoke the words as though twisting a knife—"interfere with their duty."

"See that they don't," Trask said. He stood up and left the ready room.

As the days passed the dishonor grew like tarnish on an ill-kept knife. To have someone abuse his good name in an affront to the captain, to leave the offense unavenged so long—Worf had a strong urge to carve his enemy into a human-skin rug. He would not indulge that particular wish, but once he identified his enemy . . . well, dishonor is always avenged.

The thought of vengeance made him growl pleasantly as he entered Ten-Forward. It was too bright and cheerful a place to spend the eve of a battle—assuming that Picard would relent and permit a battle—but it was a good place to judge the spirit of the crew. As he looked around he found no discouragement here, no fear, no unseemly deprecation of war.

Worf saw three familiar faces at a table: Deanna, Geordi and Barclay. The Betazoid counselor looked weary; she had been working overtime with plague-infected humans. La Forge and Barclay looked exhausted, and they picked at their dinners. Worf ordered a meal from one of Guinan's assistants and went to the table.

Geordi nodded to him as he sat down. "Your statue is fixed, Worf. You can pick it up any time."

"Thank you," Worf rumbled. The damage to his statue of Kahless annoyed him. Esthetics aside, it was a reminder of his rough handling by Dunbar. "Were the repairs difficult?"

"N-no, they were easy," Barclay said. *"Khrolat* wood is easy to work with, you'll, you'll never know the statue was broken."

"That is good," Worf said, and looked at the humans. "Is all well?"

"Yes," Deanna said, while the two humans nodded. "Geordi was just telling me about these dreams he's had lately."

"They're weird," the engineer said. "Usually my dreams are pretty mundane, but these—well, take last night. I dreamed I was a pirate, and I was digging up my office floor to get at some buried treasure."

"It is good to dream that one is a pirate," Worf rumbled.

"It is?" Barclay asked. "What, I mean, why is that?"

"Because it is good to *be* a pirate," Worf explained patiently. He reminded himself that one had to make allowances where humans were concerned. "A pirate commands his own destiny. He takes orders from no one and obeys no law but his own honor. To dream of finding pirate treasure is to view your life as a success."

"Too bad I'm not a Klingon," Geordi said. "The funny thing about these dreams is that I keep finding diamonds and other jewels in them, but I toss them away."

"Waste," Deanna said. Worf heard the playful note in her voice, which told him she was relaxing. Compared to the problems with which she had dealt lately, Geordi's dreams must have presented a pleasant diversion. "Jewels are valuable. They're beautiful and they can have historical or sentimental value."

"That isn't what I'm thinking in the dreams," Geordi said. "It's like there's supposed to be something in the diamonds, and when I can't find it, they're worthless."

"You're, you're looking for an answer to your problems," Barclay said.

"Yeah, and I'm not finding it," Geordi said disconsolately. "I'm no closer to getting Astrid off the hook now than I was when Trask locked her up."

Worf grunted. "I share this dishonor."

There was a moment of awkward silence. "I wanted to ask how you're doing, Reg," Deanna said, breaking the quiet. "You seem calmer than you did a few days ago."

"I, I, I *am* calmer," he said. "Having the p-plague isn't as rough as waiting to get it. And, and, it doesn't seem so bad. The changes, I mean."

That surprised Worf. Barclay was the last human from whom he would have expected a calm response to sunrise, much less the plague. "Your line will become one of mighty warriors," he said. "That is enviable."

Barclay shook his head. "I wasn't thinking that way," he said. "It's just, I've always been so wound up, even my shadow jumps. Nerves run in my family—well, they kind of skitter around in my family. Only now they won't. I mean, *my* kids won't have ulcers when they're ten."

Worf looked up as Guinan came to the table. She bore a perplexed look instead of his dinner. "Guinan?" he asked.

"I'm having some trouble with the replicator," she said. "Geordi, you'd better have a look. I think we've got another practical joke on our hands."

"I hope you're right," Geordi said. He went to the bar with her, followed by Worf, Deanna and Barclay.

A dinner tray rested on the bar. *Gagh* swarmed in a bowl next to a tall, cool glass of prune juice, and a roasted *targ* haunch sizzled on a platter. However, a beribboned box replaced Worf's usual slab of *rokeg* pie. "'To Daddy from Al,'" Geordi said, reading the label. "It's a joke, all right."

"Indeed," Worf rumbled. Alexander never called him anything but "Father"—and the boy was on Earth now.

"This proves Astrid hasn't tampered with the computer," Deanna said. "She definitely has an alibi."

"She, she still doesn't have an alibi for the transmission," Barclay said. "But maybe whoever did *this* sent the message, too."

"If that is so . . ." Worf mused. He picked up the box, determined to investigate it.

"Don't open it," Geordi warned. "Whatever it is—"

The warning came too late. The box fell apart in his hands, and Worf found himself holding a live tribble. He sprang back and snarled in disgust as the loathsome little parasite spat at him. *"Plakh!"* he bellowed over the laughter ringing through the lounge.

Deanna scooped up the hissing, spitting tribble and carried it out of the lounge. *"I swear vengeance!"* Worf shouted, further enraged by the chuckles. No one showed enough sense to back away from him. *"This time my enemy has dishonored MY SON!"*

"'This time,'" Geordi repeated, as if hearing the combination of words for the first time in his life. "Of course, *this* time, boy, am I an idiot!"

"M-m-me, too," Barclay said excitedly. "There's no telling how long this has been going on!"

"And the diamonds—" Geordi smacked his forehead with a palm. "So *that's* what I've been trying to tell myself. Valuable crystals, that's what the dreams mean!"

"The flight data recorders," Barclay said. "They're pseudodiamond crystals, they're, they're stored in your office—"

"What the *Hu'tegh* is this?" Worf demanded.

"You'll see," Geordi said. "Let's get down to my office."

Enterprise had just entered the Heran system when Data detected an incoming message. "Captain, we are being hailed by Hera," the android said.

"On screen," Picard said. A swarthy man with vaguely Mongolian features appeared on the main viewscreen. He appeared to be of similar size and mass as Dr. Kemal, with an approximate age of thirty standard years—although Data noted that there were uncertainties in the Heran aging rate. The file pictures of Dr. Kemal's parents showed a man and woman who appeared to be only slightly older than their daughter. He wore a beard and mustachios similar to those affected by Worf, and his slanting eyes added to the Klingon impression. "This is Captain Jean-Luc Picard, of the Federation *Starship Enterprise.*"

The man nodded. "And I am Carlos Ulyanov, Senior of the Modality. Surrender."

Oddly, Picard smiled. "We've already discussed that course of action with Captain Nkoma," he said. "Senior, I believe it is possible to negotiate a peace between Hera and the Federation. The effort is certainly worth making."

"I don't see where we have anything to negotiate, Captain," Ulyanov said. His voice grew dry. "Your people will try to exterminate us. We, of course, will dispute that."

"The Federation has never exterminated any race," Picard said. "Nor do I intend to see that happen here. Senior, time is running short, but we *do* have time. Is there any harm in our meeting to discuss possibilities?"

"Yes; I don't think you have the authority to make a binding agreement, but you might demoralize our people." Ulyanov paused, his face momentarily blank. "But I could be wrong. I'll await your arrival in my office. And if your ship doesn't attack us," he added, "we won't attack you." A starfield replaced his image.

Picard turned to Deanna Troi. "Counselor?"

"Captain, I sensed no deception or arrogance in him," the Betazoid empath said. "He believes he's the aggrieved party, fighting for survival . . . and riddled with guilt over what he sees as the necessity for some ugly decisions. He doesn't trust us, but if he sees a way to end this war, he'll take it."

"Sir," Data said, turning to face Picard, "precisely how will you negotiate a peace settlement?"

"By persuading the Senior that his planet will not be harmed," Picard said, "and that an 'unconditional surrender' will not be a draconic measure. But that will require—"

The turbolift door opened and Trask strode onto the bridge. Data found his posture and facial expression suggestive of a confrontational attitude. "Picard, the computer says you just talked to the Herans. Why wasn't I notified?"

"The Herans contacted us," Picard said, "and I deemed it wiser not to keep them waiting. I've been invited to a meeting with their leader when we reach Hera."

"You're not going alone," Trask said. "I'll be there."

"Certainly, Admiral." Picard smiled slightly. "I will also require Dr. Kemal's presence. The Herans may listen to her."

"And risk having her defect?" Trask asked. "No."

"She would not do that," Picard said. "But if I am wrong, what harm can she do?"

"Let's not find out," Trask said. He returned to the turbolift, effectively terminating the conversation.

Data puzzled over the exchange. By all rights, Captain Picard's logic should have persuaded Admiral Trask to release Dr. Kemal from detention, at least for the purpose of negotiating with the Herans. Clearly logic had been overridden by some nonlogical force. Data had noted that certain humans defended erroneous positions with increased vigor when confronted with superior logic; his research suggested that this was connected with something called "ego." Admiral Trask's stubbornness suggested that he had a large and powerful ego.

A message came through from Engineering. "La Forge to bridge. Captain, I can prove Astrid didn't send that message."

"Indeed?" Picard asked. "Meet me in the conference room. Picard to Trask. Admiral, there's been a new development. We'll meet in the conference room in five minutes. Number One, you have the bridge." Picard nodded to Data, who left the bridge with him.

"Proof," Trask said, as Worf and Geordi sat down at the conference table. Picard thought the word left a bad taste in his mouth. "Let's have it, Mr. La Forge."

"It's been in the flight data recorders all along," Geordi said. "I've been so busy trying to prove that Astrid didn't send this one particular message that I missed the obvious—that other messages could have been sent *before* she came on board the *Enterprise*."

Geordi set a pair of data crystals on the table. "These are cartridges from the flight data recorders. Each contains a day's worth of engineering and navigational data, including information on subspace transmissions. Now, neither has a direct record of any unregistered messages, but they contain housekeeping data that says that such messages *were* sent. Power consumption, antenna aiming commands, computer message routing—it's all here. This cartridge"—he held up one of the glittering rectangles—"was made while that message was sent, and *this* one has identical data, but it was made the day *before* Astrid came on board."

"You're certain this isn't a fluke?" Trask asked.

Picard saw Geordi smile. "Positive. Astrid couldn't have tampered with the records; these are holographic crystals, and any attempt to change their contents would ruin them. The same goes for replacing them with forged replicas—the structures are designed so they can't be replicated."

"Maybe," Trask said. "And maybe Herans have some trick—skip it. Tell me this. If Kemal didn't do it, who did?"

"The culprit remains unknown," Worf said. "However, we have identified a similar pattern in my assault by"—his natural grimace deepened—"practical jokes."

"So you see a connection," Picard said. "This could narrow the list of suspects, Mr. Worf. The only person who would play a practical joke on you would either be someone who is woefully ignorant of the Klingon attitude to such behavior—or a mortal enemy."

"I have been too genteel to acquire such enemies aboard the *Enterprise*," Worf confessed. "But some humans find amusement in destroying one's dignity. This behavior must be . . . corrected."

"This would explain the messages, too," Geordi said, shivering at Worf's tone. "Maybe they were just random signals meant to drive you up the wall."

"Except it's taken you all this time to notice them," Trask pointed out. "You only caught this last one because it was made when the ship was at yellow alert. Jokes are meant to be noticed."

"I agree that we should treat this as more than a joke,"

Picard said. "And we must accept Dr. Kemal's innocence. Mr. La Forge, we'll reach Hera within the hour. Would you tell Dr. Kemal that I would like to see her at her convenience?"

"Yes, sir." Geordi left the conference table, and Trask raised no objection to her release.

Worf loathed visiting a planet unarmed. He was reluctant to go anywhere without a weapon, and his distress deepened as the transporter placed him on the Heran surface with Picard, Kemal and Trask. Memories of his fight with Dunbar only strengthened his awareness that he could not prevail against a Heran. Where was the honor in being a security chief who could provide no security?

The foursome had materialized in a parklike setting. Alien buildings with white marble columns rested on grassy knolls, while tall hedges and clusters of flowering bushes provided natural cover for combatants. All of the buildings showed the restrained bulges of phaser and shield barbettes.

"That one," Astrid said quietly, pointing to a nearby structure. "That's the central Modality office."

"It resembles the Parthenon," Picard noted.

"It's an old-human style," Astrid agreed. "Greek mythology is popular here. Heran society is loosely patterned after the ancient Greek city-state as well. Everything is divided up into units of five thousand or so adult citizens."

"But with machinery instead of slaves," Picard said.

"And a dictatorship instead of a democracy," Trask said.

"I know," Astrid said. "In theory, the Modality is only a service organization that coordinates the economy and keeps the public utilities running. It's run by people who are tested for their aptitude for the job. Unfortunately, the tests were created two centuries ago by ambitious, power-hungry people."

"Old humans, no doubt," Trask muttered sourly.

"Yes, sir," Astrid said. "As I was saying, these tests place a high value on ambition, the urge to give orders, and the willingness to ignore other people's rights. We have people like that, too." The Heran shrugged. "I never said we were perfect."

Worf led the way as the humans chattered. The building's foundation was surrounded by more of the flowering bushes, which ran up to the main doorway. As he neared the building Worf saw the bushes sway toward him, almost like a time-lapse recording of plant growth. Vicious thorns bristled gorgeously along the stems.

Astrid saw it as well. "Interesting," she said to Worf. "I don't remember anything like this. It must be new."

"Moving roses," Trask said in disdain. "So what? Let's not waste our time admiring the flowers."

Worf's opinion of the admiral dropped a notch as they entered the building. He could see how the Herans would use their genetic technology to turn a rosebush into a defensive weapon. Any assailant who attempted to climb through a window or place an explosive charge next to a wall, would be ensnared in the thorny stems. It was all a part with the landscaping and architecture. The fact that the Herans had so heavily fortified their capital district intrigued the Klingon. Such preparations suggested they feared their own citizens.

The interior of the building was a marble corridor, long and large, with rows of unmarked office doors on either side. "Senior's office," Astrid said, and in response a holographic line glowed in the air. They followed it to the door at the end of the corridor. Worf felt that its size was designed to intimidate visitors by impressing them with the Heran government's power.

On the other hand, he thought with a glance at Astrid, beings of her size would need an uncommon amount of room. Perhaps this architecture was not just a childish attempt to overawe newcomers.

The Senior's office was an austere place of white

marble walls and a single barren desk. The only two chairs in the room were behind the desk, and Herans occupied them. One was a handsome man; his companion was a dark, attractive female with black hair. Both wore loose, flowing garments of white.

The man raised an eyebrow. "What do my eyes behold? Into our room of bliss advance creatures of other mold—earth-born, perhaps?"

Picard's lips twitched in cold amusement, but Astrid showed as much annoyance as Worf had ever seen on her dark face. "Oh prince, oh chief of many throned powers, who led the embattled seraphim into war—if you have to quote Milton at us, could you at least get him right?"

The man sighed. "Embellishment is a fine art. Who are you?"

Trask spoke up. "I'm Admiral Allen—"

"Not you," Ulyanov said. He gestured at Astrid. "I'm only interested in people. Who are you?"

"He's Admiral Allen Trask, of Starfleet Intelligence," Astrid said. "You've already spoken with Captain Picard. The Klingon is Worf, son of Mogh, security chief of the *Enterprise*. I'm Dr. Astrid Kemal of the Daystrom Institute."

"Ah, Kemal," Ulyanov repeated. "Your parents would be Ivan and Lenore Kemal? They were my students in college. They're well?"

"Yes. They're living on Zerkalo."

"That's supposed to be the most congenial planet in primal space," the woman said. "I'm Anya Dunbar. What happened to the *Temenus*'s crew?"

"They all died," Worf said. He owed Astrid a debt; he could not let her take the blame for Dunbar's death in front of his widow—or his sister. "Three died when the *Temenus* was sabotaged. Blaisdell died attempting to escape from a starbase. Dunbar died after attacking me." That bit of misdirection, he reflected, was quite true, and perhaps not as dishonorable as a direct lie.

The woman nodded silently. "We'll expect you to return their bodies," Ulyanov said.

"You're in no position to make demands," Trask told him. "We're here—"

"—to discuss a *peace* settlement," Picard said firmly. "To that end, we shall of course return their remains. And I believe the next step is to learn why your people attacked us, Senior. I'm not aware of any provocation."

"We've been continually attacked by primals," Ulyanov said. "Over the past twenty-one years, seven hundred thirty-two of our citizens have died in forty-five different incidents. Their only motive has been hatred of what we are. Now your Federation is moving into our sector. That can only mean an increase in these attacks."

"You're talking about criminal activity," Picard said. "The Federation has never sanctioned any such attacks, and we would want to bring the perpetrators to justice. It would be to our mutual benefit to cooperate in this matter."

"I'm curious about these 'attacks,'" Trask said. "Forty-five of them? We've heard nothing of this, not even rumors. What happened to these attackers?"

"We obliterated the attackers in thirty-nine of the incidents," Ulyanov said. "There have also been seventeen other incidents which ended without any casualties on our side."

"Dead men tell no tales," Worf said, hearing the implicit boast in the man's words. "What of the other incidents?"

"We've bribed them into silence," Ulyanov admitted. "Exposing us would end the bribes, and I doubt that a criminal would boast of his actions to your Federation."

"I see," Picard said. "Under the circumstances, you cannot be faulted for your handling of the situation. However, a strong Federation presence in this sector will mean an end to such attacks."

"After you accept our unconditional surrender," Anya Dunbar said. "With no conditions, how could we keep you from exterminating us after we surrender?"

"They wouldn't do that," Astrid said. "Old humans aren't as monstrous as some people say they are. I've had trouble"—Worf saw her glance at Trask—"but Captain Picard has risked his career to help me, and I've made friends with some of the old humans on the *Enterprise*—"

"The fact is," Trask said, "you don't have a choice, Ulyanov. Surrender now, and get off lightly. Fight, and we'll hammer you into the ground."

"Then bring your finest hammer," Ulyanov said, in a tone that filled Worf with admiration. "We stand on hard ground."

"There is no need for combat," Picard insisted.

"Not unless you're mad enough to think one world can stand against the Federation and our allies in the Klingon Empire," Trask said. "We'll have your system swarming with ships."

"Really?" Ulyanov chuckled. "You make it all sound intriguing—but 'what folly then, to boast of what arms can do.'"

"There's a large invasion fleet on its way," Astrid answered. "'Read thy lot in yon celestial sign.'"

He nodded. "'Satan, I know thy strength.' Dr. Kemal, by siding with the primals you've committed treason against Hera. If you return, we'll execute you at once."

Astrid's laugh impressed Worf. "That's the best offer I've had all week," she said.

"No, the best offer is our order that you surrender," Ulyanov said. "Captain Picard, I did not permit you to land to listen to your empty demands. I expect you to accede to *our* demands. Your portion of the human race is to submit to our authority. We plan no vindictive moves, but your people will be required to undergo genetic modifications which will bring your descendants, at least, up to our standards."

Trask looked disgusted. "You can't be serious."

"I am," Ulyanov said. "But I don't expect you to surrender. Your limited intelligence makes you stubborn and foolish. We'll have to pound you into submission. You may leave." He turned his attention to his desktop's computer display, dismissing them.

Picard signaled the *Enterprise* and the transporter took them away. "'Milton'?" Worf asked as they materialized in transporter room three.

"A Terran poet," Astrid said. "Khan Singh used to quote from his *Paradise Lost* all the time. My parents said that's a Heran tradition too, but I think that Ulyanov quoted Milton to offend Captain Picard and Admiral Trask."

"I agree," Picard said, and smiled wryly as they stepped off the transporter stage. "'Words which no ear ever to hear in Heaven expected.' I'm puzzled at his threat against you, Doctor. It seemed pointless."

"The Senior was trying to scare off a peacemaker," Worf said. He felt disgusted by the ludicrous position in which the mission had placed him. Picard, his commander, had been plotting to create execrable peace, while the dishonorable Trask had struggled for war. Sometimes it seemed there was no justice in the universe.

"I'd say you're right, Lieutenant," Trask observed. "Those monsters want war. I wish I knew if they're just arrogant, or if they've got more tricks to pull on us."

The intercom signaled. "Bridge to Picard," Riker's voice said. "Captain, we've just intercepted a message from Hera to Nkoma. The Heran fleet has been ordered to destroy Admiral Hoskins's task force."

Riker sounded scornful of the orders, but it was news to gladden the heart of any self-respecting Klingon. "Now there will be no peace," Worf observed happily, before he recalled that he was not supposed to want a war here. He found enough good grace to look abashed.

"No," Picard said. "The Senior is trying to thwart efforts for peace, which suggests he thinks peace is still possible."

Astrid nodded. "He knows that'll be harder once the shooting starts, but we can do it. I *know* there are people down there who want to deal with the Federation, even if I haven't seen them in eighteen years. They—"

"You're guessing," Trask said.

"I'm not guessing that somebody sabotaged the *Temenus*. I'll have to—" She stopped and fought down a massive yawn. "Sorry. I'll have to go back down there. Later, after I get some sleep. If you'll excuse me?"

"Wait a minute," Trask said. "What have you got planned?"

"Right now I plan to get two or three hours of sleep," she said. "In a real bed, with sheets and pillows. In quarters with a shower, and a private bathroom, and without a sleazy Pa'uyk guard who keeps asking me if I think Klingons make better lovers. Then I'm going to—"

"Listen," Trask said angrily.

"No, you listen," Astrid said, looking down at him with eyes as cold as space. "I've had it with you pushing me around and interrupting me, and the next time I hear you use the words 'Heran' and 'monster' in the same sentence it had damned well better be an apology!" She turned and strode out of the transporter room.

Molyneux's pocket computer showed the situation outside the system. The five Heran ships had formed into a tight cluster and were accelerating toward the Federation's sixteen troop transports. A combat force of five capital ships and eight destroyers had deployed between the two groups, screening the transports. It was getting dark, and the display seemed to glare in the waning daylight. Marla was glad when Molyneux dimmed the display.

Squatting under the rock ledge with Marla and Molyneux, Dallas idly scratched Koshka's head as he watched the holographic projection. "We can't stop them, can we?" he asked.

"No," Molyneux said. "But if we do enough damage, they may retreat."

"And come back with a world-wrecker," Marla said. All she could feel was the futility of fighting hundreds of billions of old humans. The future might come to what she had now—hiding in a cave with other stragglers, not knowing what had become of her children, waiting for the old humans to destroy Hera with a single bomb.

"Shhh," Dallas said. A thin voice whispered from the display's speaker, reeling off attack directives. They meant nothing to Marla, but she saw Molyneux nod in approval. She hoped that meant they had a chance.

The Heran squadron seemed to pause in a last moment of peace before it turned and accelerated toward the invaders. The squadron opened fire at extreme range with its missiles, which raced ahead and tore into the attackers. The data matrix alongside the display showed the results: a missile dodged here, a shield crippled there, another missile destroyed by a well-placed phaser shot. One Federation destroyer lost all of its shields to a direct hit, but it came on with a dogged persistence. Then it entered a wide turn at warp eight, clearly out of control. "One down," Molyneux muttered. And how many people did we just kill? Marla asked herself. She had seen battle-damaged ships land at her spaceport, and she knew what those bright lights and precise figures meant: mangled bodies in shattered hulls, lives ruined beyond any hope of repair. She forced herself to dismiss those thoughts. This battle was the only thing that would keep the old humans away from Hera—and her children, wherever they were now.

The invaders moved to intercept the Herans, answering their attack with volley after volley of photon torpedoes. They concentrated their fire on one ship, which dodged and turned under the relentless attack. The steady barrage detonated in a ripple of flashes, and the frigate went dark as its power failed. Then the four remaining ships were amid the invasion force, and the range was too close for missiles and torpedoes. They converged on the largest ship, battered its shields down and turned away from it. The Federation ship flew on for a moment, then spun out of control. "That was their flagship," Molyneux said quietly. "That may disrupt them."

If that loss had any effect on the old humans it ended in a matter of seconds. The invaders regrouped and again positioned themselves between the transports and the frigates. At least they don't understand our tactics, Marla thought. There was no need to attack the troopships. They were lightly armed, and by themselves they could never penetrate Hera's perimeter defenses. Only the larger ships could hope to take on the defense satellites and the ground-based missiles. Without the front-line ships the transports could not land their troops.

She drew thin satisfaction from that thought as the two forces reconverged. The bulk of the old-human fleet concentrated its fire on a single Heran ship, and the frigate found itself caught amid five Miranda-class ships. The three split apart and went in pursuit of a second frigate. Their target staggered and spanned as its shields overloaded under the attack, but then another frigate homed in and dealt a fatal blow to its power plant. The puny frigate was turning toward a destroyer when a burst of torpedoes from another cruiser, fired at dangerously short range, knocked out its warp coil. Wallowing under impulse power, it became easy prey for the Federation ships, which dispatched the damaged ship in a matter of seconds.

The last frigate fought on, stubbornly dodging amid the warships that held it at bay. One old-human ship was lost to a reflected phaser beam which sliced through its weakened shields and reduced its warp nacelles to scrap. Then, while engaging a destroyer at point-blank range, the last frigate's shields collapsed. In the display, the Federation ships rejoined the transports and resumed their advance on Hera.

Dallas reached out and turned off the computer. "We did our best," he said. "It wasn't enough."

"Yes." Molyneux squeezed his eyes shut as he leaned back against the rock ledge. " 'See with what heat these dogs of Hell advance, to waste and havoc yonder world.' "

The sun was down, and Marla was astonished to find that the battle had lasted almost an hour. She felt stunned; some of the people on the lost ships had been her friends. Jane Nkoma had introduced her to her husband; Joachim Liu had helped her get her first job at the starport.

"We may hand them a few more surprises," Molyneux said. He took his computer, folded it and slid it into his hip pocket. "If everything went well, we'll have a few hundred prisoners to use as bargaining chips. Or a few thousand."

Marla felt alert. So that was why the Hephaestos Institute had wanted to borrow a courier on the day the *Temenus* left. "The transporter experiments?"

"Yes." Molyneux's smile was wolfish. "It's not over yet."

Chapter Seventeen

TRASK FOLLOWED PICARD into his ready room when the message from President Jaresh-Inyo arrived. "Captain Picard," he said, as soon as the screen had cleared, "I've just spent a very difficult afternoon with the Zerkalan ambassador. She demands that we immediately remove Kemal from any possible danger. I want you to put her on a shuttle and send her to the nearest starbase."

"That might not be safe, Mr. President," Picard said. "A lone shuttle would be vulnerable to attack by Heran raiders. In addition, Dr. Kemal has volunteered to help us negotiate with the Herans. We have evidence of an active resistance to the Heran government. If she can help persuade the resistance to side with us and overthrow its government—"

"If there's a resistance," Trask noted. "We only have Kemal's say-so about that."

"We also have the evidence of our eyes," Picard said. "The Heran capital is rather heavily defended against internal attack. It seems the Modality does not trust its

194

own people. And somebody on Hera sabotaged the *Temenus.*"

"I see," Jaresh-Inyo said. "So you think you can drive a wedge between the Modality and its citizens."

"That's why I need Dr. Kemal," Picard said. "She may help me find that wedge."

Jaresh-Inyo nodded. "I agree, but the Zerkalans are becoming impossible. They want Kemal out of danger."

"Or else what, Mr. President?" Trask asked.

"Or else they'll withdraw their request for Federation membership, and negotiate an alliance with the Romulans."

"A bluff," Trask said.

"I can't count on that," Jaresh-Inyo said. "This incident is turning into a major embarrassment for the Federation. We do *not* want to drive a potential Federation member into the Romulan camp. Captain, you are to do everything you can to protect Kemal. You may also inform her that we've dropped all legal proceedings against her." The transmission ended.

"Well, Picard?" Trask asked. "What are you going to do about Kemal?"

"I intend to allow her to return to Hera," Picard said.

"Against your orders to protect her?"

"She's probably safer on the ground than on a starship in a war zone," Picard said. "And the danger will vanish once a peace is negotiated."

"If it can be negotiated," Trask said. "Picard, have you considered the impossibility of enforcing a peace here? The Herans believe they're superior to us, so why should they subjugate themselves to us? And with their brains, how long would it take them to find a way to slip out of a peace treaty and attack us again?"

"I'm willing to assume they'll negotiate in good faith," Picard said.

"Why?" Trask asked. "Because Kemal's a nice kid?"

"Because I have no reason to think otherwise, Admiral," Picard said. "Despite the Senior's words, I think the Heran people want nothing more than to live in peace. There must be a way to make that possible, and I will find it."

Trask said nothing in response, but the cold look in his eyes warned Picard that he would do everything in his power to prevent that.

The air in holodeck three was thin and cold and filled with blowing snow. Ice covered the craggy cliffs; to Geordi, it looked as though the chamber had been adjusted to simulate the high Himalayas. Starfleet uniforms were designed to keep their wearers comfortable under a variety of conditions, but Geordi still shivered in the biting cold. "Astrid?" he called. He felt out of breath, and he realized the simulated altitude must be extreme.

Almost lost in the mist, several massive humanoid shapes loomed on the ridge above him. Geordi was thinking of the yeti legends just before one of the figures clambered down the rocky slope and turned into Astrid. "Computer, reconfigure program, set weather to mild, air pressure to standard," she said. The storm was replaced with orange sunlight in a clear, frigid sky, and as the air thickened Geordi swallowed to relieve the sudden pressure in his ears. Shaggy Kalars looked down at him from the ridge. "This is my favorite camping spot back home," Astrid told Geordi as she came down the rocky slope. She idly brushed snow from her bare forearms. "All the time I was cooped up in the brig, I kept thinking how much I wanted to come here, feel real weather and stretch my legs."

Geordi nodded; he'd never heard anyone say that the brig was oversized, and someone with Astrid's physique would need an enormous amount of exercise. "I don't know if you've heard the news," he said. "Those Heran ships fought our task force about three hours ago."

"How bad was it?" she asked.

"The Herans were wiped out," Geordi said. "But we lost seven ships, including the *Eando Binder* and the

Raymond Z. Gallun. We've got almost fifty people known injured and over two thousand missing."

"Long-range transporters," Astrid said. "It's possible for a transporter to operate over a range of light-centuries; the Triskelion gamesters could do it."

"So can a few other races," Geordi said. And so, he decided, could the Herans. "But what's the point in abducting—oh. Prisoners."

"They'll make great bargaining chips," Astrid said. "Failing that, they could make Starfleet reluctant to hit Hera too hard. We wouldn't want to hurt our own people."

Geordi nodded. That explained the Heran tactics; instead of destroying ships, the frigates had veered off as soon as a Federation vessel had lost its shields. Without shields, there was nothing to keep somebody with a transporter from abducting crew members. It was the sort of mild tactic he had come to expect from the Herans. "Astrid, I talked with Captain Picard a while ago," Geordi said. "He says you want to go back down there. Do you think you can accomplish anything?"

"Yes. If we can get in touch with the resistance, maybe we can find a way to end this war. And the way they took prisoners suggests they want to talk. You only need bargaining chips if you plan to bargain."

"You're going to need help," Geordi said. "If you can use me, I'll go."

"I was hoping you'd ask," she said. "Kemal to Captain Picard. Sir, would it be possible to meet with you, Lieutenant Worf and Mr. Data in the conference room."

They walked out of the holodeck. "Worf told me you had an argument with Admiral Trask," Geordi said as they went down the corridor. When she nodded he went on, "What happened? Losing your temper isn't like you."

"I didn't lose it," she said. "I threw it away. I'm an anarchist, remember?"

"And you're not supposed to let the government push you around," Geordi said. "Is that it?"

"It's more than that," she told him as they entered the turbolift. "I realized something in the brig. If I have to spend the next couple of centuries in the stockade on Jarus Two, I don't want to have to tell myself that I didn't fight it."

"I understand," Geordi said. He tried to think. "Astrid, right now people are scared and confused, and Trask is taking advantage of that. But once this blows over, everyone will come to their senses and he won't be able to exploit their fear. So don't do anything now to make things worse."

To his surprise she laughed, a sound with a nervous edge to it. "He wants to lock me up for the rest of my life and have me used as a guinea pig. How can he make things worse?"

"He'll find a way," Geordi said. "Something tells me he's good at that."

"I see your point." She looked thoughtful. "Geordi, can you tell me something about Captain Picard? Something personal?"

The change of subject surprised him. "I can try. What is it?"

"What's wrong with his heart? I can't hear his pulse when I'm around him. Just this strange rushing noise. It's been driving me crazy."

"He has a bionic heart," Geordi said. "I don't know how he lost the original—an accident, I guess. I know it's strange. Every time I look at him, I can see the pump's electric fields instead of the usual body-electric fields."

"That must be wonderful," she said. He thought she sounded wistful. "All the things you can see."

"I like it," Geordi said. "Having the VISOR helps in my work, but what's really fun is to look at the sky. People say the sky is black, but that's because they can't see radio waves and gamma rays and neutrinos. It's like . . . like . . ." He fumbled for words, then gave up. "There are no words for it. And people—there are these electric fields that surround everyone, that make it look like life is a force as real and solid as gravity. Dr. Crusher keeps trying to convince me to get 'normal' eyes, but I don't see how I can give up what I have." Even as he said that Geordi felt surprised. He rarely admitted that to anyone.

The ship's full command staff was in the conference room, along with Admiral Trask, who seemed less pleased than usual to see Astrid as she entered the room. Geordi wondered just what had happened down on Hera; if there had been trouble beyond the failure to make peace, Worf and Picard had not mentioned it.

Data opened the meeting. "At Dr. Kemal's request, I have made a survey of biological research installations on the Heran surface. Although there are fifty-seven such facilities scattered around the planet, there is only one which appears to be dedicated to biowar research. Dr. Kemal, am I correct in assuming that it is this facility that interests you?"

"It is," Astrid said. "If there's a cure for this plague, or the information that could make a cure possible, it's there. That makes it the most important place on Hera to us. The Modality knows that and so does the resistance. If they want to deal with us, they'll have someone waiting in the area to meet us."

"That seems our best chance," Picard agreed. "Do you intend to go alone, Doctor?"

"Geordi's volunteered to go with me, sir," she said. "And I'd like to take Worf along, as well as Commander Riker." Geordi noted Riker's surprise at that request.

"Why them?" Trask asked.

"Geordi can handle their technology, and Worf knows security systems," she said. "If things don't work out, that would give us a better chance of grabbing the secrets behind their genetic technology. Commander Riker—I don't mean to cast any aspersions on him, but he's not too trusting of Herans in general, or me in particular. That could be useful."

"Why is that?" Riker asked.

"Suppose I'm wrong," Astrid said. "Suppose I'm

leading us into a trap. With your experience, you're more likely to spot it than I am. That could save us."

"I don't know," Trask said. "La Forge is one of Starfleet's best engineers and Worf is an outstanding tactician. Riker is a valuable, well-informed command officer, and a key element to running this ship. The Herans could learn a lot from them if you turned them over. That's a lot more credible than your story about meeting the Heran resistance."

"I find her logic persuasive," Picard said.

"I don't," Trask said. "She makes too many assumptions. One is the good intentions of this so-called resistance."

"I could be wrong," Astrid admitted. "If you want me to go alone, I will, but—"

This time the intercom broke into her words. "Bridge," Ensign Rager said. "Captain, we're picking up a transmission from Hera. It's Admiral Hoskins," she added in surprise.

"Pipe it down here," Picard ordered.

Admiral Hoskins appeared on the briefing room's screen. He seemed uninjured to Geordi. He was flanked by two Herans. One looked rather like a Klingon, while the other was a woman who might have been Astrid's sister. "Hoskins to task force," the admiral said. "Who has command?"

A woman's voice answered. "Captain T'Kir, on board the *Titov*. Are you under duress, sir?"

"No, but I'm still a prisoner," Hoskins said grimly. "Carry out the task force orders, Captain. Link up with the Klingons and hit 'em hard."

"If you do that," the Heran man said, "you may endanger our prisoners. We have twenty-one hundred and seventeen Federation citizens in our custody, including two hundred and fifty-three civilians."

"Understood," T'Kir's voice answered. "Are you threatening to place your prisoners in a combat zone?"

"No," the woman said. "But it seems our entire world

is to become a combat zone. We'll keep them as safe as possible. If they're harmed, it will be your doing."

"Understood," T'Kir repeated. "Out."

Geordi looked to Picard. "Captain, a while ago Astrid figured out that the Herans had long-range transporters, and that they took prisoners to serve as hostages. I think we can rely on her assumptions."

"I agree," Picard said. "And if we are to negotiate with the Herans, we'd better hurry. The Klingons will be here in an hour. Mr. La Forge, Mr. Worf, Commander Riker, you will accompany Dr. Kemal on her mission."

"Thank you, Captain," Astrid said, and stood up. "Let's go."

While Beverly Crusher, Deanna Troi and Data left for the bridge, Geordi accompanied the others to the nearest transporter room. Once there Geordi checked out a tricorder. He wasn't too thrilled by the thought of beaming down into an impending war zone, but that was part of the job.

"I don't think it's a good idea to take that along," Astrid said as Riker picked out a phaser. "This is a diplomatic mission, and if a Heran sees you with a weapon, you're dead."

"Maybe," Riker said grimly, "but I'm not going into a combat zone unarmed. Regulations," he added.

Astrid looked to Picard, who seemed about to speak. "Captain, please let me handle this," she said. When Picard nodded she stepped over to a bulkhead and leaned against it, crossing her arms in front of her. Her manner seemed casual, almost lazy. "All right, Commander, if you can shoot me, I won't question your decision to take that phaser."

"I'm not about to shoot anyone," Riker said.

"Try it," she urged him. "I won't move until you draw, but I guarantee I'll take it away from you before you can pull the trigger." Riker merely looked stubborn. "Come on, try it, little fellow. It's open season on Herans; shoot! *bImoH 'ej SoSlij DutuQmoH tlhaQ!*" she snarled in Klingon.

Riker glared at her goading. "I won't shoot an unarmed—"

201

Geordi barely saw what happened next. Trask had been carrying a phaser. He drew it, and Astrid moved with a speed and agility Geordi would have sworn was impossible. She seemed to bounce off the admiral, and as he slammed against a bulkhead she came away with his phaser. She stopped in front of Riker and held the weapon's business end scant millimeters from his nose. Riker had barely begun to draw his phaser, and with her free hand Astrid took his weapon and tossed it to the transporter chief. Then she ejected the power cell from Trask's phaser and crushed the weapon in her hand. Her face remained impassive throughout the entire action, which lasted less than three seconds.

"Impressive," Worf muttered to Geordi, as Astrid handed the ruined phaser back to Trask. "I would have to use both hands."

"What did she say to Will?" Geordi asked.

"'You are ugly and your mother dresses you . . . funny.'" Worf looked pained by the feeble insult. Geordi decided that offensive behavior wasn't Astrid's forte.

Her next words confirmed that. "I'm sorry if I embarrassed you, Commander," Astrid told Riker, "but you had to see how dangerous a Heran can be. You could have shot me at a greater distance, but at close quarters an old human doesn't stand a chance against a Heran. Your reflexes aren't good enough."

"You've made your point, Doctor," Picard said. "If you're ready to leave—"

The transporter room door opened and K'Sah sauntered in. "You are not wanted, Ensign," Worf said. "Depart."

"Okay," the Pa'uyk said. He stepped onto the transporter stage. "I'll depart with you. You need me. Doesn't it make you happy to hear that?"

Suspicion burned in Worf's eyes. "Why would you volunteer for a dangerous mission?" he demanded.

"What, and miss a chance to loot a brand-new world? Besides," he added proudly, "if there's anything worth stealing down there, I'm your spider."

Astrid spoke to Picard. "I'll take him, Captain," she said. "I can use him."

"As *targ*-bait," Worf muttered.

"Make it so," Picard said. "And good luck, Doctor."

Geordi stepped onto the transporter with the rest of the away team. "Astrid," he asked quietly, "why would you want to take him along?"

"For the same reason I'm taking Worf and Riker," she said, and gestured to the transporter chief. "You see—"

The transporter came to life, and the team materialized in a ravine. Overhead, the sky was dark with night.

"—they aren't old humans."

"No, Admiral, I do not usually tolerate such behavior among my crew members." Picard kept his eyes fixed on the turbolift door. K'Sah's last-minute offer to join the away team might have been amusing in a less dangerous situation. "But I do make allowances for Pa'uyk cultural behavior, and as an exchange officer, Ensign K'Sah is not a normal crew member."

The turbolift stopped and the two men stepped onto the bridge, where an image of Hera's surface filled the main screen. "I still don't like the idea of sending Riker, La Forge and Worf down there with Kemal," Trask said. "I don't think she was telling us everything. She was too logical about this."

"She *did* have a hidden motive, Admiral," Deanna Troi said, as Picard and Trask seated themselves. "She isn't consciously aware of this, but she feels safe around Geordi. She's hanging on to him like—"

"—a security blanket?" Trask suggested.

"More like a life preserver, Admiral," the counselor said. "He was friendly to her when other people wanted nothing to do with her, and he did everything he could to get her out of the brig. In a way, she's falling in love with him."

"Only in a way?" Trask asked. "Did her makers leave that emotion out of the package?"

"She's capable of love, Admiral," Deanna said. "But she still fears what she calls 'old humans.' What's worse, her belief that she's some sort of weapon gives her a feeling of worthlessness. That limits what she can let herself feel for Geordi."

"Incoming message from the *Titov,*" Ensign Rager said.

"On screen," Picard said.

A Vulcan woman appeared on the main viewer. "Captain Picard," she said. "In the interests of coordinating our attack, I am placing the task force under the command of the Klingons. Pursuant to task force orders, you will also place your ship under the command of Admiral Vorkhas."

"That's not possible, Captain," Picard said. "We are engaged in negotiations with the Herans. It would be inappropriate to engage in battle with them."

"Captain, a refusal to obey this order could be construed as insubordination," T'Kir replied evenly.

"I'm aware of that, Captain," Picard said. "But I am on a mission of peace. I understand that Surak took even greater risks in the pursuit of peace."

"Correct." Although the Vulcan's face showed no emotion, Picard thought he heard approval in her voice. Mentioning Surak, who had led the Vulcans into the ways of peace and logic, had been a sound move. "Peace and prosperity," she said, raising a hand in the Vulcan salute.

Picard returned the gesture. "May you live long and prosper."

A view of the Heran globe replaced T'Kir's image, and the peaceful scene filled Picard with melancholy. The Heran fleet had fought Hoskins's task force with desperate courage as they stood between their homes and invasion. That battle had been a foretaste of horrors to come, if the away team could not make peace with the Herans.

* * *

"What do you mean, I'm not human?" Riker demanded as the away team materialized in the ravine. Geordi heard the anger in his voice. "Is this your idea of a joke?"

"No," Astrid said quietly. Geordi noticed how she pulled away from him, as if she were afraid of him—or of hurting him, he mused. "And quit shouting. Half the planet can hear you."

"I wasn't shouting," Riker said.

"What's he griping about?" K'Sah asked Worf. "The enemy spy finally says something nice to him—"

"Silence," Worf growled.

Geordi scaled the side of the ravine. He raised his head over its edge and looked around, scanning the terrain in infrared light. The ground was rough and rolling, and cluttered with heavy shrubs and thick grasses. There was no one in the area—wait, his VISOR was picking up a patch of distortion in the distance. It might have been from a jammer that didn't quite cover all of his VISOR's frequencies.

"Company," Geordi said, dropping back down the side of the ravine. "I think somebody's about one kilometer east of us."

"They can wait," Riker said. "Let's have an explanation."

"I'd like to hear one, too," Geordi said, still looking at Riker. He was never going to forget the look on Will Riker's face. "Astrid, if this is your idea of getting even, it's a doozy."

"It is?" she asked, sitting down on a flat rock. Geordi sat next to her, while Worf and K'Sah remained alert. She seemed just as puzzled as Riker had seemed insulted. "Am I supposed to get even with him for something?"

"Well, not really," Geordi said. "Let's talk about it later."

"Okay," Astrid said. She looked to Riker. "Commander, I didn't say you weren't human, just that you aren't old human. Not entirely, to be precise. Do you know much about the Khans?"

"Only what everyone knows," Riker said. His anger had faded rapidly, but it was clear that he felt far from amused. "Most of the Khans were wiped out after the Eugenics Wars. A few of them tried to make it to Tau Ceti, but eventually they were killed, too. Are you saying that some of them survived?"

"No," Astrid said. "Maybe you don't know that a lot of them took old-human spouses. The Khans loved these people enough to make formal, public marriages with them, and to raise children with them. The Khans may have been genetically engineered, but in the matters that counted they were as human as anyone else. They loved as well as you can, Riker, and they never stopped to ask if their mates were genetically superior. They knew how unimportant that is.

"After the war, many of the men and women who had married Khans were hunted down and lynched. Their children were killed just as ruthlessly. But the Khans did not love foolishly. Their husbands and wives were people of high intelligence. Most of them found ways to survive.

"Ask yourself this, Commander," Astrid continued. "If you had a child, and if you and that child lived under a death sentence, what would you do?"

Geordi answered for Riker. "I'd hide."

Astrid nodded. "You'd go someplace where you weren't known. Someplace where life was so difficult that your intelligence would be an asset and people wouldn't question your background or ask awkward questions about your children. You'd go to a frontier— the Sahara Reclamation Zone, Mars, the Moon, Alaska—"

Geordi laughed suddenly. "Sorry," he said, seeing the baleful look he drew from Riker. "Astrid, I'm not sure I buy that. A lot of people lived in Alaska before the Eugenics Wars. Even if what you're saying is right, these half-Khan children would only be a small portion of Will's ancestors."

"Alaska was almost abandoned during the wars," Astrid said. "And there wasn't much immigration afterward. The several hundred half-Khan children who were brought there formed a respectable percentage of their generation's population. Quite a few of them are bound to be Commander Riker's ancestors. That's why I shut up in Ten-Forward," she said to Riker. "I figured you knew; your talk about *homo arrogans* sounded like some sort of verbal camouflage. That was the only explanation that made sense to me."

"So you were trying to protect me?" Riker asked. Geordi thought he sounded incredulous.

"I didn't want to get you in trouble," Astrid said, and shrugged. "But I guess you didn't know?"

"And I don't believe it, either," Riker said.

"Why not?" Astrid asked. "I've looked at some Terran census records, and there are some odd omissions in them that are best explained by people in the early twenty-first century covering up their Khan ancestry. And you're well above normal by old-human standards—larger, stronger, smarter."

"Why tell me this?" Riker asked coldly, while Geordi struggled to keep from laughing. Astrid looked perplexed by Riker's reaction, and Geordi wondered if she thought she was flattering him.

"Two reasons," Astrid said. "One is that you should know who and what you are. In addition, if the Herans think you're only part old human, they may be less hostile to you. That could make negotiations easier."

"Oh, really?" Riker demanded.

"Yes, really," she said patiently. "Old humans designed us as weapons. You can't understand how much we resent that. Unless you like the idea of being an expendable killing machine?"

Riker let out a Klingon-like grunt. "No. But why is it important to have nonhumans here?"

"They seem less threatening than old humans," she said. "You heard how my parents acted when those Intelligence agents visited them. *I* know you mean well, but between the Modality's propaganda and these outlaw raids, things could be awkward."

"Point taken," Riker said. "What about Geordi?"

"Name one person who doesn't like Geordi," Astrid said. "There's something about him—look, we need an old human who can show Herans that he can deal with us on an equitable basis, and that's Geordi. Besides . . . well . . . it seemed like a good idea."

Geordi thought she looked flustered, and he decided to change the subject. "You make it sound like Khan Singh is a folk hero on Hera," he said. "I guess you wouldn't look at him the way we do."

"We've got a lot in common with him," she said. "Such as being created by a bunch of raving maniacs, and having certain people try to wipe us out. And you find a lot of people named after him and his followers—my dad's father was named Khan. But the Modality has slanted history to make the Khans sound a lot more civilized than they were."

"Like they weren't really products of the twentieth century?" Geordi suggested.

Astrid nodded. "Or at least as though they were better behaved than their creators. The Modality's aim is to make enmity between us and you seem inevitable. Some of the things they teach—" She paused, then stood up. "Worf, I hear three or four people out there."

The Klingon nodded. "Three humans and a large animal," he said. "They are downwind of us."

"I can still smell 'em," K'Sah complained. "You wanna go meet them, Lieutenant?"

"Let them come to us," Worf said. "And be silent. They may hear our words."

"Don't worry, Worf," Astrid said. "They can hear our breathing a hundred meters away—" She stopped. "We're from the Federation *Starship Enterprise,*" she said to the empty air. "We're here to negotiate an end to the war . . . no, we're not going anywhere . . . yes, but we're all unarmed . . . okay."

"What's all that?" Geordi asked her. It was baffling to hear only one side of a conversation.

"I guess you couldn't hear them," Astrid said. "Those three people and their cat are from the resistance. They said they've been waiting for someone to show up."

"So you were right again." Geordi lowered his voice. "How are you holding up?"

"Fine." Astrid shook her head. "Scared. Maybe I shouldn't have come here."

Geordi could guess what was on her mind. "Nothing's going to make you switch sides," he said, putting an arm across her shoulders. Her size made him feel awkward, but she clearly welcomed the gesture. "You stood up to the Senior, right? Whatever the originators did to you, they didn't turn you into a puppet."

"I hope you're right." She sighed. Geordi thought she might put an arm around him as well, but something seemed to hold her back.

Geordi heard footsteps. There was only a little starlight, but in infrared light his VISOR let him see two men and a woman come down the side of the ravine. From the way they moved Geordi could tell that they had no trouble with the near-total absence of visible light. They were big, and two of them seemed even larger than Astrid. "You're sure they're from the resistance?" Riker asked uneasily.

Astrid chuckled as she and Geordi stood up. "I don't think the Modality would send only three people, and especially not a fourteen-year-old."

"I'm thirteen," the smallest of the trio said. Whatever his age, he was as large as Worf. He approached Geordi and Riker and stared down at them as though they were the most peculiar creatures he'd ever seen. Then he faced Astrid. "These are old humans?" he demanded.

"Geordi is," Astrid said. "The bearded one, Will Riker, is part Khan. The Klingon is Worf, son of Mogh. That's K'Sah. I'm Astrid Kemal."

The man nodded. "Are you in charge?"

Astrid shook her head. "No, Commander Riker is. He's also the *Enterprise*'s executive officer. Is something wrong?" she asked the boy, who was still staring at Riker.

"No." The boy shook his head in bewilderment. "It's just that . . . I guess I wasn't sure what I expected old humans to look like. I mean, they're so *little* . . . ."

Worf looked amused as the Heran man stepped up to Riker. "I'm Alistair Molyneux," he said as he shook Riker's hand. "My friends are Marla Sukhoi and Dallas Thorn. You're looking for this, of course." He handed a tricorder to Riker.

Geordi joined Riker and looked at the instrument. "This has the data on your genetic plague?" Riker asked.

"That, and several alternate cures," Marla said. "It can synthesize the corrective viruses, assuming we've made the right guesses about your physiology."

"You probably have," Geordi said, glancing at Astrid. He hadn't placed a lot of confidence in her plan to find the resistance, which had involved more guesswork than he'd liked. Now he saw how badly he had underestimated her intelligence. "But why are you just giving this to us?"

"Maybe to give you a reason to trust us," Molyneux said. He looked up at a low, feline growl. "Yes. We'd better move before Central Security locates us."

Geordi saw something move on the ridge above his head. A tawny shape flashed through the starlit air toward the boy, who caught it in his arms. Astrid had mentioned a cat, but this animal was the size of a mountain lion. "I suppose the cat's been genetically altered?" Geordi asked the boy.

"Not Koshka," Dallas said, draping the animal over a shoulder. It began purring loudly. "He's natural-born. But his ancestors were synthesized from different Terran felines, and they were given enhanced intelligence and psychic talents," he added. So don't try fibbing around him, Geordi finished silently. As if in response the cat turned its head and gave him a look of feline smugness.

Molyneux started leading the company down the ravine. "Where are we going?" Riker asked him.

"There's a tube station forty kilometers north of here," the man said. "We can be there in an hour, and—"

"An hour?" Geordi asked.

"We can't move any faster over rough ground like—" He paused and looked over his shoulder. "Oh. How fast can you travel?"

"If I push it, I can do that in four hours," Geordi said. "But why walk? The ship can beam us there, or anywhere else."

The boy snorted in derision. "And Central Security would show up in a minute. You can't miss a transporter beam."

Riker smiled grimly. "Your secret police are going to be too busy to bother with us soon. The invasion force will land in less than an hour."

Molyneux sighed. "That still gives CS more than enough time to react, but we'll have to risk it."

"There's something we can try," Geordi said. *"Enterprise,* eight to beam up."

The transporter beamed up the group in two separate parties. Geordi came up last, and as he stepped off the transporter stage he felt that four oversized Herans, a Pa'uyk and a Klingon made the transporter room seem unusually cramped. Worf, who was standing next to Dallas and his cat, began to sneeze. "Sickbay," Worf said, touching his combadge. "Send a medical technician to transporter room three."

"Is there a problem?" Beverly Crusher asked. When Worf answered with more sneezes, she went on, "Understood, Worf."

Geordi went to one of the wall panels, opened it and started rearranging its circuit modules. "Our transporters use a subspace pulse to lock on to a transport site," he explained to Dallas, who joined him and peered over his shoulder. "I'm going to code this to give several thousand pulses, spread all over the near side of Hera."

"They'll still pick up our energy trace when we beam down," the boy said. He pointed to one of the modules.

211

"Heterodyne that resonator with the main coherer. Central Security uses a polyphase detection system—"

"—and the multiple resonances will make our beam down look like a random energy flux," Geordi concluded. "Good thinking."

Molyneux had joined them. "That should buy us an extra fifteen minutes before they can pinpoint us," he said. "By then we'll have our own defenses set up."

Geordi nodded. "Just where do you want to beam down?" he asked.

"There's a communications complex two kilometers north of the capital," Molyneux said. "When we take it, we can communicate with everyone on Hera and block most of the Modality's communications at the same time."

"What about Central Security's backup systems?" Astrid asked.

"We staged an uprising a few days ago," Molyneux said. "We managed to destroy the backup networks. CS won't have restored more than a third of its emergency systems by now."

Geordi closed the circuit panel. "Ready here," he said.

"Then let's go," Riker said. He took one step toward the transporter stage, then stopped dead in his tracks. He looked at his empty hands in bewilderment.

K'Sah let out a piercing whistle, then held up the tricorder that Molyneux had given Riker. "Lose something?"

Riker seemed ready to explode. "Ensign, how in *hell* did you get that away from me?"

K'Sah snickered. "Now why would an honest, upright Starfleet officer want to know how to swipe something?" He tossed the tricorder to Worf, who had just received an injection for his cat fur allergy from a medical technician. "But if you're really interested, I give lessons."

Worf growled at K'Sah, then handed the tricorder to the orderly. "Give this to Dr. Crusher," he ordered.

Geordi noticed that Astrid had fixed K'Sah with a

sharp, suspicious look, an unusual display of emotion for her. "We're wasting time," she said. "Let's move."

Geordi stepped onto the stage with Astrid, Riker, Worf and Molyneux. "Energize," Riker ordered, and seconds later they stood in a clearing near a white dome. The sun was low on the horizon, but still bright in the clear blue sky. The air's warmth told Geordi it was late evening here rather than early morning.

K'Sah and the other two Herans materialized a few seconds later. "What now?" Geordi asked.

Dallas checked a tiny instrument that he pulled from a pocket, then pressed a signal button. "Our people will be here in a few minutes," he said. "Then we'll take that." He nodded at the white dome.

Riker looked the dome over. "Is anyone in there?"

"Just some workers and the automatic defense system," Dallas said. "It's too tough for me to crack by myself, but—"

Thunder and lightning rumbled in the distance. "What the heck?" Geordi wondered; he had seen a lot of strange things on various worlds, but a storm in a clear sky was new to him.

Riker had his tricorder out. "It's a Klingon space raid," he said. "They're invading."

Chapter Eighteen

CONCERN FOR THE SAFETY of his ship had led Picard to order the *Enterprise* to pull away from Hera as the first wave of ships broke into orbit. As the *Enterprise* waited in a high orbit Picard paced his bridge and consulted different tactical and navigational displays. It was clear that the Herans had never expected an assault on this scale, and the combined Klingon and Federation forces quickly overwhelmed their defensive satellites.

That action carried a high cost. A Klingon battle cruiser was so badly damaged that it was forced to withdraw, limping away from Hera at warp two. A Federation destroyer was smashed by one of the last Heran satellites, and the *Enterprise*'s sensors told Picard that this time the Herans were unable to beam off any survivors before the ship's reactor blew up.

The invasion force began making pinpoint attacks on Hera itself, cutting at ground defense installations with phasers and disrupters. Meteors in reverse, clusters of torpedoes rose from the surface and tore into the fleet. A Federation cruiser lost one of its warp nacelles to the attack, and a Klingon scout ship was left drifting without power.

The defense was futile. Screened by the combat ships, the transports began beaming down their troops even before the last installation was destroyed. Picard called for a tactical surface display, and the bridge's main viewer showed that the Klingon commander was concentrating his force around the Heran capital—and around the *Enterprise*'s away team. It would be far too easy for a stray shot to destroy the team, Picard thought, and while such teams were in theory expendable, that theory overlooked years of friendship and the value of each individual. "Mr. Data, who's in command of the Klingon task force?" Picard asked.

"General Kateq, sir," Data responded from his post. "He was one of Gowron's main supporters in the Klingon civil war. He is an expert at leading ground assaults. He is now on the surface."

"Hail him," Picard said, taking his command seat.

Trask occupied Riker's usual seat, from which he had watched the assault in stony silence. "You're worried about your away team," Trask said.

"I'd like to make certain there are no accidents," Picard said.

A stout Klingon with graying hair appeared on the main viewer. He stood on the Heran surface, in an open-air command post set up on the side of a grassy hill. Other Klingon warriors bustled around him as they set up equipment. "What do you want?" Kateq demanded.

"I have an away team in your area," Picard said.

Kateq grunted. "We will try not to kill them."

"They're trying to bring the Heran resistance movement on to our side," Picard said.

"Good," Kateq said. "That will make their surrender easier."

"They may not surrender," Trask said. "Herans are tough, General. You may have to fight them to the death."

"Good," Kateq repeated. *"Qaplah!"* He broke the contact abruptly and vanished from the viewer.

Deanna Troi had listened quietly from her seat at Picard's left. Now she looked at him in concern. "Why do you want to exterminate the Herans, Admiral?" she asked.

"I don't," Trask said.

"Perhaps not consciously—" Deanna began.

"Counselor, what I want to do is win," Trask said. "If the Herans surrender, fine. If they insist on fighting to the death, well, better them than us." He stood up and left the bridge.

Deanna spoke as soon as the turbolift door had shut on him. "Captain," she said urgently, "he doesn't just want to win. He wants to wipe out the Herans."

Picard didn't doubt her, although that was a monstrous thing to find in a human. "Can you say why?" he asked.

She shook her head. "It's not resentment over the plague. He doesn't hate the Herans, either. He's motivated by something cold and calculating."

"Is he looking for a way to advance his own career?" Picard asked.

"No, sir," Deanna said. "If anything, he's willing to sacrifice his own career in exchange for exterminating the Herans. I don't understand it."

"Neither do I." Picard rubbed his chin in thought. He had believed Trask to be what he appeared to be: dedicated to the Federation's well-being, opposed to the injustice of the Heran actions—and nothing more than that. The captain would have liked to maintain that belief, but he knew better than to doubt Deanna Troi's wisdom. "I can think of nothing more evil than genocide. Is he insane?"

"Morally, yes, but not legally," Deanna said. "He doesn't regard the Herans as people, which makes this decision easy for him."

Picard nodded. "He's consistently spoken of the

Herans as monsters, and that would explain his eagerness to arrest Dr. Kemal. Isolating her from the crew would make it that much harder for us to see her as a person."

Data had been quietly working at the conn. Now he turned around in his seat. "Captain, I have lost contact with the away team."

" 'Lost contact'?" Picard repeated. "Can you find them on sensors?"

"No, sir," Data reported. "Sensors and communications are being jammed from the surface. I can find nothing."

"We're in the middle of a triangle," Riker said as he checked his tricorder. Geordi saw him point in different directions. "Klingons that way, Federation troops that way, Herans that way, and all of them in a bad mood."

"Plus there's some kind of subspace jamming in effect," Geordi said as he checked his tricorder. He'd never seen jamming like this, but whatever it was, it meant communicators and transporters wouldn't work. It was also screwing up his VISOR, although he could still use enough frequencies to see by. "We're surrounded and cut off."

K'Sah cringed and looked to Worf. "Don't you just hate it when that happens?"

"Silence," Worf said. "I see no problem. We are not at war with anyone."

Geordi heard the regret in his voice. "And we've got to stay that way," he said.

"Correct." Molyneux turned toward Riker. "We've got less than a day to end this, Commander. There are three couriers on the way into old-human space. They'll reach their destinations tomorrow, and when they do, they'll infect Earth and two other planets with the Unity virus."

"We know about the couriers," Riker said. "I take it that 'Unity' is your name for the plague?"

"Yes," Marla said. "And there's only one way to stop those ships. That's to depose the Modality, put the resistance in charge, and hope that those ships accept orders from us."

"That doesn't sound like much of a hope," Riker said.

"If you've got a better idea, I'm open to suggestions," Molyneux said.

"I'm the one who wants suggestions," Riker said. "We kick out the Modality and put you in charge. What's to keep you from turning against us?"

"What's to keep you from wiping us out after we surrender?" Marla countered. "Nothing. But you could wipe us out anyway. And you will, if this war goes on. Or if we renege on a surrender."

"We aren't going to wipe you out," Geordi said. "The Federation doesn't work that way."

The cat made mewling, rowling noises. "Maybe he's telling the truth, Koshka," Dallas said. "But he doesn't make Federation policy."

Worf eyed the boy. "You can read minds?" he asked.

"No," Dallas said. "I just know Koshka's language."

"bIjeghbe'chugh vaj biHegh!" a Klingon voice roared from nearby. Although Geordi's command of the language left much to be desired, he recognized this phrase, which was a useful phrase to know when dealing with Klingons: surrender or die.

Astrid snarled an answer: *"yiyach'qu jay' yiH!"*

Geordi looked to Worf, who shook his head in disgust. "Do I want to know what that means?" Geordi asked.

K'Sah snickered. "Translated into human, it would be 'go pet a tribble,'" he said, and snickered again as Worf's glower deepened. "Just the thing to tell a bunch of kill-crazy Klingons. Damn, Worf, she really is your kind of woman."

"She must learn worse manners," Worf said, and muttered a few Klingon words that might have enhanced Astrid's vocabulary.

A skirmish line of Klingon warriors crept into the clearing, weapons at the ready. They looked wary; being insulted in a war zone was enough to put them off-balance. "Identify yourselves!" one commanded.

Riker stepped forward. "I'm William Riker, first officer of the *Starship Enterprise*. I want to see your commander."

The leader grinned nastily. "General Kateq will want to see *you*, prisoner. This way." He gestured with his disrupter.

To Geordi's relief none of the Herans tried to argue. Worf, however, demurred. "We are *not* your prisoners," he grated.

"Oh?" The leader grinned again. "We have weapons and you do not, and I find you consorting with Herans in a war zone. So what does that make you?"

Worf straightened. "I am Worf, son of Mogh. What are you?"

The leader thumped his chest with a gauntleted fist. "I am Commander Kharog—and *I* am not unarmed." The other Klingons laughed at his wit.

Astrid tugged at Worf's sleeve. "Worf, if you want his weapon . . ."

"No," Worf said. He looked as though he were near the end of his patience. "His weapon is dirty."

"Let's skip the unpleasantries," Riker said, while Kharog glowered at Worf's insult. "Kharog, these Herans are our allies. Take us to Kateq. Now."

Kharog glowered at Riker, but he barked a command at his men and pointed east. Klingons, Federation personnel and Herans started walking. They marched in silence for a half hour, until they came to a group of Klingons in a meadow. Geordi saw that the grassy field was busy with the invaders' activities. While Klingon technicians fussed and hammered at large pieces of equipment, a small cluster of officers shouted at one another over a portable disrupter cannon. Other officers bellowed at one another across a map projecting table.

Kharog led the group to the table. "General Kateq," he said, amid the outraged howls of the Klingon command staff. "This is Riker, from the *Enterprise*. He is—"

"Shut up," Kateq said. He looked up from the table and glared at Riker. "What treachery is this? We land, we deploy, our weapons fail!" He slammed a fist on the cannon, denting its projector. "Nothing works!"

"Central Security," Molyneux said. "They had a lot of tricks up their sleeves."

Geordi and Astrid already had their tricorders out, and Geordi felt pleased that he beat her to the answer. "Nanites," he said as he scanned the clumsy-looking weapon. The *Enterprise* had once been infested by similar virus-sized robots, and Geordi was painfully aware of their destructive potential. "They've disabled the power links."

Kharog gaped. "These people contaminated their entire planet?"

Geordi shook his head. "Herans aren't stupid," he said. "I'll bet these nanites are programmed to attack nothing but weapons, and deactivate themselves after a certain length of time."

"You think well," Molyneux said, and sighed. "If all the invaders are disarmed, we'll have a harder time overthrowing the Modality."

"The—" Kateq peered at Molyneux. "Who *are* you?"

"Alistair Molyneux, former head of Heran Combat Operations. Let's see. You'll need weapons. Shields, too. They're a dead giveaway to our sensors, but you probably don't need to hide. How are your communications holding up?"

Kateq looked as though Molyneux were several jumps ahead of him. He turned to Riker, who as a Starfleet officer was at least a familiar object. "What is this?"

"Molyneux leads the resistance to the Heran government," Riker explained. "There's been a change in plans, General. Molyneux's people have joined us. They intend to overthrow the Heran government, then form a provisional government and surrender."

"We still must fight," Worf said, assuring the Klingons that their visit to Hera would not be wasted.

"I'm afraid you're right," Molyneux said, as he pulled a handkerchief from his pocket. He draped it over the cannon's flat upper surface. "Stunner," he said, and a hand weapon appeared on it.

"Oh, wow," Geordi muttered, as Molyneux tossed the weapon to Kateq. Portable replicators were supposed to be impossible. He wanted the war to end right now, so he could find out how the Herans managed that trick.

Marla Sukhoi and Dallas had produced their own pocket replicators and were helping to arm the Klingons. Most of the Klingons looked pleased to hold live weapons again, but Kharog looked at his gun in disgust. "A stunner," he said. "No warrior fights with *veQ* like this."

Kateq ignored his comrade and turned toward Molyneux, not quite aiming his new weapon at the Heran. "Weapon parameters?" he demanded.

"It has a range of fifty meters," Molyneux said. "At that range, it will incapacitate a Heran for at least a minute. Point-blank, it'll knock one of us out for an hour. It won't penetrate a wall, but the government forces can't interfere with its functions."

"Good," Kateq said.

"Bad," Kharog sneered.

"You talk too much," Kateq said in irritation.

Kharog ignored that. "Are we to trust our enemies' weapons?"

"Yes," Worf said.

"And invite betrayal?" Kharog threw his weapon to the ground. "Never!"

Worf almost purred as he spoke to Kharog. "You know much of betrayal."

"You *toDSaH!*" Kharog snapped. He would have said more, but Kateq punched him in the face, silencing him.

"Later," Geordi muttered to Astrid, when she gave him an inquiring look. Now he saw why Kharog had taken an instant dislike to Worf. During the Klingon civil war Worf had been instrumental in helping Supreme Councilor Gowron defeat the Duras family. Worf had helped expose the Duras family as traitors who worked with the Romulans, the blood-enemies of the Klingons. Kharog might swear loyalty to Gowron now, but it was clear he had sided with the Duras family. He wouldn't forgive Worf for exposing the dishonor of his side.

Riker was looking at the stunner Dallas had given him. "Fighting Herans can be a problem," he said. "Kateq, have you been warned what they're like?"

"I heard Worf's report," Kharog said, and grinned at Worf. "You lost a fight with a Heran, didn't you? Well?"

"Yes!" Worf spat.

"No wonder they impress you," Kharog said. He chuckled and turned to Kateq. "The losers always exaggerate their enemy's strength. It makes their defeat look less dishonorable."

"You are not one to speak of dishonor," Worf said. "General, we need a plan. I suggest—"

"You suggest?" Kharog sneered. "Why should we listen to one who wears the uniform of a child?"

Worf clenched his fists. "Do you fear my words?" he demanded.

"Fear you?" Kharog laughed. "One who lives with humans? Do you also visit dentists? Do you like opera, too?"

Geordi thought that Riker looked as offended as Worf, and even the other Klingons seemed annoyed by Kharog's boorish opinion of opera, but before anyone else could respond Astrid reached out, grasped Kharog's leather-clad shoulders, and raised the warrior until his feet dangled a half-meter above the ground. Eyeball to eyeball with the enraged Klingon, Astrid bared her teeth, snarled and broke into a Klingon shriek:

> *"Be silent, weak and foolish one!*
> *At battle's start we saw you run!*
> *Oh, how to punish such a one?*
> *Tell me, Klingons,*
> *   what shall be done?"*

Kharog squirmed and kicked as he tried to break free of Astrid's grip, a struggle she easily ignored. The other Herans cringed and covered their sensitive ears while Astrid sang, and the cat raised his head to wail at the sky. Worf, however, beamed in delight at the stirring lyrics. He and the other Klingons roared into the booming chorus with her, their fists swinging to the rhythm:

> *"Give him to Fek'lhr, who sees his dishonor!*
> *Lock him in Gre'thor, pit of the horror,*
> *To rot in shame forevermore!"*

Astrid dumped Kharog on the ground and looked down at him. "I like opera," she said. "Now please pick up your stunner."

Kateq and the other Klingons bellowed their approval as Astrid turned away from Kharog, who hastily picked up his stunner. Geordi's ears felt bruised, although he knew that his universal translator had shielded him from the worst of it. "How's your throat?" Geordi asked Astrid.

"Intact," she said. "Think I should sing that for Trask?"

He chuckled. "Still working on this getting-even stuff?"

Astrid nodded. "Everybody needs a hobby."

"Yeah—hey, you're hurt," Geordi said in dismay. Her knee was bleeding from where Kharog had kicked her with his spike-toed boots. As she sat on the grass Dallas came over and made some medical instruments with his replicator. The tools were similar to their Federation counterparts, and Geordi looked over the boy's shoulder as he tended Astrid's injuries. A trimensional scan showed only cuts, bruises and a small fracture in her kneecap. All of the injuries were easily treated.

The Klingons ignored the first-aid work. "You had an idea, Worf," Kateq said. "Talk."

"The Modality would wish us to attack their stronghold," Worf said. Geordi nodded at that; attacking a strong point was always a tough mission. "It is bad to do what the enemy wishes."

Kateq mulled that over. "Talk more," he said.

Worf talked. "Let us surround their stronghold and wait. While we wait, we will declare that we have neutralized the Modality, and that we recognize Molyneux as the new ruler of Hera. Then our enemies must attack, to prove us wrong and restore their power."

"And we attack when they come into the open?" Kateq laughed evilly. "Not a bad plan . . . for a Starfleet lapdog."

"*We Klingons* are the ones to attack!" Kharog protested. "Leave these others out of it."

As if in response, Kateq eyed Astrid. The sight of a mere human toying with a Klingon warrior had clearly made him thoughtful, which, Geordi realized, must have been exactly what Astrid had had in mind. "I said we would attack when they come into the open," Kateq said in a decisive tone. "We will. Let's go. Where is the enemy?"

Marla pointed. "The Modality's headquarters are that way."

Chapter Nineteen

WORF THOUGHT the central Modality building looked undefended, but Molyneux refused to let anyone approach within a hundred meters of it. "They've got other tricks beside stunners," Molyneux said.

Kateq looked unimpressed. "Such as?"

"A mental suppression field," Molyneux said. The parklike setting held a scattering of marble benches, and he sat down on one. "It inhibits neural activity. Get within range while it's on and your brain will cease to work, permanently."

"A dangerous weapon," Kateq conceded, and glanced at Kharog. "For some."

"It's not much of a weapon," Dallas said, while Kharog glowered at his commander. The boy let his cat drop to the ground. "It's too big to be portable, and it doesn't have much range."

"But it will force us to keep our distance," Worf said. The cat approached him and purred as it rubbed against his knees. Worf wished it would go away. The orderly's injection had alleviated his cat fur allergy, but the *ghay'cha'* drug had left him with a dry mouth and an unwelcome feeling of sweet mellowness. Worf had to fight to maintain his emotional equilibrium. "Have you any portable weapons?" he demanded of the boy.

The boy shook his head. "None that will work here. Central Security has defenses against every type of weapon you can name: nuclears, explosives, biochemicals, nanites, the works. Even a starship's phasers couldn't get through to them."

"You said they could not interfere with a stunner," Worf said.

Dallas nodded. "They don't need to. Those walls are a half-meter thick. You could fire a sonic cannon at them all day and all night, and it wouldn't do any good."

"We are not going to fight them on those terms," Kateq said. "The plan is to make them attack. Kharog, deploy our forces."

"At once," Kharog said.

"Of course at once, you idiot," Kateq snarled, as Kharog strode off. Kateq looked away from his subordinate, and Worf heard him mutter something that involved in-laws, inbreeding and political infighting. Meanwhile Kharog started shouting and waving his arms, and groups of Klingons began to move into position.

Worf looked around the area. Aside from Astrid, Molyneux and his two companions, there were no other Herans in sight. According to Molyneux the civilians had evacuated this area. Despite that he picked up the distinctive scent of humans coming from the target building—quite a few of them, in fact. If they chose to launch a sally, they might overwhelm the Klingons. It would be glorious, but it wouldn't last long.

Molyneux stood next to him. "There's another problem here, Worf," he said. "The whole planet is going to watch this attack. If it turns bloody—"

"*Turns* bloody'?" Kateq chuckled. "We *start* bloody, human."

Dallas snorted. "That's why the primals sent them,"

he said. "A bunch of bloodthirsty maniacs. Just the thing to exterminate a planet."

Kateq look pleased by Dallas's words, but Astrid put a hand on his shoulder. "No one wants to exterminate us."

"Prove it," he said.

"We can't," Geordi told him. "You're just going to have to believe that we aren't as vicious as your originators were."

Marla Sukhoi stared at him in surprise and anger, Worf saw. He found the sight of Heran anger to be impressive, and he had to respect the engineer for not flinching. "What would you know about them?" she demanded, in the few seconds before her calm demeanor returned.

"Just the obvious," Geordi said. "There's something evil about people who would design their own children to be weapons. You must hate them, and considering the trouble you've had, you can't be blamed for thinking we're like them."

Dallas's cat made a strangely modulated mewling noise. "He means that," the boy said in blank astonishment.

"Enough pleasantries," Worf said. "Molyneux, you must capture the communications station."

Molyneux nodded. "Of course. Commander Riker, you should be present for this." He gave Kateq a cordial nod. "If you'll excuse us, General?"

"By all means," Kateq said, evidently deciding it would be unwise to show the normal Klingon curtness to a Heran.

After Molyneux left with Riker and Marla Sukhoi, Worf sat down on the grass and contemplated the Modality building. It looked like nothing more than an ornate heap of marble, but that said nothing of its defenses. It was heavily defended, to be sure, yet there had to be a way to assault it, in case the siege failed.

Worf looked at the feline. It had sat down two meters in front of him, and it watched him with eyes far too intelligent for an animal. Displeased by the thought that it was reading his mind, Worf growled at it. The cat growled back, then stood, arched its back and raised its hackles. Envying the display, Worf bared his teeth. The cat hissed loudly at the Klingon and showed its claws. Worf snarled at it. The cat crouched and prepared to leap on Worf.

Dallas walked over and picked up the cat. "Forget it, Koshka," he said. "He's bigger than you are." The cat growled nastily. "Sure, but what if he ate you first?"

"I might," Worf said. "I have not eaten today."

"Oh, right," the boy said, as if eating were the sort of thing anyone might normally forget. He let his cat jump to the ground, after which he pulled a replicator cloth from his pocket. "I can only synthesize terran-stock foods. What sort would you like?"

Worf grunted. Most Earth foods struck him as bland, but the planet *had* spawned a few taste treats. "Prune juice and goat meat," he said.

"Okay," the boy said. "How do you want that cooked?"

Worf did his best to look blank. "'Cooked'?"

"Never mind," Dallas said. He lay the replicator on the grass and spoke a few words. A slab of red meat and a jug of prune juice appeared.

Worf sat back and ate while he continued to watch the Modality building. He didn't doubt that its defenses were too sophisticated for him to defeat. Perhaps the *Enterprise* could blast away the building with her phasers, but that destruction would only harm the Federation's cause here.

On the other hand . . . "That building," he said to Dallas as he finished eating. "How is it constructed?"

"The building itself?" Dallas shrugged. "It's pure marble, just like the original Parthenon back on Earth."

"No reinforcement?" Worf asked.

"No," Dallas said. "It doesn't need any. Why should it?"

"Defense," Worf said, and stood up. "I have a plan."

Dallas looked interested. "What is it?"

Worf flashed a ferocious smile. "Trust me," he said. He looked around, found a stone and hefted it. The cobble gave his hand a solid, gratifying feel. Worf gauged the distance to the building, then hurled the stone. It sailed through the air and smacked harmlessly into one of the building's windows, A second later the window opened. A Heran leaned out, waggled a finger at the Klingon as though he were a naughty child, and then graced him with a forgiving smile.

Kateq laughed at Worf as the window slid shut. "Well-done. You have struck the first blow. Already their morale sags."

Worf ignored him. What mattered was that the building was not protected against inert projectiles; the Herans clearly had not expected an attack by such a crude technique. It was a poor opening, but better than nothing. "I need your replicator," he told Dallas.

Geordi and Astrid walked up to him as the boy handed Worf the cloth. "What have you got in mind?" Astrid asked as Worf spread the cloth on the grass. "A gun? They've got a damping field against explosives and shock waves."

"I bet I know," Dallas said as Worf grunted. "And a pocket replicator won't be big enough. Medium construction replicator." A thickly folded cloth appeared atop the replicator. Dallas shook it out and spread it on the grass, covering an area of a dozen square meters. "Mind a suggestion, Worf? Use tritanium-osmium spheres with a twenty-centimeter radius. They'll give you higher density and the best kinetic energy yield."

Worf grunted in acknowledgment of the suggestion. "Catapult," he said.

"I'll be damned," Astrid said, as light glared and a massive wooden framework appeared on the replicator. "Worf, that's so simple, it's brilliant."

"He's never at a loss," Geordi said in admiration, while several Klingons walked over to join Worf. Growling in approval, they lifted the catapult and turned it to face the building. Worf ordered the replicator to produce one of the spheres that Dallas had suggested. The high-density metal sphere weighed more than a hundred kilos, and he did his best not to look strained as he carried it over to the catapult. The other Klingons were grunting and straining too as they wound the siege engine's elastic band around its capstan. As Worf had surmised it would, the replicator had delivered a machine best suited to Heran muscles, and it was all the aliens could do to arm the catapult.

Worf dropped the sphere into the holding cup at the end of the catapult's arm. He inspected the machine, pretending to judge its aim and abilities while he looked for a trigger. "Stand clear," he said at last, finding a likely looking mechanism. He pulled the rod, and the machine kicked as it flung its load toward the building. There was a quick hiss as the ball sped through the air, followed by an explosive *crack!* as it struck its target. White chips flew through the air as a small fracture appeared in the marble wall.

The Klingons roared in delight at the damage they had done. "I could get to like fighting Herans," one said as he began to rewind the catapult.

Worf grunted in agreement and went for another projectile. The large replicator was in use, however; Kateq and several other Klingons had decided to join the fun by making their own catapult. Worf was glad for that. It would speed up what promised to be a long process.

Riker often exercised by sharing holodeck adventures with Worf, and those strenuous battles—the Klingon liked to fight hand-to-claw with synthetic monsters twice his size, and with dispositions even he considered vile—kept the *Enterprise*'s executive officer in superb condition. He was doubly glad for that now. The Herans walked at a rapid pace, and he was able to keep up with them without huffing and puffing.

Even so, he knew they were accommodating him by

traveling at a rate they considered slow, and they had more than enough breath for conversation. "It must be difficult for you," Marla Sukhoi said, as they followed a narrow trail through some woods. "Being part Khan among old humans."

"I'm not sure I believe what Kemal said," Riker told her.

Sukhoi looked over her shoulder at him. "No?"

"No," he said. "This is her idea of a joke. Even if it were true, after three-hundred-plus years that sort of ancestry would be so diluted that . . . hell."

"What?" Molyneux asked.

"Maybe I wouldn't be so annoyed if I didn't think it's possible," Riker admitted. He didn't like the idea of being even partly descended from the Khans; it was like being asked to share the guilt for what they had done. It was as galling as the sympathy the Herans were showing him.

"I can see why you'd feel upset," Sukhoi said. "I've read some old-human history books. They aren't objective about the Khans."

"It's hard to be objective about mass murderers," Riker said.

"I know what the Khans did in your Eugenics Wars," Sukhoi said. "They used their old-human subjects as cannon fodder, and they were pretty casual about slaughtering their opponents. But they did other things that you don't have to feel ashamed of."

"Such as?"

"Think," she said. "Before the Khans appeared, the old humans only had one space station, they used rockets to get into orbit, and they could barely reach their moon. By the time the Khans were defeated, Earth had ships good enough to reach the stars, except nobody gives the Khans credit for contributing to Zefrem Cochrane's experiments on warp drive.

"Maybe," Riker said. "But that doesn't cancel out what they did."

"Nobody said it did," Sukhoi said. "Although if it matters, the Khans weren't any more brutal than some old humans, and they didn't try to wipe out humanity. And the Khans managed to end a lot of the old humans' tribal and religious conflicts."

"Only because it suited their needs," Riker said. "And I suppose that deep down you think we primals should thank you for this Unity plague—"

Her face blank, Marla stepped in front of Riker, blocking his path. "Listen, little man," she said coldly. "My husband died trying to stop Unity. The Modality took away my children and sentenced me to death because I tried to stop it. They've killed many good people who tried to stop it. You may not like us, but by God you will respect us."

Riker looked up at her. "You're right," he said. "I apologize."

Marla nodded at that, and they walked on. Molyneux broke the silence after a long moment. "If you're from a ship named *Enterprise,* you're probably familiar with Mrs. Sukhoi's namesake, Marla McGivers."

The name jogged a memory. "She married Khan Singh," Riker said, "after the original *Enterprise* rescued him." That had been a well-kept secret until after the notorious Genesis incident.

"And after she committed mutiny to aid him," Molyneux said. "The story is famous here. All sorts of dramatists, composers and artists have created works based on their love. The theme of these works is that we can get along with old humans. That's not a popular idea with the Modality—"

"—but your people don't always agree with your leaders," Riker concluded.

Molyneux raised an eyebrow. "Do yours?"

Despite himself Riker had to smile. *"Touché,"* he said.

Molyneux smiled back as they entered a clearing. Riker stopped and held up a hand; there were a dozen Federation assault troops in the clearing. "Don't shoot,"

Riker said as they looked at him. "I'm Commander William Riker of the *Enterprise*..."

Riker's voice trailed off as he looked at the troops, who milled about in obvious confusion. "What in hell?" he muttered. He found a man with lieutenant's pips on his collar. "Report," Riker ordered him.

"I'm, uh, ensign, I mean—" The man shook his head. "I'm an officer. From the *Crazy Horse.* We've captured a prisoner, sir," he added proudly. "She's around someplace, but she won't escape, because we're guarding her, so don't worry about her escaping."

"What's your name, Lieutenant?" Riker asked.

"Was I promoted? Oh, right. I've got a name, sir. And a prisoner. You've got, let's see, one, two—well, a lot of pips on your collar, so, uh, you outrank me, right?"

"That's right," Riker said. Baffled, he turned to Molyneux. "What happened to him?"

"I'm not sure," Molyneux admitted. "It could be confusion gas, a neural stunner or a psionic scrambler. The effects will wear off in a few hours."

The lieutenant nodded. "That's right, there was some gas, but it didn't do anything, even if we did get gassed, because we're all okay despite the gas we're all on top of the situation is under control. Say, you're in Starfleet, right?" He watched Riker nod, then drew his phaser and casually pointed it at Riker. "What am I supposed to do with this?"

Riker felt faint, even after he saw that the weapon's power cell had been removed. "Just put it back," he said.

"Oh, thanks," the man said in evident relief. "Say, are you in Starfleet?"

Riker turned away from him as a Heran entered the clearing with two more Federation soldiers. She looked harried. "Please give me a hand," she said to Molyneux and Marla. "There are at least twenty more primals lost in the woods around here. A couple of them have hurt themselves, too."

"We can't stay," Marla said. "There's a communications station in the area. We're going there."

"It's about two hundred meters that way," the woman said, pointing. "Tell them I need help. The primals keep wandering off."

"No one's wandering off," the lieutenant said.

The woman nodded. "That's right, I'm your prisoner and you have to stay here to keep me from escaping. Hey, you with the beard!" she said, as Riker started to leave with Molyneux and Marla. "You have to stay here and make sure I don't escape!"

"It's all right," Molyneux said. "He's with us."

They took a different clearing out of the trail, and returned to the clearing where they had beamed down. Phaser marks now scorched one side of the dome. "We can go in," Molyneux said as he made a scan with his tricorder. "Our people have neutralized the defenses."

Riker and Marla followed Molyneux through the door. Three Herans worked at control panels inside the building's main chamber, and as Riker came in all three of them pointed hand weapons at him. "It's all right," Molyneux said. "Commander Riker is here to help end the war."

"Oh," one of the technicians said. They all looked mildly embarrassed as they put their weapons aside. "Sorry," one man said, "but we had some trouble with other Federation people a while ago, after our defenses failed."

"Was anyone hurt?" Riker asked.

"I don't think so. Is the war really over?"

"It will be shortly," Molyneux said. "We're surrendering to the Federation."

The technicians looked puzzled. "Is that a good idea?" one of the two women in the station asked. "The Modality claims we're winning."

"We're winning this battle," Molyneux said. "But the Federation has more resources than we do, and they've wiped out our fleet and ground defenses. We can't stop a second assault, especially not if they decide to use a world-wrecker."

"You're saying we don't have much of a choice," the

first technician said. "I'm not sure I like the idea of surrendering to the primals. I know how they act."

"No, you don't," Riker said. "Not all of us." He looked to Molyneux. "And we wouldn't destroy Hera. That's one thing we won't do—exterminate an entire people."

"Commander Riker is living proof of that," Marla said. "Some of his ancestors were Khans. He even *looks* a bit like Khan Singh, don't you think?"

Riker tried not to appear affronted while the technicians looked at him. "Well, maybe," one of them said grudgingly. "What happens if we surrender?"

"The resistance has formed a provisional government," Molyneux said. "The Federation is willing to deal with us, which implies they'll accept Hera's continued existence."

"And you need to broadcast that message," the woman said. She gestured to the other technicians. "Jackson, Kwame, let's get set up."

The Klingon and surviving Federation ships had undisputed control of the space around Hera. The tactical display on the bridge's main viewer proved it. No Heran weapons remained operational in space, and the starships covered the planetary starports with their weapons, while several small Klingon ships formed a loose perimeter at the edge of the Heran planetary system. Despite that Picard felt ill at ease. Something in the tactical situation felt wrong. It was as though the Herans had conceded the first round, but had not yet begun the next phase of their assault.

Five ships, Picard thought. Five small ships and their crews had devastated one of the largest Federation forces since the battle of Wolf 359. A dozen satellites and surface installations had done still more damage to the invading fleet. He had to wonder why the Herans hadn't fielded a larger force, with more potent weapons. With the resources of their world, they could have done so easily.

Admiral Trask paced back and forth in front of the main viewscreen. It showed an overhead view of the Heran capital. Individual humans and Klingons appeared as dots on the edge of visibility. "Can't you get a better image?" he asked, stopping in front of Data's station.

"No, sir," the android said. "The Herans are generating interference all across the spectrum. I cannot even ascertain that we are viewing actual events."

"You mean we could be looking at a hologram?" Picard asked.

"That is correct, sir," Data said. He paused as new information appeared on his instrument board. "I am picking up a Heran transmission."

"Put it on the main viewer," Picard ordered.

Will Riker and two Herans appeared on the viewer, seated at a table in front of a bare wall. Riker appeared dwarfed by the man and the woman who sat with him. "I am Alistair Molyneux," the Heran man said, "acting head of the resistance. Speaking on behalf of the resistance, I hereby declare that the Modality no longer has authority to govern our world, and that the resistance will serve as a provisional government until a democratic replacement system can be organized.

"My first order is that all hostilities against the Federation and their allied forces cease, both on the ground and in space. The Federation has offered peace terms that are acceptable. We have every reason to believe that the offer is made in good faith." He nodded to Riker.

"I'm Commander William T. Riker of the United Federation of Planets," he said. "This war is being waged in response to an attack made by the Modality against the Federation. Our only goal is to ensure that Hera will not launch another attack. After the surrender your world will be administered temporarily as a Federation trust territory—"

Trask's jaw sagged. "Who gave him permission to make Federation policy?" he demanded.

"No one," Picard said. "Commander Riker is merely citing well-established Federation policies."

"It may not be our policy this time," Trask said. "Dammit, he could be committing us to anything!"

"—assure you that it is not our intention to harm anyone," Riker continued on the screen. "The Federation is not founded on violence or extermination. One of our first missions here will be to prevent the sort of trouble you've had with old-human outlaws. Furthermore, our presence will be as unobtrusive and limited as possible. We are confident that cooperation is possible between Hera and the Federation . . ."

Static drowned out his voice as the image dissolved into a jagged raster pattern. The screen cleared and Carlos Ulyanov appeared. "Well, well," Trask said acidly, recognizing the leader of the Heran government. "Now for the rebuttal."

"I am the Senior of the Modality," Ulyanov said formally. "As such, I assure our citizens that the Modality is intact and functioning, despite certain inconveniences. Although Hera has been invaded and the primals control the skies above us, 'the issue remains in doubt.' As I speak a relief fleet is on its way and will arrive within a matter of hours. More to the point, we have other weapons at our disposal. We anticipate that within the day we will force the primals to surrender. Continue to fight; we shall survive." He vanished from the screen.

Picard looked to Troi. "Counselor?"

"That's no bluff, sir," she said. "The 'other weapons' must mean those ships we tracked leaving Hera."

"And the 'relief fleet'?" Picard wondered. "Mr. Data, begin a long-range scan for Heran ships. I think we can expect company soon."

The catapult assault had gone on for almost three hours when Riker, Molyneux and Marla Sukhoi rejoined the away team. Geordi thought Riker looked a bit winded, but he was obviously working to hide that. "What's up?" he asked Geordi.

"We're trying to get into their headquarters," Geordi said. Another metal ball cracked into a battered wall. "Worf decided to try knocking on the door. Once we get it open—"

A triumphant Klingon bellow cut off his words. Geordi looked at the building and watched a large chunk of the outer wall fall away, exposing a room and a half-dozen Herans. It was obvious that the Herans had anticipated this. They immediately broke out into the open and ran pell-mell toward a group of Klingons. Stunners knocked two of the Herans to the grass outside the building, but the others dodged and weaved too rapidly for the Klingons to strike them with their shots. In seconds the three remaining Herans were in the midst of a dozen Klingons.

Kateq glowered as his men were pummeled and tossed about like rag dolls. "The Romulans would die laughing," he muttered in disgust. Nearby Klingons fired their stunners into the melee, but one Heran escaped their barrage. Picking up a Klingon, he used the man's body to shield himself as he dashed back into the damaged building.

Geordi watched as the man and his prisoner vanished through a doorway. "Now why did he do that?" he wondered.

"You didn't hear?" Dallas asked. "Naguma—she's the acting head of Central Security—told them to bring back a prisoner."

"Old-human hearing is not acute," Worf said. He drew a veil of silence over Klingon hearing; if anyone had called an order from the building, Geordi doubted Worf had heard it.

One of Kateq's aides spoke to him in a quiet, intent whisper. "Rescue a prisoner?" Kateq snarled at him. As if in answer to his own question he spat on the grass.

"It must be what they expect," the aide said. "This means they must have lowered that mental-suppression field. This *could* give us a chance to rush in and overwhelm them."

"With their own laughter," Kateq grumbled. "Shut up before somebody confuses you with my *Qip* son-in-law."

There followed a long moment of silence, after which a door opened in the building and the captured Klingon was shoved into the open. He walked stiffly across the ground toward Kateq, who looked mortified. "Kharog," he muttered.

Kharog looked enraged as he reported to Kateq. "They offer to surrender," Kharog said.

Geordi thought the Klingon general looked as astonished as he felt. "They do? Why?" Kateq demanded.

"They *say* they would like to avoid further bloodshed," Kharog said. "They *say* they have fought honorably and will surrender their world to the Klingon Empire. They—" He cursed in Klingon.

"It's a trick," Astrid said. "The Modality is angling to hold on to its power."

Worf grunted in agreement. "Surrender to the Empire, and the Modality remains in power as its servants," he noted. "A clever move."

"And they don't have to worry about what the old humans might do to us," Molyneux said. Geordi couldn't read his impassive face, but he thought the man sounded tempted by the idea.

Kateq's aide spoke quietly in the general's ear. "Sir, I say—accept! We would become mighty indeed, if we absorbed them into the Empire."

Kateq chuckled, grabbed the man by the throat and pulled his face close to his own. "And what if *they* absorbed *us?*" he demanded, before he shoved the man away. "This offer is a trick. Let them surrender to the Federation." He chuckled again. "Let humans handle a human problem."

"I say destroy them!" Kharog shouted. "Butcher them! Slaughter them! Vaporize them!"

With an exasperated snarl Worf grabbed Kharog by the shoulders, faced him and slammed his forehead into Kharog's ridged scalp. Geordi winced at the thud of the impact. "*Thank* you," Kateq said in heartfelt Federation Basic as the unconscious Kharog fell to the grass. He turned to Riker. "This is a human problem, human."

"So it is." He looked at the shattered building, then gestured for the rest of the away team to follow him. "Let's go."

Chapter Twenty

"THERE IS STILL NO SIGN of Heran ships, sir," Data told Picard. He checked the instruments at the helm station again. "Sensors detect no activity within two light-years of the Heran system."

"Maybe Ulyanov was bluffing," Trask said. "Unless . . . Data, how much interference are you getting from Hera itself?"

"Large parts of Hera are still masked by interference," Data said. "However, the jamming is limited to the surface and does not affect our long-range sensors."

"So far as you know," Trask said.

"I have independently verified sensor reliability, sir," Data said. "We are receiving accurate data—just a moment. There is activity approximately ten light-hours from Hera."

"What sort of activity, Mr. Data?" Picard asked.

"A ship has just emerged from a transwarp duct," the android said. "Its configuration resembles that of the *Temenus*. It is bearing three-seven-nine, mark zero three and accelerating to warp nine-point-five."

"Another courier?" Trask asked.

"No, sir," Data said. "It appears to be heavily equipped with sensors. This suggests it is a scientific survey vessel."

"What is its course?" Picard asked.

Data consulted his instruments. "It is on an intercept course with a Klingon ship. Intercept in sixteen seconds."

Data put an image on the main viewer. A small Klingon Bird-of-Prey appeared, its image rendered indistinct by distance. As it began a turn a sleek white shape flashed past it, easily dodging a spread of photon torpedoes from the Klingon vessel. The Heran ship fired no weapons of its own, but seconds later the corvette began to dissolve like a lump of sugar dropped into water.

"Incredible," Ensign Rager said in awe, staring at the screen from her seat at the conn. "What happened?"

Data had already surmised the answer from his instrument readings. "It appears that the Heran ship attacked the Bird-of-Prey with nanite disassemblers," he said. "They took the ship apart atom by atom."

"But . . . so quickly?" Trask asked.

"The nanites could have converted the ship's material into more nanites, which would cause the rate of destruction to grow geometrically," Data said. "It is an intriguing and irresistible weapon. Shields are not designed to stop nanites." He saw new activity on his sensors. "Detecting a second Heran ship. It is at bearing three-twenty-nine-mark-fifty-zero-five, and moving to intercept a second Klingon ship."

"On screen," Picard ordered.

The main viewer now showed a second Heran ship as it flashed toward, and past, a Klingon vessel. The Klingon ship fired its disrupters as the Heran craft neared it. Then a gaping hole appeared in the Klingon ship's engineering section, and it began a slow tumble as its power died. "More nanites?" Trask asked.

"No, sir," Data said, as he slowly deciphered his sensor readings. "It would appear that the Heran ship struck the Klingon ship with an antigluon beam. Gluons hold together the quark packets which make up most subatomic particles—"

"I've studied physics," Trask said sourly. "I take it that our shields are useless against antigluons."

"That is correct, sir," Data said.

"And I take it that this second Heran ship was a modified science vessel," Trask said.

"The readings do suggest that, sir," Data said. "Its weapon system was not an integral part of the vessel. Indications are that it was"—he found an appropriate term—"jury-rigged."

"They're showing off," Trask muttered. "Letting us know that they can invent new weapons in a hurry."

"Incoming message, Captain," Rager reported. "It's from the Heran ship."

"Put it on the main screen," Picard ordered.

A space-suited Heran woman appeared on the screen. "Enemy fleet," she said. "We have more ships on the way. Surrender or be destroyed. You have thirty minutes to decide."

"Hail them," Picard said as the woman vanished from the screen.

Rager touched her controls, then shook her head. "They're ignoring our hail, sir."

"Damn," Picard muttered. "We can't go away and leave our problems unresolved."

"I concur," Trask said. "Hail that Klingon admiral, what's-his-name."

"Admiral Vorkhas," Rager said.

The commander of the Klingon task force appeared on the main screen a moment later. "The peacemakers," he said in contempt, seeing Trask and Picard. "What do you want?"

"We've got less than thirty minutes to settle this issue," Trask said. "If we don't do it now, we'll never be rid of the Herans. Beam up your forces—then bombard every military and industrial site on Hera."

"And what about these attacking ships?" Vorkhas asked. "We cannot resist them."

"We can be done and gone before they show up," Trask said. "There's no time for debate, Admiral. Our peace mission has failed."

"It has not," Picard said. "Admiral Vorkhas, my away team is still trying—"

"The mission has failed," Trask said firmly. "Picard, follow your orders."

"Admiral," Picard said in a level voice, "we are too close to a peaceful solution to throw it away."

"There *is* no peaceful solution," Trask said. "You've seen how these monsters fight. Give them a replicator and they can create any weapon they like. We've got to disarm them."

On the screen, Vorkhas grunted. "Sensible talk. What is an industrial site? Every house with a replicator?"

"I intend to issue General Order Twenty-Four to the Federation ships of the task force," Trask said. "Captain T'Kir on the *Titov* will supply you with the appropriate target parameters. *Enterprise* out." Trask turned to Picard. "You'd better get your away team out of there."

Data looked at Picard and decided that it would be an appropriate metaphor to say that his face had turned to stone. "Admiral, I refuse to obey that order. I also refuse to allow you to contact the *Titov*."

"I knew you'd say that," Trask said. "Computer, General Order One-Eighteen. Authorization—"

As the admiral spoke, Data moved his hands across his control panel and entered a command of his own.

"—Trask seven-gamma-twelve, initiate."

"What is this?" Picard demanded. "General Order One-Eighteen—"

"—is only to be used in case of mutiny," Trask finished. "Which is what we call it when a junior officer refuses to obey a direct order in a combat situation. The *Enterprise* is now under my command. We're bringing this war to an end now—the only way it *can* end. Computer, hail the *Titov*."

"Order denied," the computer answered.

Data turned to the admiral and spoke in a regretful tone. "I locked out your command authorization before you could complete your order, sir."

Trask seethed. "This is mutiny!"

"That is correct, sir," Data said. "However, I cannot be a party to an act as immoral as the one you would order."

"What does a machine know about morality?" Trask demanded.

"Genocide is never moral," Picard said, as though repeating the obvious to a backward child. "And that is obviously what you want."

"For the good of the human race," Trask said. "Picard, *think*. How did the Khans take control of a quarter of the Earth? There weren't enough of them to grab it by force. No, they *swayed* people into following them. With their charisma and intelligence, they were irresistible, natural leaders. And now we've got a whole world of Khans on our hands! What happens if they decide to take over? Do you think we'll have the strength of will to resist them?"

"I cannot say," Picard told him. "But I cannot condemn an entire people merely because you fear what they might do. And even if you are correct—good! The human race demands challenges. There is no better way to develop character."

"This *challenge* could destroy us," Trask said. "Or enslave us. We need to exterminate them."

Those words hung in the air. "I would rather see the human race enslaved than commit genocide," Picard said. He nodded to Ensign Kellog, who stood at Worf's post. "Ensign, remove the admiral from my bridge."

Data turned to Picard as Kellog led the admiral into the turbolift. "Captain, there is the possibility that Admiral Trask is correct."

"Perhaps," Picard conceded. "But I think of 'humanity' as a characteristic we could not maintain if we exterminated a foe. Such an act would cost us our souls."

"I understand," Data said. "However, this does not obviate the possibility that Admiral Trask is correct."

Picard nodded. "In that case, we'll have to be very careful, won't we?"

"You haven't won yet," Ulyanov said as Riker led the away team along with Marla Sukhoi and Dallas Thorn into his office. Riker noted how Worf looked around the room as though searching for traps. K'Sah searched the room as well, then looked irritated when he found nothing worth stealing. Geordi took a chair next to Astrid Kemal. "And you can't win," Ulyanov continued. "We have a dozen ships coming in from our outposts. They'll reach Hera in a matter of minutes."

"Those are civilian ships with improvised weapons," Marla said. "And with crews who aren't trained to fight and kill. They may not be a match for the Klingons and Starfleet. And what happens when the Federation sends another task force?"

Ulyanov smiled. " 'Hast thou turned the least of these to flight'? The relief fleet will buy us enough time to finish building a fleet of robot warships. Then we'll overwhelm our enemies."

"Don't bet on it," Riker said. He seated himself in front of Ulyanov's desk. The chair was scaled to fit Herans and it almost dwarfed him. "You may win this battle, but you'll lose the war."

"Will we?" Ulyanov asked. "We have three ships inside Federation space. They'll spread the Unity virus to several old-human worlds—including Earth. You may exterminate us on this world, but you'll accomplish nothing."

"Don't count on that, Senior," Riker said. "Your plague ships haven't succeeded yet. Even if they get through the different planetary defenses, we'll find a way to reverse Unity's effects."

"And even if everything goes as you plan," Astrid added, "have you thought about what a victory will look like? The old humans and their children will hate you as much as we hate the originators. You'll find yourself at war again in another generation, and *this* time you'll be fighting your equals."

"You can't know that," Ulyanov said.

"It's a high probability," Marla said. "But I guarantee you won't live long enough to see the outcome. The Modality brought this war down on us, and you've forced us to fight and kill, as though we were nothing but weapons. Now nobody trusts you. Either surrender or see how long decent people let you live."

"You're out of power, Senior," Riker said with a nod at Marla. "Give all the orders you please, but nobody will take them anymore. All you can do is cause more ruin."

Ulyanov was silent for a long moment before he finally looked at Riker. "What are your terms?"

"First, a cease-fire," Riker said. "Recall your ships. Release your prisoners. Hera will be placed under the authority of the Federation, in accordance with Chapter Twelve of the Articles of Federation."

"So we're to be a trust territory," Ulyanov said. "As though we were a tribe of savages."

"Not quite," Riker said. "Eventually you'll be allowed to join the Federation—"

"—where you can keep us under your thumbs," Ulyanov said. He scowled, then touched a pad on his desk. "Naguma. 'The brazen throat of war has ceast to roar.' Issue an order to all ships. Cease fire; we have surrendered. Contact the invaders and transport all prisoners to their ships."

That took Riker by surprise. He had expected more arguments from Ulyanov; this capitulation came as suddenly as a chess player resigning from a lost game. "You're surrendering?" he asked.

"It's either that or be destroyed," Ulyanov said. "Not that conquering us will do you much good. We won't stay surrendered, *primal*. You may loathe us, but we hate you with a strength you can't imagine, because this is an intellectual hate, based on what every Heran knows to be true."

"They aren't the originators," Astrid said quietly. Riker saw her move closer to Geordi.

"They're no better than them," Ulyanov told her. "They've killed at least five hundred people in this assault. They've left us defenseless. They aren't going to protect us from outside attacks, or even from their own criminals."

"We can trust them," Astrid said.

"I doubt that Hera will agree," Ulyanov said. "We know what primals are like."

"Do we?" Marla asked. The look on her face reminded Riker of the blank expression Data showed while processing a complex problem. "Let's look in the archives."

"'The archives'?" Ulyanov repeated.

Marla nodded. "During my interrogation you mentioned an 'originator file.' I think it's time to see what you've been keeping secret."

Chapter Twenty-one

PICARD BEAMED DOWN ALONE, materializing in front of the shattered Modality building. Despite his trust in the Herans he felt uneasy. The situation was precarious, and given the depth of Heran fears about human behavior, it would not take much to provoke more fighting.

And Admiral Trask would love that, he thought as he entered the building. Picard feared that the man might yet find a way to resume the war. In that case, the extermination of the Herans might become inevitable. That had to be avoided at all costs.

He found the away team and several Herans in the building's basement. The basement was a long, marble-walled chamber that held several thousand white metal cabinets filled with data cartridges, as well as several display machines. Worf and K'Sah both looked alert and were holding Heran weapons in place of their deactivated phasers. Riker and Geordi La Forge aided the Herans in their search of the cabinets. "You said you had something, Number One," Picard said as he approached Riker.

"Not yet," Riker said quietly. "Mrs. Sukhoi is looking for a classified document about the originators."

"Except that we can't locate it," a Heran woman said. She spoke without looking up from the cabinet tray she had been searching. "It has to be in here somewhere, but it's been deliberately misfiled."

Picard nodded thoughtfully. "Which suggests that this document is dangerous to the Modality," he noted. He recognized her as the woman who had appeared with Molyneux and Riker in the transmission. "You're Mrs. Sukhoi?"

"Yes." She spoke without looking up from the tray. "Please excuse my manners, Captain Picard, but the recent past has been rather trying."

"I quite understand," Picard said, unsurprised that a Heran would apologize for not being perfectly cordial. Of the other two Herans in the room, one was a young boy who introduced himself as Dallas Thorn. A feline the size of a mountain lion sat by his feet, and the boy introduced the animal as though it were fully sentient. Seeing the way in which the animal eyed him, Picard found that a distinct possibility.

Geordi was growing exasperated with the search. "Maybe they destroyed what we're looking for," he said.

"No," Astrid said. "They wouldn't do that, no matter how dangerous the file was to them. The Modality had to know the truth. But something that important should be accessible. They should have hidden it some place obvious."

"Except they didn't," Dallas said. "The Senior knows where it is, but he won't say, and even Koshka can't get it out of him. We may have to read every file in here."

Marla Sukhoi looked at the endless ranks of cabinets. "That could take days," she said, and shook her head. "There's a pattern to everything the Modality does, even in the way they keep secrets, but they haven't followed the pattern this time."

"Perhaps the Modality didn't hide this file," Picard

suggested. When the Herans looked at him in confusion he pressed on, "If this secret file concerns your creators, it might have been filed before your people came to power, perhaps even before your ancestors came into existence. The current Modality would only have to know where they placed it."

"That makes sense, Captain," Astrid said. "Our old-human ancestors didn't think they way we do. They weren't exactly open-minded and reasonable."

"Vicious, secretive, power hungry, bloodthirsty—" Dallas chopped off his own words, an embarrassed look on his face. "But how are we supposed to figure out how people like that thought?"

Picard could have sworn that Worf smiled. "Allow me," the Klingon said. "What became of your originators?"

"They were executed for treason," Marla said. "They tried to engineer us to be absolutely loyal to them. As slaves," she added in barely controlled disgust.

"That's what the history books say," Dallas said. "The loyalty modification they had planned wouldn't have worked, but the Modality executed them anyway, for trying it."

"This seems improvident," Worf said. "What if the rulers had required their services again?"

"They gambled that they wouldn't," Marla said. "In fact, the Modality destroyed the records that told how genetic engineering worked, to make sure that nobody could repeat the originators' treason. They wanted to keep power to themselves."

"Was there a trial?" Picard asked. "Perhaps this 'originator file' is the record of their trial. It might be filed as a legal document."

"Hera doesn't have trials," Astrid told him. "Not like the Federation. If you're suspected of a crime here, you're interrogated under truth drugs. You either convict yourself or clear yourself." Picard saw Marla nod in agreement with that.

"But there will be a record of this interrogation somewhere," Worf said. "And you say these genetic-engineering records were destroyed."

"Not all of them," Dallas said. "I saw a reference to some records of failed gengineering work. They must have been overlooked, maybe because they wouldn't have any useful information about genetic engineering."

"Exactly," Worf rumbled. "Let us see these records."

"This way," Dallas said. Picard had thought he might need to check the filing system, but evidently the reference he had glimpsed was enough to tell him where to find it. The boy led the others down a passageway between a double row of towering cabinets, each equipped with a dozen primitive slide-out drawers marked with labels. But no locks, Picard noted, or any other security arrangements to protect the files. It seemed an odd omission for the security-conscious Modality.

Dallas stopped in front of a cabinet identical to the thousands of others that filled the basement, but it was Geordi who spoke first. "Don't touch anything," the young engineer said. "The molecular pattern in the floor looks like it's taken some phaser hits."

"A booby-trap," Riker said. He, Picard and Worf looked around, and Picard spotted a security monitor in the ceiling. The captain pointed it out, and Worf shot it with his weapon. Picard had expected only a small puff of vapor as the monitor was destroyed, but it went up in a shower of high-energy sparks as a phaser power system exploded. A few seconds later, Worf destroyed a second phaser system, which had been concealed in an air vent. That certainly explains the lack of locks, Picard mused.

"We must be on the right track," Riker said. "They're certainly protecting something important."

"And I'd hate to be the clerk who opened the wrong drawer here," Geordi said as he scanned the cabinet with his tricorder. "I can't find any more traps."

Dallas opened a drawer and extracted an old-style data cartridge. "This has to be it," he said. "It's labeled as a blueprint file of a failed genetic-engineering virus, but it looks like an audio-visual recording instead. Let's see what we have."

Dallas handed the cartridge to Astrid. Picard and the others followed her to a computer workstation, where she sat down and placed the cartridge in a reader slot. Geordi took the chair next to her, and they fussed with the controls for a moment.

"This might take a minute," he said. "This is an antiquated recording, so we need to reconfigure this machine to play it back.

"There," Geordi said at last, as a group of people appeared in the holographic tank.

A pale, haggard man sat strapped to a chair in a barren gray room. Picard thought the restraints were unnecessary; he seemed too frail to offer any physical resistance to his captors. The two people who stood by his side did not look any healthier; one was a middle-aged woman wearing a respirator mask, while her companion, a dark, white-haired man, wore crude power-assist bands on his legs and arms as he checked a medical display in the chair's side. Picard realized that these people were the unmodified ancestors of the present Herans—and it was a small wonder that they had developed genetic engineering. Astrid had said that they had severe health problems, but the sight of the three ailing people in the holographic tank told Picard how bad the situation had become on Hera.

"That's Ivan McGinty," Marla said to Picard, with quiet hatred in her voice. "The man in the chair. The head of the damned originators. The others were Jana Olsen, the Senior, and Khan Sabha, head of Central Security."

Picard nodded as one of the people in the recording spoke. *"He's under,"* Sabha said, his voice scratchy with static. *"One hundred percent."*

"Good," the woman said, her voice muffled by her respirator. The anger in her words came through clearly as she spoke to the man in the chair. *"McGinty—why?"*

"Had to," he mumbled. *"Protect our children."*

"You've ruined everything!" Olsen said. *"Hera's whole future, our destiny, our—"* She stopped and wheezed until she had her rage under control. *"You've destroyed our future."*

"Yours, not theirs." McGinty shook his head feebly. *"What sort of a future is it . . . for our children . . . design them to fight and die?"*

"These aren't your children we're talking about," Olsen said to McGinty.

"All of them are our children," McGinty said. *"We designed them, created them. Day after day . . . poured our life into them. And the experiments . . . the malformed babies we euthanized, the painful failures that had no love . . . too much to bear. We want an end to the evil."*

"'We,'" Sabha repeated. He leaned over the man in the chair. *"Which members of your team are involved in this conspiracy?"*

"I think it's more a question of which ones aren't *involved,"* Olsen said. *"I'm not sure if there are enough loyal scientists to reconstitute the project."*

"You can't," McGinty said. *"No one will help you . . . and when you started rounding us up, the ones you didn't catch . . . erased records, sabotaged equipment—"*

"Terminate him!" Olsen said. Sabha touched a control on the chair, and McGinty faded out of consciousness. *"We're ruined,"* the woman said as McGinty slipped into death. *"When the rest of the Modality learns about this, they'll kill us."*

"They don't have to learn," Sabha told her.

"They'll learn!" Olsen said. *"When they see how those children act, they'll know* those weaklings *aren't going to conquer anything. No aggression, no xenophobia— they're nothing!"*

"Think this through," Sabha said. Picard heard the electric hum of his power-assist bands as he hobbled back and forth in the holotank. *"The superchildren aren't normal humans. So why should anyone expect them to*

act human? And behavior is determined as much by training as by heredity. They can be trained *to behave the way we want."*

"The two of us can't do this ourselves," Olsen said.

"I know." Sabha's smile looked wolfish. *"But there are other people who have the same stake in this as we do. They'd hate to have the rest of Hera rise up and hang them."*

"Or you execute them," Olsen said, to which Sabha nodded in agreement. *"Speaking of which, you'd better terminate McGinty's fellow conspirators, before one of them talks to the wrong person. Put it out that we have ironclad proof of the conspiracy and don't need any more investigations—and classify the recording of this interrogation."*

The recording ended, and Picard found himself facing an empty viewer. As he looked at the Herans in the chamber with him he saw that Dallas looked thoroughly bewildered. Astrid was still seated next to Geordi; Picard saw her turn, bend down, rest her head on his shoulder and start to weep in relief, while Geordi put an arm across her broad shoulders to comfort her. "I don't get it," Marla said. "Is this a forgery? A decoy to keep us from finding the real secret?"

"No," Picard said. "It's the key to a very complex puzzle."

"We were so close," Riker said. "When Worf suggested that someone had sabotaged the genetic engineers' work, he was right, but it never occured to us that the engineers themselves could be the saboteurs."

"Or that their sabotage was a deflection instead of destruction," Picard said. "A very subtle form of sabotage."

"I don't understand," Marla said. She had the horrified look of someone who doubts her own sanity. "What are you saying?"

"That your people weren't born to be weapons," Picard said. "The clues lay before us all the time. Your lack of xenophobia might be explained as a tool to prevent you from fearing your enemies, but the effect is to keep you from feeling motivated to fight—in fact, to make you want to *like* the people you might otherwise attack. Your strong sense of guilt would restrain you from unjust acts of aggression. Your self-confidence would temper any aggression you might feel."

"But we're made to be aggressive!" Marla said. "We have to take classes to control it."

"Astrid's never taken an aggression class," Riker said. He looked only slightly less bewildered than the Herans. "And I've seen her back away or even freeze up when I would have expected her to lash out. Face it, these classes don't teach you how to *control* aggression; they teach you to *be* aggressive."

"Yes," Marla said, and Picard saw that she had already regained her mental balance. "The class structure and content fit that theory. And the classes are a good way to spot people with a high natural level of aggression. When we investigate, I think we'll find that the Modality screened its highest members to make certain they were highly aggressive."

"By Heran standards," Picard said. And it was no wonder that they had never spotted the deception, he mused. Take a child, raise him to believe he is stupid and worthless, and he will grow up believing that; no amount of success in later life will persuade him otherwise. The Herans knew they had been genetically engineered, and they thought they knew the motives of their creators. With no old humans around for comparison, it had been easy for them to see what little anger and aggression they could actually feel as monstrous levels of rage.

Dallas shook his head after Picard had explained this. "Then . . . then we aren't weapons," the boy whispered. He leaned against a marble wall as though no longer able to support his own weight. "The originators weren't monsters."

"The Modality has been lying to you," Riker said. "Just to make it easier for them to hang on to power."

"No," Picard said. He could understand how upset the

Herans felt. While they had just heard good news, it had wiped away something they had always believed. Even relief can be disturbing under such circumstances. "I think they sincerely believed we threatened Hera. They withheld the truth to make their people fear us. The Modality needed to motivate its citizens to fight us."

"Or to avoid you," Marla said. "If we had known about this, we wouldn't have avoided contact with your Federation. We would have learned the truth sooner."

"So everything that happened . . ." Dallas still looked dazed. "You mean . . . we went through all this . . . for nothing?"

"No," Riker said. "You had good reason to feel afraid. But that's over and done with."

Not entirely, Picard thought. If nothing else, Admiral Trask was still determined to eradicate the Herans. "Releasing this recording may dispel some of the animosity Herans feel toward us, but that is only a first step—on their side. We have work of our own in this matter." And he thought he knew what had to come next. Picard looked to Astrid, who held Geordi but no longer leaned on him; she had evidently regained her self-control. "Dr. Kemal, I may have a solution to our problems."

Riker had intended to go straight to the bridge upon his return to the *Enterprise,* but as soon as he had solidified on the transporter stage Beverly Crusher called and ordered him to sickbay. When he entered sickbay he found that the doctor looked harried, but pleased. "We've got the corrective for the Unity virus," she said, holding up a hypospray. "The tests show that it works perfectly. Twelve hours from now you'll be back to normal."

"Is this going to make me sick?" Riker asked as the doctor approached him.

"You'll experience the same symptoms you did with the original plague," she said. "That won't kill you."

"Can it wait a while?" he asked. "I have some unfinished business waiting for me. We've got to beam up our prisoners from Hera, set up communications with their provisional government—"

"This can't wait," Beverly said. "All of the infected crew members have to be treated simultaneously, before one of you can reinfect the ship. Now hold still," she insisted. "Honestly, Will Riker, you're as much trouble as Reg Barclay."

Riker grimaced as he was injected. There was no pain, but he didn't relish the notion of being sick again, even in a good cause. "What was Barclay's problem?"

"Every time I called him into sickbay to be cured, it seems there was a communicator malfunction, or he had a work assignment in some remote crawlway, or the computer couldn't locate him," Beverly said. "The truth is, he didn't *want* to be cured. Somebody finally cornered him in holodeck two. Can you believe that he programmed the holodeck to create a hundred replicas of himself? Dr. Par'mit'kon had to inject all of them, and even then he wasn't sure he got the real Barclay. I still don't understand that man."

Riker chuckled, recalling what Worf had said about Barclay's reaction to the plague. "How long will I be sick?" he asked.

"You should be better in twelve hours," Beverly said. "Enjoy it; you need the rest. Now go to your quarters."

Riker left the sickbay. At least I'm getting back to normal, he assured himself. He decided he could sleep through most of the illness. And after a day like this, he knew he could use some sleep.

But when he got to his quarters he decided there was something that needed his attention first. He sat down at his computer console and accessed the ship's library. *Paradise Lost* appeared on his display.

Geordi went into the Ten-Forward lounge, picked up a drink and joined Astrid at the table she'd reserved. "How are you feeling?" he asked her.

"Very strange." She spoke quietly. "Finding out that

I'm not a weapon, that I don't have to be afraid of old humans . . ." She shook her head. "I still don't know how to react."

"It's got to be a relief," Geordi said. Having her cry on his shoulder had been a strange experience, but not an unpleasant one. "I'm just glad I can't imagine how big a relief it must be."

"It's something I can get to like, though." She toyed with her glass. "Like drinking with a friend. I could never do that before."

"But now you don't have to worry about saying the wrong thing." Geordi picked up his drink. "Astrid, there's something I've been wondering about. Everyone was carrying on about how they felt about the plague . . . uh, the Unity virus. Only, nobody ever asked how you felt about it, did they?"

"Are you asking?"

Geordi nodded. "You don't have to worry about saying the wrong thing," he repeated.

Astrid looked thoughtful. "At first I couldn't understand why everyone was so upset. From my point of view, you, or at least your potential children, were getting a lot—better senses, better minds, better health, everything I've always taken for granted. If Blaisdell and Dunbar had come to me and confided in me, I might have helped them.

"But I thought about it while I was in the brig, and then I wasn't so sure. For one thing, I would have been doing exactly what I hated the originators for doing. More than that, what they were doing was taking away everyone's right to decide their own future. I still think that rejecting the Unity virus was the wrong decision, but it wasn't a decision I wanted to take away from billions of people."

"I don't think Unity would have been good for us," Geordi said. It surprised him that he could discuss this without feeling anger or fear. It was a pleasant surprise, as though he had freed himself of a burden—or a limitation. "Sometimes I think we're defined by our limitations, and sometimes"—he fingered the golden rim of his VISOR—"those limits force us to be more than we ever thought we could be."

"We Herans have our limits, too," Astrid told him. "We find them just as challenging as you find yours, and we wouldn't want to accept lesser limits." She smiled at him, an expression as soft and warm as the bioelectric fields that he saw surrounding her face. "You might want to remember that the next time you have to persuade Dr. Crusher that you don't want to replace your VISOR with 'normal' eyes."

"Fair enough," Geordi said. He wondered about the sort of limits a Heran might have. "Maybe some day we'll be ready for greater limits," he said. "When we are, Hera will still be there, to offer them to us."

Astrid raised her glass. "To greater limits, then."

Geordi returned the toast as the intercom signaled. "Dr. Kemal, Commander La Forge, please report to the conference room."

They put down their drinks and headed for the conference room. Picard, Riker and Dallas Thorn were already present and seated as they entered. "Where's Mrs. Sukhoi?" Geordi asked Dallas, as he and Astrid sat down.

"She's trying to locate her children," the boy said. "President Molyneux asked me to take her place today."

Geordi nodded at that. Having a thirteen-year-old boy sit in on a political conference was irregular—by our standards, Geordi thought. He knew that the boy was intelligent and educated, and that he had been an active participant in the Heran revolt. Geordi decided that his brains and experience made him better qualified for this task than some adults he could name.

Trask entered the room alone, as if to make clear his separation from the others. "Computer," Picard said, "contact Vice President Chandra . . . and President Stoneroots."

Chandra and Stoneroots appeared in a split image on the conference room's viewscreen: Chandra in her office, and Stoneroots in its workshop, up to its tentacles in a broken robot. It straightened up and switched on its computer translator as Chandra spoke. "Captain Picard. Aré the Herans prepared to formally surrender?"

"They are, Mr. President," Picard said, and nodded at Dallas. "Mr. Thorn has been authorized by their provisional government to accept our terms."

"Very well." Chandra accepted the boy's presence without comment; she seemed more interested in Stoneroots's involvement. "But why are the Zerkalans sitting in on this?"

"I've asked the Zerkalan government to participate in this affair because I think it will help persuade them to join the Federation," Picard said.

"Really?" Stoneroots asked. Geordi thought that the leafy anarchist sounded annoyed. "Why should we hang around?"

"For one thing, sir, the Federation has need of a world with your attitude," Picard said. "Your defense of one of your citizens speaks highly for your ethics."

"You're calling me a good example?" it asked, affronted.

"It's nothing personal, Mr. President," Geordi said.

Picard smiled slightly. "What I propose is this. The Federation is to administer Hera as a trust territory, until such time as it can become a full member of the Federation—"

"No," Trask said. "Vice President Chandra, we can't coexist with them. Everything we've seen in this war proves that. I know I was wrong about their intentions, but even with the best of intentions they could still overwhelm the human race."

"They aren't going to start another war, Admiral," Geordi said. He reached out and patted Astrid's hand. "The last thing they want to do is act like weapons."

"I believe that," Trask said. "But you're forgetting that Herans were designed to be intelligent, imaginative and charismatic. They're natural leaders, Vice President Chandra. There may be ill will over their attack now, but what happens when that fades? You could see a Heran taking over your office. You could see them persuading us to accept this Unity plague, and that would be the end of the human race as we know it."

The master chess player, Geordi thought, trying one last gambit to win his game. He could see how Trask had pitched his words to appeal directly to Chandra, and she was clearly mulling it over. "What do you propose, Allen?" she asked.

"Keep them out of the Federation," Trask said. "Establish a neutral zone between Hera and the Federation. They stay on their side of the border, and we stay on our side. With no contact—"

"Admiral," Picard said, "are you saying that the human race is so primitive that we need to be protected? Are you invoking the Prime Directive?" The captain paused as Trask's final effort went down amid chuckles; Geordi saw that Chandra was doing her best not to laugh. Picard resumed speaking when a sense of decorum had returned to the conference room. "As I was about to say, according to Chapter Twelve of the Federation Charter, a trust territory is to be administered by a member planet of the Federation. Vice President Chandra, I propose that we assign the trusteeship of Hera to Zerkalo, once it joins the Federation."

"A planetful of anarchists—" Chandra began, and chopped off her words. "This is an irregular suggestion, Captain."

"But one with certain advantages, Mr. President," Picard said. "The Herans are apprehensive about being ruled by human beings. As the population of Zerkalo is largely nonhuman, they might feel more comfortable with Atrician supervision, and the Zerkalans have a citizen who would make an ideal planetary commissioner for the trusteeship."

"Dr. Kemal?" Chandra asked. Geordi glanced at Astrid and saw that the suggestion had not taken her by surprise. He wondered if Picard had had any trouble in getting her to agree to this course. It was an obvious move and, he thought in regret, one that would take her off the *Enterprise.*

"Her presence would show the Herans that we wish to be fair," Picard said. "Mr. President, all of the evidence suggests that the Herans are a peaceful people. So long as they do not feel threatened, they will not pose a threat to anyone."

"Picard, there's something wrong with your plan," Stoneroots said. "A lot of my citizens are ticked off at the way the Federation treated one of our citizens. Why should we stick around?" It weaved several tentacles into a cat's cradle. "What's in it for us?"

"Business," Dallas said. "As our administrator, your planet will control our foreign trade operations. We'll probably maintain those links even after we join the Federation."

"I get the picture," Stoneroots said dryly. "I doubt anyone here will turn down an offer like that. But it will require that we join the Federation, won't it?"

Picard affected an innocent smile. "Why, so it will, Mr. President. I look forward to seeing a Zerkalan sitting on the Council."

"Could be fun," Stoneroots conceded, while Chandra tried not to cringe. "I can put it to a Board vote later today, but I'll want something extra."

Chandra looked chagrined. "If you require an official apology for Dr. Kemal's mistreatment by Admiral Trask . . ."

"I do," Stoneroots said. "I'll expect it on a general subspace broadcast to the whole Federation. But there's one other thing. Starfleet Intelligence seems to think it can just waltz in and abuse our citizens. I want a permanent liaison with Starfleet, somebody who will live here and do his best to make sure this kind of thing never happens again. And since Allen clan-Trask already understands the sort of problems we had . . ."

Trask looked affronted. "You wouldn't," he said in a chilly voice.

"I'd suggest you volunteer for that duty, Commodore," Chandra said. "If you do, we'll forget about court-martialing you and jailing you for the next fifty years."

Trask's look of anger deepened as his demotion sank in. "On what charge?"

"On a charge of attempted genocide," Chandra answered. "Your attempt to issue General Order Twenty-Four is a matter of record. I think that a few decades of keeping anarchists happy might be just what you need. Captain Picard, I see no objection to the course of action you've outlined. I'll let you work out the details with Mr. Thorn. Out." She vanished from the screen. Stoneroots turned off its translator, then made a few sign language gestures to Astrid before it broke contact.

Trask growled, and Geordi saw how frustrated anger made his face burn with infrared light. "This will never work."

"I think it will," Astrid said. She stood up and looked down at Trask as she towered above him. "Let this be a lesson to you, Commodore. Next time, pick on somebody your own size."

Chapter Twenty-two

Captain's log, stardate 7332.1 The cease-fire is holding, and Zerkalo has just voted to join the Federation. Mr. Data is now briefing Commissioner Kemal on the legal and technical aspects of her new post, which she will assume when the peace negotiations are finalized. The Herans have released their Federation prisoners, who appear unharmed by their experiences. They are returning to Starbase 389 aboard the remnants of the task force, in the company of Commodore Trask. The Herans have supplied a corrective treatment for the Unity virus, and the last effects of the plague have been eradicated. Mr. Worf continues his investigation of our idiosyncratic computer problems, but he admits to being no closer to a solution now than he was in the beginning.

THE HERAN SURVEY SHIP *Rhea* was a small vessel, not much bigger than the *Temenus*, but it seemed comfortable to Geordi. Part of that was due to the ship's interior, which had been scaled to fit Herans; Geordi found its cabins and central corridor expansive. The ship's crew was also friendly, which helped. They seemed to bear no resentment over the war, even though all of them had lost friends in the battle—an attitude that baffled him.

"I'm not sure what you mean," Joachim Nkoma said, as he and Geordi had lunch on the *Rhea*'s bridge. "I miss the people who died . . . especially my sister. But we all did what we thought was right, and it's over now. What's to resent?"

"Never mind," Geordi said. Explaining resentment to a Heran was about as hopeless as telling Reg Barclay how to unwind. "I was wondering—"

An alarm began to flutter on the conn. Keyed to the acute Heran senses, Geordi found its indications barely noticeable. "Odd," Nkoma said. "I'm getting signs of a cloaked ship."

"Maybe it's one of the Klingons," Geordi said. The Klingon task force had headed home, but they might have left a ship behind to watch Hera—and the Federation, just in case something suspicious happened. "Or could it be an outlaw raider?"

Nkoma shook his head as he checked the instruments. "It's not Klingon," he said. "And it's not one of yours. I don't recognize the configuration."

Geordi looked over Nkoma's shoulder. "Same here—wait. I've seen readings like that before."

"Where?"

"A couple of times recently the *Enterprise* has picked up partial readings on a cloaked ship," Geordi said. "These readings match what we saw. We thought it was a cloaked Heran ship pacing us."

"That power utilization curve is too inefficient to be ours," Nkoma said. He ran his fingers over the control panel as he worked the sensors. "And it's heavily armed. It could wreck a planet if it weren't careful."

"I see." Geordi rubbed his chin as he thought. "Captain, get your ship's weapon ready."

"What for?" Nkoma asked. "That ship is just sitting there."

"I know, but I don't trust heavily armed, cloaked ships," Geordi said.

"If you say so," Nkoma said with a shrug. He powered up the *Rhea*'s improvised quantum inverter. Through principles Geordi was struggling to understand, it could cause antimatter to undergo a simple quantum change and transmute itself into matter. At first glance that seemed harmless, but it had deactivated the antimatter in several Klingon ships, leaving them without enough power to fight. If the Herans had used such weapons against Hoskins's task force, Geordi thought, that battle would have been a total disaster for the Federation. The Herans, however, had not seen a reason to arm their ships with anything more sophisticated than phasers and missiles until the invaders had actually landed on their planet. Then, of course, their inventiveness had created weapons that could have obliterated the Klingons and Federation forces, but they had preferred a peaceful surrender to further carnage.

Nkoma adjusted the weapon, then spotted something on a sensor panel. "It looks like they're friendly after all," he said.

"Why's that?" Geordi asked.

He pointed. "Well, somebody on your ship is sending them a signal. You don't talk when you're going to fight, do you?" he added in uncertainty.

Geordi didn't answer. The transmission was in code, and the code looked very familiar. He felt certain that Worf would have approved of the suspicion he felt. "Lock weapons onto the target," he said.

"'Target'? Oh." Nkoma gave Geordi a peculiar look as he worked the weapon's improvised controls. "You were a holy terror in aggression class, weren't you?"

"'Aggression class'?" After a puzzled second Geordi almost laughed. "I never took a single class, Captain. I'm a natural genius." He settled back in his seat and waited to see what the cloaked ship would do next.

"I don't know," Reg Barclay said disconsolately to the people in Ten-Forward. Will Riker thought he seemed as awkward as ever. "I, I wouldn't *want* to pass on a disease, but, well, I was getting used to the idea of all those changes. I sort of liked it, you know, the thought of having super-kids some day."

"So I'd heard," Riker said. He picked up his drink and tasted the synthehol. "I can't say that I miss it."

Worf grunted, although Riker couldn't tell if that was in sympathy or disagreement. "The attack was dishonorable," he said, as though discussing the only point that mattered.

He seemed about to say more when Astrid entered the lounge. Instead of going to the bar she went straight to Worf. "Come on," she said in properly curt Klingon. "You have an arrest to make."

Worf looked irritated, although Riker was certain the Heran had just made his day. "Who?"

"The *taHqeq* who made the transmissions," she said. "And pulled the practical jokes."

That was all Worf needed to rise to his feet and follow her out the door. Riker got up and hurried after them; whatever was going on, he wanted to be in on it. "Who is it?" he asked.

"K'Sah," Astrid said.

"I thought he wasn't a suspect," Riker said.

"Apparently you assumed he couldn't do a brilliant job of manipulating the computer," Astrid said. "But I just caught him at it. Deck eight, section three," she said as they entered a turbolift.

Riker nodded as the lift started. "Somehow I'm not surprised. He's had a problem with Worf all along. He seems the perfect target for a troublemaker like K'Sah."

"There's more to it than that," Astrid said. "One time, he asked Geordi and me about the Klingon idea of honor. When I was in the brig, he kept pestering me with these really rude questions about, uh, Klingon romantic customs. He's been rude to Worf, even though he minds his manners around everyone else. And when we beamed up from Hera and he stole that virus-creator from you, Will, he gave it to Worf."

"Proving what?" Riker asked. "He had to give it to somebody."

"Without at least trying to sell it back?" Astrid asked. "I think he did that so he could see what Worf would do with it."

"Why?" Worf asked.

"Because I think K'Sah is interested in you," Astrid said. "What you do, what you think, what you feel. He seems to be studying you."

"That would explain the practical jokes," Riker said to Worf. "They show how you react to dishonor."

Worf muttered a Klingon curse in reply. Riker could understand his feelings. K'Sah was the last creature any self-respecting being would want for an admirer. As the elevator stopped Worf drew his phaser and set it on heavy stun. "He shall see *exactly* how I react."

K'Sah was holding a knife in each of his four chitinous hands as they came in. "Hey, Lieutenant," he said cheerily. "You've got a hell of a knock there."

Worf growled at him. "Drop your weapons," he said. "Or disembowel yourself."

K'Sah's serrated mandibles opened and shut several times. "You know, that's not much of a choice."

K'Sah raised his knives. The next thing Riker knew was that Astrid stood behind the Pa'uyk, with one arm around his throat and her other hand holding his knives. "You aren't a nice person," she said to him.

Riker sighed, while Worf and K'Sah looked equally exasperated by her words. "The captain will want to see you," Riker told K'Sah. "Let's go." Astrid virtually carried K'Sah, her arm still locked around his throat in case he produced more weapons.

Riker led the others to the bridge, where Picard watched their arrival with interest. "Dr. Kemal caught our 'exchange officer' making one of those secret transmissions," Riker told him.

"So you are a spy?" Picard asked him.

"A scientific observer, baldy," K'Sah muttered.

Ensign Rager spoke. "Captain, we're being hailed."

"On screen," Picard said.

The bridge of the Pa'uyk ship *Throatcutter* appeared on the main screen. Its control stations looked like a cluster of tiny lairs, with each spidery crew member virtually encased in his or her position. The screen was centered on the Pa'uyk captain, who seemed ready to leap from her lair to capture her prey. "Enemy ship," she said in a dangerously pleasant tone. "Return Dr. K'Sah to us now, or we'll destroy you."

"You and who else?" Riker asked coldly.

"She can do it, chucko," K'Sah said.

"That's right," the Pa'uyk captain said. "And if you don't obey me, I'll destroy your ship, you soft-skinned, fluffy—oh, why bother wasting good insults on you?" She waved a couple of her hands in a chopping gesture. "Blast them!"

The *Enterprise* shuddered as a particle beam shot out of the Pa'uyk ship and slammed into the shields. The Pa'uyk captain laughed—a sound which ended as her ship rocked around her. She shouted an order in her language, while her bridge crew reacted in frantic haste to failing lights and the howl of warning klaxons.

Data spoke as he studied his instruments. "The Pa'uyk ship has been struck by a quantum inversion field," he reported. "It has turned the antimatter in their power systems and torpedo warheads into ordinary matter. The Pa'uyk ship appears to have lost its power."

"That would be Mr. La Forge's doing," Picard said. He looked to the creature on the screen. "Well, Captain, it would appear you're no match for Heran weaponry."

"Okay, okay!" the Pa'uyk captain said, fluttering her mandibles in consternation. "Look, plug-ugly, we *need* Dr. K'Sah. Give him back and we'll go home. We won't even think about annihilating you, even though we could."

Riker spoke quietly to Picard. "Captain, she's being rude. That means she's ready to negotiate."

Picard nodded. "That *does* fit what we know of Pa'uyk behavior, Number One."

"Yes, and I'm in the right mood to handle these negotiations. With your permission?" At Picard's bemused nod he addressed the *Throatcutter*'s captain. "If you really want K'Sah back, you spawn of a Melkotian sea slug, you'll tell us why you're here. *Now,* damn it."

"A mangy, dimwitted tree climber like you couldn't possibly understand," the Pa'uyk captain said.

"And maybe you're too mindless to explain, you blight on the fabric of the space-time continuum," Riker countered.

The Pa'uyk captain sighed. "It's a matter of survival. I hope that even a species as underbrained as yours can understand that survival is a very good idea. K'Sah, it was your stupid idea that brought us here. *You* tell him."

"I will if this idiot will quit strangling me!" he said. At that, Astrid removed her arm from around his shaggy throat and pushed him away. He stumbled, then stood up on his four legs. He looked at Riker and Worf, who both held their phasers on him. "It wasn't *my* idea to come here," he said. "I just had the bad luck to get a sky-high score on the self-control tests, which meant I could work with you. I've had the displeasure of your stomach-churning company ever since."

"Serves you right," Riker said coldly. "You were spying on Worf. Why?"

"It's a matter of survival, you flea-eaten fool," K'Sah said. "We do a lot of fighting among ourselves when we aren't busy exterminating inferior races like yours. Every so often, like now, we manage to build up a society, one that takes us out of the caves. Then, sooner or later— usually sooner—we destroy ourselves. Blast our planets, wipe out the fleets, that sort of thing. Then the survivors spend the next half-million years trying to establish a new civilization. We've done that sixty-three times so far." He shrugged. "Maybe we've done it more. Who knows? The records usually get wiped out."

"So you blow yourselves to Hell, over and over," Riker said. "I feel sorry for Hell. What's that got to do with the Klingons?"

"Shut up and learn, tiny," K'Sah said. "We evolved from creatures like your trap-door spider, which makes us about as sociable as hermit crabs. Our usual way of saying 'hello' to a stranger is to stick a knife in him. Working together is a real trick for us; we've never had the knack for making long-lasting societies the way other people do. And as Captain Cpuld can tell you, we're on the verge of blowing ourselves away."

"That's true," the Pa'uyk captain said. "There's already fighting in the Outer Marches. We just received word that the Mrav and Grost systems were vaporized within the past lunation."

"Aw, *snork,*" K'Sah grumbled. "I knew people on Mrav. They owed me money."

"They're gone now, sucker." Cpuld leaned forward in her seat. "We always thought these collapses were inevitable because of our nature. But recently we heard rumors of a people much like us, fierce warriors who live to fight—who somehow did *not* destroy themselves."

"Klingons," Data observed.

"Right," K'Sah said. He looked to Picard. "We've been spying on the Klingons to see how their society works. There's not another race in the galaxy like them, and if we can learn the virtues that make them so superior, then maybe, just *maybe,* we can find a way to stave off our next collapse. This concept of 'honor'—" He shook his head. "It's weird, it's sick, but it has a certain appeal."

Cpuld looked at him in fascination. "You've learned something, lackbrain?"

"I think so, powermouth." His faceted eyes glittered with what might have been excitement. "They use a concept called 'honor' to make things work. Worf is an especially good example. He's a total warrior, but 'honor' lets him cooperate with anyone, even the most bizarre and disgusting aliens you can name."

"Humans," Cpuld said.

"I wasn't going to name any names," K'Sah said, "but, yeah, he can live with them without trouble. It's uncanny. I was going to bring him home for some lab tests, but—" He bit off his words and growled in frustration.

"Maybe we won't need him," Cpuld said, "if you've

learned enough already. Of course, now that you've gotten yourself captured, you ugly dimwit . . ."

"You can have him back," Picard said. "I wouldn't want to deny your people a chance to survive."

"You wouldn't?" Cpuld looked blank. "Why not?"

Picard sighed. "Never mind. Captain, we humans have some experience at avoiding self-inflicted catastrophes. We could offer you the benefit of what we know."

"Really?" Cpuld's faceted eyes glittered in curiosity. "What about that, Doctor?"

"He doesn't know what he's talking about," K'Sah said. "His idea of a horrible catastrophe is something like the war they just fought here."

"They just fought a war?" Cpuld blinked. "You're kidding."

"Nope!" K'Sah said. "A real devastating war."

"I didn't see any war," Cpuld said. "How many planets did they destroy?"

"None."

"None? How about battle fleets? How many were wiped out?"

"I think a dozen or so ships were destroyed, all told."

Cpuld's razor-edged mandibles quivered in what could only be a smirk. "Some war. How many billions of people did they slaughter?"

"None. There were a thousand killed, tops."

Cpuld laughed. "That sounds like a quiet morning back home."

Picard seemed more bemused than offended by Cpuld's mockery, but Riker could tell that he'd had enough. He waited until the Pa'uyk stopped snickering before he spoke again. "My dear Captain Cpuld—" he began pleasantly.

"Watch your mouth!" the Pa'uyk said, snapping her mandibles for emphasis.

Picard ignored her. "We've done our best to deal with you on your terms," he went on. "Now I think it's time for you to extend us a similar courtesy—"

"Courtesy!" Cpuld made the word sound like a shocking obscenity.

"It's one of *our* customs," Picard said. "You've attacked us and otherwise inconvenienced us, and Dr. K'Sah's secret transmissions led to Dr. Kemal's incarceration. I think you owe us something for that. So, if you want Dr. K'Sah back you'll have to say 'please'—and be polite about it."

"*'Polite'?*" On the screen, the Pa'uyk's head swiveled as she looked around her bridge. *"In front of people?"* She sounded aghast, while her bridge crew managed to convey a spidery sense of shock.

"It's the only way you'll get him back," Picard asserted. "Of course, we could arrest him on a charge of espionage, and then you could explain to your superiors how you lost him, his knowledge, and your people's hope of survival—"

"You wouldn't," Cpuld grated.

"Why not?" Picard asked. "Mr. Worf, would you be so good as to break contact with—"

Cpuld made a sound that suggested she wanted to curl up and die. "May we . . . *please* . . . have K'Sah back?"

"Why, certainly, Captain." Picard looked pleased as he settled back in his seat. "Mr. Worf, escort Dr. K'Sah to the transporter room and send him home. Mr. Worf?"

The Klingon didn't seem to hear Picard. Riker looked at him and saw that he wore an expression of exalted surprise on his face. "I'll take care of it, Captain," Riker said. He nudged K'Sah with his weapon's muzzle. "Move it, targ-breath."

"Whatever you say, shorty." The Pa'uyk preceded Riker to the turbolift, then paused at its door. "Just one question."

"What?" Riker demanded.

"You've been making all this noise about primals and genetic monsters," K'Sah said. "Would you mind explaining the difference between Herans and the rest of you? For the life of me, I can't see it."

Chapter Twenty-three

Captain's log, stardate 7325.9. The Pa'uyk ship has departed, and we have successfully concluded our peace negotiations with the Heran provisional government. Hera is now a trust territory of Zerkalo. After we leave Commissioner Kemal on Hera the Enterprise will resume her original beacon-laying mission in this sector, although due to some temporary crew reassignments in the engineering, medical and science divisions we shall be rather shorthanded during the next four weeks. Although we will no longer have Dr. Kemal's assistance with the buoys, she assures me that they are fully operational and ready for deployment.

"WE'LL HAVE TO REMAIN in the sector for the next month no matter what," Picard said to Riker, as they rode a turbolift to transporter room two. "The Federation wants its flagship here as a show of force, in case any Heran hard-liners consider resuming the war."

"But you don't think that's likely," Riker said. "Captain, I'm curious about something. Why did you assume that the Herans would be so willing to accept peace?"

"Because I believe qualities the originators gave the Herans could only strengthen their essential decency. And the Herans' behavior supported my belief. An agent who apologized while trying to kill his victim, combat ships that fought to disable rather than to destroy, the abduction of prisoners during battle—and how many human worlds defend themselves with only five warships and a dozen installations?"

"Not many," Riker admitted. Most worlds built layer upon layer of defenses, instead of just enough to do the job. The Herans seemed to lack that fascination with weaponry and combat. "We may not impress the Pa'uyk, but we're still not a very peaceful people."

"No, we're not," Picard said. "But as bad as this has been, Will, it could have been worse. Even a few centuries ago we might very well have impressed K'Sah's people by annihilating the Herans, and their originators might have felt no qualms about making them into true warriors. Perhaps we've made a little progress over the centuries."

The turbolift stopped and released them into a corridor, where Worf was waiting. The Klingon looked . . . intent, Riker decided. His eyes gleamed. He also carried a data pad, an uncommon sight. "Mr. Worf," Picard said. "I thought you were packing for your leave."

"I am packed, sir," Worf said. Earlier that morning he had asked permission to spend a month on Qo'nos. Picard had granted the request and authorized Worf to take a long-range shuttle. "I shall depart later today, but first, I wish to ask Commander Riker's opinion on a . . . a personal matter, sir."

"In a few minutes," Riker said. "Come on; we're going to see Astrid off."

Worf grunted and joined them in the transporter room, where Astrid was placing her luggage on the stage. Riker saw that she was carrying a bundle of preserved roses, which must have come from the ship's arboretum. "I'm ready to leave now, Captain," Astrid said. "But I wanted to say good-bye . . . and thank you for everything you did for me."

"The Federation owes you its thanks as well, Commissioner," Picard said. "And—unofficially—you have new orders. The Federation Council wants Hera ready for Federation membership within one year."

"It does?" Astrid looked thoughtful. "That shouldn't be a problem, not on Hera. But what about the rest of the Federation?"

"You mean the old humans?" Picard smiled wryly. "We can be reasonable at times. Starfleet Command is concerned about the possibility of a return visit from Dr. K'Sah's people."

Riker nodded. "We scanned the *Throatcutter* as it left the Heran system," he said. "It had restored full power within an hour of the engagement, and it had better weapons than anything the Federation has. Given the ease with which that science ship defeated the *Throatcutter,* the Federation can use a member like Hera."

"That makes sense," Astrid said.

"There are other, better reasons to invite Hera into the Federation," Picard said. "I for one would welcome a people who are not naturally combative."

The transporter technician spoke. "Hera is signaling, sir. They're ready to receive the commissioner now."

"Very well." Picard shook hands with Astrid. "And if you'll forgive one last misquote of Milton, Mr. Commissioner—'Well done, well have you fought the better fight.'"

For a few seconds her composure seemed to fade as her lips trembled. "Thank you, Captain," she said, when she had regained her equanimity. Astrid stepped onto the transporter stage. "Good-bye, Will. Die well, Worf."

The transporter energized and she faded out. "Your words sounded odd, sir," Worf said to Picard, "as she helped to *end* fighting."

"No, it's appropriate," Riker said. He thought the Klingon seemed nettled to have heard a peacemaker praised. "In *Paradise Lost,* when Satan incited his followers to revolt, one angel refused to follow him, despite all threats and arguments. That quote was the congratulations he received for remaining loyal to the forces of good."

Worf grunted in understanding, while Picard raised an eyebrow. "Number One, you continually surprise me. I had no idea you were a Milton scholar."

"I've . . . developed an interest in him lately," Riker said. He didn't believe Astrid's suggestion about his ancestry, and after all these centuries it wouldn't matter, but, well, he told himself, it never hurt to be open-minded. And whatever else the Khans had been, they had also been human; the human race couldn't escape responsibility for their deeds by denying them. "Anyway, does she know Geordi is down there?" he went on. "She didn't seem surprised when he didn't show up to say good-bye."

"It's rather hard to tell with her, isn't it?" Picard asked. The *Enterprise* had left a team of scientists and engineers on Hera, to begin the investigation of the planet's scientific and technological advances. Geordi had arranged to stay with them while the *Enterprise* completed its beacon-laying mission in the Heran sector. He had professed an interest in Hera's inventions; Riker had refrained from teasing him about his obvious interest in a certain Heran. "But no one told her," Picard said. "Mr. La Forge wants to surprise her—if that can be done."

Worf cleared his throat; he had waited through the farewell and discussion with what little patience he could muster. "If you'll excuse us, Captain?" Riker said. At Picard's nod Riker led Worf out into the corridor. "What's this personal matter?" Riker asked.

Worf thrust the data pad into Riker's hands. "I want your opinion."

Riker activated the padd and read the Klingon words that flooded its display. "What is this?" he asked.

"It is a . . . libretto," Worf said, as if challenging Riker to laugh.

"A libretto?" Riker didn't recognize the word; it didn't even sound Klingon—wait. "The lyrics for an opera?"

Worf grunted in agreement. "I began work on it last night, not long after K'Sah made his . . . statement. I felt . . . " The Klingon groped for a word. "I felt . . ."

"Inspired," Riker suggested.

"Yes." He smiled slightly. "I believe the galaxy is ready for an opera about the virtues of the Klingon people."

"And you're going home to find a composer," Riker said.

Worf nodded. "I have some ideas for the music, but I need the help of a genius. For now, I need advice on the libretto."

"I'll let you know," Riker said. He studied the data pad in bemusement as Worf walked away from him. "'World of genius, great and strong,'" he muttered in translation, "'honor's emissary to the galaxy, listen to a tale of glory' . . ."

As if in reply, Worf's voice came ratcheting down the corridor: *"qo' wIgh, Dun je HoS, batlhDaj Duy qIbvaD, bI'Ij lut—"* The hiss of a turbolift door cut off his singing like an axe blow.

Riker touched his comm badge. "Riker to shuttle bay one."

"Shuttle bay," a woman's voice answered.

"Is Lieutenant Worf's shuttle ready for departure yet?"

"No, sir, we're still prepping it for long-distance flight."

Riker sighed. "Well, get it ready—and *hurry.*"